Truth Digger

Truth Digger

THE BEST OF
SHOVON CHOWDHURY

EDITED BY

URMILA CHOWDHURY
AND
SANDIPAN DEB

ALEPH

ALEPH BOOK COMPANY
An independent publishing firm
promoted by *Rupa Publications India*

First published in India in 2022
by Aleph Book Company
7/16 Ansari Road, Daryaganj
New Delhi 110 002

This edition copyright © Aleph Book Company 2022

All rights reserved.
The sources on p. 253 constitute an extension of the
copyright page.

This is a work of fiction. Names, characters, places,
and incidents are either the product of the author's
imagination or are used fictitiously and any resemblance
to any actual persons, living or dead, events or locales is
entirely coincidental.

The views and opinions expressed in this book are
those of the author and the facts are as reported by
him, which have been verified to the extent possible,
and the publishers are not in any way liable for the
same.

No part of this publication may be reproduced,
transmitted, or stored in a retrieval system, in any form
or by any means, without permission in writing from
Aleph Book Company.

ISBN: 978-93-91047-91-7

1 3 5 7 9 10 8 6 4 2

This book is sold subject to the condition that it shall
not, by way of trade or otherwise, be lent, resold, hired
out, or otherwise circulated without the publisher's prior
consent in any form of binding or cover other than that
in which it is published.

CONTENTS

FOREWORD	vii

COLUMNS

THE INVESTIGATOR	3
WE THE PEOPLE	39
THE 4-MINUTE MANAGER™	62
WHAT IF	82
ASK UNCLE	106
HEALTH IS WEALTH	115
42	146
A FEW OF MY FAVOURITE THINGS	172

FICTION

THE COMPETENT AUTHORITY	199
THE MAN WHO TURNED INTO GANDHI	212
I LOST MY TROUSERS IN TILJALA	231

POEMS

MIDDLE MEN	242
TOMORROW NEVER DIES IN DELHI	243
BIG RED FLASHIE LIGHT	244
MAMA'S PIZZA	245
MAN OF GLASS	246
STITCHING	248
THE GRUMBLIES OF THE NO-NO	249
UNCLE'S INVENTION	251
LIFE	252

SOURCES	253

FOREWORD

I possibly met Shovon—'encountered' may be a better word—for the first time on 19 June 1986, the day we arrived at the Indian Institute of Management Calcutta campus. I would imagine that his rich baritone would have caught the attention of all of us standing in queue for registration and allotment of hostel rooms. In any case, over the next couple of weeks, he had become an essential member of our friend circle of about a dozen young people who worked (or did not), played, and lived together for the next two years.

To the rest of us, Shovon appeared intriguing, perhaps even weird. He was the only person we knew who was still reading Marvel comics and was quite unembarrassed about it. He could talk about the origins of the X-Men and the Avengers and the connections between the various series that built the all-conquering Marvel Universe of today. Not only did he know the backstories of all the lunatics whom Batman fought but also how different teams of writers and artists had interpreted and altered the dark knight character over time.

And he actually listened to The Carpenters! What grown man ever did that? All right, he also listened to Pink Floyd and the Doors, but still, his tastes in music were distinctly suspect.

We soon discovered that he was exceptionally well-read. He could hold forth on the idioms and metaphors in *Hamlet*, and the arcane allusions in T. S. Eliot's poetry. He was an authority on every great science fiction author we had never or barely heard of. He also seemed to have read most of the classics in Bangla literature. This was quite extraordinary, since he was born and spent the first ten years of his life in England, and had been relocated to India with hardly any familiarity with his 'mother tongue'.

He had a deep knowledge of military history, from Julius Caesar to the tank battles in the Second World War. He could distinguish Manet from Monet and knew the name of the only painting that Van Gogh had managed to sell in his lifetime. He was acquainted with the various strands of European philosophy of the last 300 years, and looked at them all with a touch of disdain.

Shovon was well-known in Kolkata quiz circles, had done amateur theatre and had a big repertoire of comic songs. He also knew that comedy is all about timing. He could do a very authentic Tarzan yell and could sing 'Edelweiss' at the most inappropriate—that is, the most comically appropriate—moment and have everyone in splits in a way that Rodgers and Hammerstein could never have imagined. The only area of the arts and popular culture that he did not have a clue about was Hindi films. I don't think that he ever managed to overcome that lacuna.

I need to put all this in context here. Shovon was technically an engineer, as were most of us, and it was very unusual for a fresh engineering graduate to have already developed such a broad range of interests and such a rich life of the mind.

Yet, the most striking thing about him was that he did not take himself seriously. He had a terrific sense of humour and that humour would often be directed at himself. He could laugh at himself as hard as he laughed at some of India's fumbling politicians. In the thirty-five years that I knew him closely, I don't believe I ever heard of him saying anything that could remotely resemble the slightest boastfulness. All of us have known people who cultivate humility as mere good manners or a cover for real self-doubt or as a useful tool to advance one's interests. In Shovon, it seemed to be ingrained; for him, it was quite simply, the right thing to do.

In fact, his modesty and cheerful self-deprecation may not have been an unalloyed good thing, especially in his chosen profession of advertising, where a little self-aggrandisement or, at the very least, talking of one's achievements, can certainly do no harm.

When we were done with IIM, or IIM was done with us, Shovon's life and mine stayed interlinked. We joined the same advertising firm in Mumbai, working late nights on weekdays and living it up on the weekends. We got married within a fortnight of each other. Later, when I was working in a consumer finance company in Kolkata, I was handling the company's advertising, and he was the executive in charge of our account at the agency. I moved to Delhi in December 1990, and he was posted there in 1994. And there we remained, we and our families sharing many ups and downs together.

After ten years as a wage-slave, Shovon turned entrepreneur and co-founded an ad film making company. A few years later, he launched his own advertising agency, Street Life. I happened to work with him on a couple of assignments and he brought a rare combination to the table—the ability to meaningfully analyze very large amounts of data, and a quirky but focused creativity. I speak here as a client and not as a friend.

But at his core, Shovon was a writer. He loved words, and he actively tried all his life to make sense of the world around him. When something happened in India or elsewhere on the planet, he would carefully marshal the facts, study the opinions expressed from all over the political, social, and moral spectrum, and attempt to reach an objective viewpoint. And that viewpoint would often surprise and illuminate. It was only natural that 'The Investigator', the column he wrote for many years in the newspaper the *Hindu Business Line,* carried the tagline: 'We dig for the truth. So you don't have to.'

Two qualities underpinned his view of the world. One, a deep empathy for the underdog, the less privileged, and the weak. Two, his acute sense of irony, which would often spot the farcical in the tragic and could put a magic-realist spin on reality. These two qualities were hardly mutually exclusive. In fact, they intertwined and fed each other and gave his best writing considerable power, without ever being preachy.

Shovon always claimed that he was not a natural writer, in the sense that the words did not flow easily off his keyboard. It took a lot of hard labour. We will not know whether this was true or his customary self-effacement, but to support his claim, he would point to the fact that he had taken eleven years to write his first novel, *The Competent Authority*. There were days, he said, when a thousand words would cheerfully gush out on to the page, and there were others when he could produce only a sentence or two. But one should remember that he was writing his book while working at a very demanding day job.

In *The Competent Authority*, Shovon's aim was to project a near-future scenario that would be a logical development if certain events take place. All good speculative fiction starts from a few base assumptions—that surveillance technology will enable an all-powerful Party to control people's actions, language, thought, and memories (*Nineteen Eighty-Four*); or that our rulers will be able to brainwash us into full subservience by keeping us mindlessly content (*Brave New World*, where technology is used for the same purpose but by means entirely reverse of those that Orwell predicted in *Nineteen Eighty-Four*). Shovon imagined an India after much of its northern and western parts had been destroyed in a nuclear war with China, and in the east, West Bengal is a Chinese protectorate.

He had always instinctively hated self-serving bureaucracy and the corruption in India's police machinery. In *The Competent Authority*, the arrogance, stupidity, and venality of these two forces are taken to extreme lengths. But this is not entirely incredible. One of the reasons why the novel took so long to write was that some of the wild ideas that he had thought up for a dystopic future came true even as he was writing about them, making extensive revisions of the text necessary.

Into this tapestry, he wove in some classic science-fiction themes like telepaths and time travel. What if agents could be sent back into the past to change three key events in the twentieth century—what would India look like then? Would it be better? He had been a history buff, and like many history buffs, had been fascinated with alternative histories. He would later be commissioned to write a number of 'What If' articles for a magazine—what would our current reality be if Mohandas Karamchand Gandhi was not ejected from the train in South Africa, or the Marathas won the Third Battle of Panipat?

The Competent Authority was a big critical success and was shortlisted for four prestigious book awards. Calling it 'charmingly self-assured and ruthlessly funny', one reviewer saw the novel 'stirring a heady cocktail of the real and the imagined, and proving, as all successful satires do, how laughter can spring from the darkest corners of our souls'. Another described it as a mixture of the best of Philip K. Dick and Tom Sharpe, who, incidentally, happened to be two of Shovon's favourite writers.

Requests for newspaper columns and regular invitations to literary festivals followed. Festival audiences loved him since he could—unlike most panelists—make them laugh even while making a perfectly serious point. The columns too were very popular. As could be expected, they expressed outrage at the goings-on around us, but the anger was overlaid with often-bizarre hilarity. Though deeply observant, they were also very often surreal, and paradoxically, rang even truer for being that, and touched a chord in thousands of Indians.

Bold protests disguised as fantasy, they spare no one who is hypocritical or exploitative. Bureaucrats plan to use moth-eaten files as missiles to be fired from ships and aircraft in case of war. Citizens are not allowed to use public toilets if they fail to provide their Aadhaar details. To reduce pendency of court cases, the government launches a mobile app, on which people can examine the evidence against themselves, judge their case on merits, and sentence themselves accordingly. Chief executives keep themselves fit by shouting daily at subordinates.

Shovon's was a voice of sanity that pretended to be half-crazed. It was a constant reminder that absurdity was very often hiding in plain sight all around us.

One of his lifelong loves was theatre, which, he argued, was a higher form of art than cinema. Film sequences can be reshot many times, edited carefully by selecting from a host of takes and camera angles, wholly transformed through computer-generated imagery, and the final product stays static and unchanging for all time to come. In theatre, however, live human beings perform for the audience, and every show is unique, because every show is made up of living creatures, who are by definition both fallible and capable of reaching unpredictable highs.

Shovon considered stage actors as people who *serve* the audience. It was for him a profession that embodies humility and a working-class ethos. And among all the theatre archetypes, he admired 'the clown' or 'the fool' the most. All actors serve the audience, but he saw the fool as providing the most selfless service. He seeks laughter and even derision as his immediate tangible reward, even if he often acts as a trigger for introspection and a reality check for the pompous and the deluded.

It is important to recognize and appreciate these beliefs when we look back at Shovon's work.

In the last year of his life, he had to be hospitalized several times. He did not tell anyone, unless he thought it absolutely essential, and forbade his family to tell anyone that what he was suffering from was a disease with an extremely high fatality rate. He had a deep distaste for being a subject of pity. Ironically, the covid lockdowns and the restrictions on social gatherings helped. This was certainly the longest period since we had first met in 1986 that we did not see each other.

In those months, I spoke to him several times on the phone. Though I had not been officially told of the true nature of his illness, I could very well guess it from what he unconsciously revealed in these conversations. I believe that all of us, his friends, deeply respected his sense of privacy. We could see that he wished to limit our interactions to the telephone and did not want to meet in a physical space. He ended the last chat we had by saying that he was feeling terribly fatigued and needed to rest, he would call me later. He never did, and a month or so later, early on the morning of February 26, 2020, he passed on. Some of us had been expecting the worst, but this did not in any way reduce the shock when we received the news from Urmila. I felt a great confusion. How could Shovon not be there anymore?

One of his last published articles ('Pancreatic Diaries II', included in this volume) was written during his second long stay at the hospital. He was in acute pain, but he laughed at himself for screaming. He joked about enemas and stents that were being inserted in his body ('I am now half human, half plastic, like a budget cyborg') and strict nurses whose heavily-accented commands he could not decipher. By this time, his test results had come in; Urmila knew that he had been diagnosed with pancreatic cancer at an advanced stage. Shovon had not been told but it is almost certain that he had a pretty good idea what his ailment was. Yet the vast majority of his readers would never have suspected that he was writing under the deepest shadows. A re-reading of the piece today reveals a man of steely courage who could not dream of imposing on anyone's sympathy.

A friend remembered him thus: 'He questioned every assumption we had and we ended up learning from him.' Another: 'He lit up the room with his wit and intelligence every time he entered.'

Three and a half decades ago, one night, sitting by the lake in front of our hostel in IIM Calcutta, Shovon had told me: 'What I find really interesting about Leonardo da Vinci is that he spent the last few years of his life trying to sketch water. That became his mission—how to freeze on paper something that never stays still and changes every moment.' My friend's passion too was to know the truth about the nature of things and capture it in words and explain it, to himself, and to anyone who cared. The truth kept shifting shape, but he never gave up.

In the end, perhaps, to quote Kurt Vonnegut, a writer he dearly loved, 'so it goes'.

Sandipan Deb
Gurgaon
August 2021

COLUMNS

THE INVESTIGATOR

'The Investigator' was Shovon's longest-running column. It appeared fortnightly in the *Hindu Business Line* for more than six years with the lofty promise: 'We dig for the truth. So you don't have to.' It reacted to the happenings of the day with irony and an imagination that took matters to absurd lengths, perhaps because he believed that only bizarre metaphors could shine a keen light on what was going wrong all around us.

No one escaped unscathed—politicians, celebrities, and, of course, the most frequent causes of Shovon's dismay: bureaucrats. And the humour was often merely a camouflage for the horror he felt.

DEFENCE MINISTRY AUTHORISES
USE OF FILES AS WEAPONS

I try not to sneeze as the bearer puts the files on the table and backs away. They should have given him gloves. The files are dank and mottled, and covered in years of dust. I can see mould and fungus. Some of the thicker files could well be breeding other forms of life. As chemical weapons, these would be lethal. If deployed in bulk, they would be weapons of mass destruction. The Defence Ministry babu smiles at me from across the table. 'As you can see, we are well-prepared,' he says.

'What led you to take this step?' I ask.

'In 2014, China's defence budget increased by 12 per cent to $132 billion, the biggest increase since 2010,' he says. 'We increased ours by 5 per cent, to $37 billion. As a result we've been unable to do certain things, like buy new batteries for submarines. For the army and the navy, the modernisation budget has shrunk by 4 and 3 per cent. Given the depreciation of the rupee, the reduction is much more. This is helping us defend the country better.'

'Against the Chinese?' I ask.

'No, against our armed forces. Our primary function in the ministry is to prevent a coup. Our penal code is from the nineteenth century. The forces have weapons from WWII. They are ahead of us. If they become too advanced, they could get ideas. There's been no coup since 1947, so our strategy must be working. We also have a contingency plan for external defence.'

He picks up a file. I try not to look. Small creatures are crawling all over it. 'This file pertains to submarine purchase,' he says, 'It has been untouched by human hands for 11 years. It contains bacteria that can eat through steel. We have developed a variety of delivery systems. In case of a naval attack, ministry officials will paddle into the ocean in rubber dinghies and hurl them at enemy vessels. They will also be fired from guns of naval destroyers, launched from submarines, and dropped from Indian Airlines aircraft, lent by the Aviation Ministry.'

'Supposing you run out of files?' I ask.

The babus laugh uproariously. 'There is little risk of that. As a last resort, some of us are willing to become ammunition. Since the Bofors guns have no ammo, feasibility studies are being conducted to evaluate if babus can be fired from them.' I tuck my pencil behind my ear and leave his room, reeling from the horrifying image of babus descending from the sky, en masse, at high velocity. If that doesn't beat the Chinese, nothing will.

Hindu Business Line, 14 March 2014

GOVT TO PROVIDE LIST OF
WORDS TO DESCRIBE 'GOVT'!

The Deputy Secretary is studying the *Oxford English Dictionary*, Volume 3, D-F. An assistant stands by his desk, holding it up for him. At a gesture from the Secretary, the assistant licks his finger and turns the page. 'D for Delightful. That's very good. Delightful!' says the Secretary. He is delighted. He points to his stenographer, who makes a note. 'Is this one of the approved words?' I ask, pencil poised on my notepad. 'It will have to be submitted to the Committee for Approved Terminology,' says the Secretary, 'but I am very hopeful. After all, we aim to provide service, and the main objective of service is Customer Delight. We would like to make this compulsory. This is part of our Phase 2 action plan, which will gradually be revealed. In Phase 1, we have created a preliminary list of words, which are now officially permitted for usage by patriotic citizens, while describing anything to do with the government. Words such as 'thoughtful', 'innovative' and 'staggeringly brilliant' are highly recommended.

'Historic', 'heroic' and 'heart-touching' are also good. Some other words will be strictly regulated. For example, use of the word 'Emergency' will only be allowed, after taking written permission from a gazetted officer of the rank of Under Secretary and above, so long as they are not on special duty. 'Unnecessary dragging in of Constitution' will attract a maximum penalty of seven years' rigorous imprisonment. 'Gratuitous references to free speech' will lead to poetry reading sessions with Kapil Sibal. Meanwhile, a delegation of Joint Secretaries has been posted to Oxford, where they will consult the writers of the dictionary regarding other good words. We have also looked into the area of ratings, which are becoming increasingly common at the grassroots level. We have issued guidelines and indicated penalties. For example, 'excellent', and 'very good' are allowed while rating government services, but 'average' will lead to delay in receipt of LPG, while 'poor' will lead to instant transfer of domicile to Kashmir. Use of emojis will also be carefully regulated. Thumbs-up and smiley faces are permitted. ROFL will be judged on a case-to-case basis, and inappropriate application could attract penalties. Sharing of emojis with threatening expressions in the context of governance will be strictly disallowed. 'Do these regulations extend to the police as well?' I ask. The Secretary shakes his head, smiling. 'They are simple fellows. They have specified that they want the public to use only one word to describe them, and that word is "uncle".'

Hindu Business Line, 11 November 2016

27 RESOLUTIONS FOR 2017!

Before providing some humble suggestions, which together form the best list of New Year resolutions ever, it is necessary to study the history, geography, and etymology of the underlying concept, because we cannot move forward unless we feel our backsides.

A New Year resolution is like a politician—it's slippery and it gives us hope for a better future. Very often we make these under the influence of alcohol, so the future tends to be hazy. This is why it's a good idea to write them down, assuming you can still grip a pen at the time. I made some really good ones in 1998, but unfortunately I forgot to do this, so they remain a mystery. In fact, the only resolution I have ever kept was one that I made in 2006, when I fell down flat on my face around midnight. I promised myself that I would sit down more. On the whole though, resolutions make us feel good early on in the year, cost nothing to make, and cause very little harm to others. They are a good thing.

Like many other things, good and bad, this practice was started by Julius Caesar, who decided one day that January 1 would be first day of the year. He ensured this by extending the previous year to 445 days, which must have been extremely annoying for everyone who had signed an annual contract. But they had to put up with it. Unlike us, they lived under an imperial system, and the word of Julius Caesar was law. Thankfully, we live in a democracy, where one man can never make sweeping changes as per his whims and fancies like that. The Romans were not so lucky, so when Caesar said, 'Next year the year will be 50 per cent longer', nobody argued. Non-compliance would have led directly to consumption by hungry wild animals, cheered on lustily by roaring crowds, who somehow always missed the point that they could be next. This was before the invention of trolls. It marked out January 1 as a special day. On this occasion, all Romans were expected to make promises to the gods, detailing what they would do to become better

Romans. Most of these involved rendering unto Caesar in a wide variety of ways, but a few had to do with other forms of self-improvement, such as lying less, and not beating the children.

Over the years, the practice was adopted by others, such as Jonathan Swift, who promised in 1699 that when he was old, he would 'not marry a young woman', 'not keep young company unless they really desire it' and 'not tell the same story over and over to the same people'. On December 31, 1929, on the banks of the River Ravi, the Indian Tricolour was unfurled for the first time, and we made a resolution to build a nation, causing sundry Britishers to choke on their gin. In 1942, American folk singer Woody Guthrie promised to 'wash teeth if any', 'change socks', 'play and sing good' and 'keep hoping machine running.' Nowadays, resolutions are like an epidemic. We're all doing it. A 2014 survey by NDTV revealed that 41.3 per cent of nearly 30,000 Indians surveyed had promised to exercise more. A follow-up survey was not conducted. A 2015 survey in the US by Statistic Brain revealed that close to 60 per cent of Americans make some form of New Year resolution, the most popular ones being lose weight, get organised and spend less. Achievement levels vary, from 14 per cent for people over 50 to 39 per cent for people in their 20s, from which we can deduce that people in their 20s in America lie more often in surveys.

How is young India doing on this front? If you believe, like me, that the children are our future, then this is an important thing to explore. What are their dreams and aspirations? What are their hopes and challenges? How will they shape the nation? How will they mould its contours? What does the future hold for India? A brief study of a 2016 Reddit thread reveals that 'getting a girlfriend' is the number one priority, closely followed by 'having saxx'. Learning Urdu, eating less sugar, and reading more also feature, so there's still some hope for the future.

Inspired by their list, I decided to make a list of my own. The sands of time are running out for me, and I have decided that nothing short of a complete makeover will do. So I sat down very carefully and analysed myself. I thought about the year gone by, and what I had learnt from it. I asked a few people I trust what they felt I should be doing. I decided that I should align myself with current national priorities as much as possible, in order to avoid arrest and/or savage beatings. On the basis of these factors, I have evolved a roadmap for a better me. This is what I will do. Most of these are self-explanatory. One or two, I have explained.

1. Learn the words to the national anthem. I've been looking down at my shoes and mumbling since I was in school, but this will no longer do. I'm no fool; I can see where this is going. They're coming for the mumblers next. When the time comes, I'll be articulating clearly.
2. Reduce my carbon footprint.
3. Reaffirm my commitment to India's secular values.
4. Stay away from policemen.
5. Stay away from fried chicken. (I have episodes. It's a thing. I don't like talking about it.)
6. Call someone a presstitute on Twitter.
7. Keep better track of celebrity baby names. We have to be vigilant.
8. Remember everyone's birthday.
9. Learn how to cook.
10. Donate one toilet. Or perhaps even two, budget permitting.
11. Do Rapidex Course in Mandarin.
12. Make friends with a joint secretary or other gazetted officer of equivalent rank, provided they are not on Special Duty.
13. Resist brainwashing by Arundhati Roy.
14. Become proficient in Surya Namaskar.
15. Ask the editor of BLink for more money.
16. Learn how to make that contemptuous samosa twirling gesture (à la Arnab Goswami) with my fingers.
17. Conserve water by pulling flush less often.
18. Support dilution of the Prevention of Corruption Act.
19. Fight harder for gender equality.
20. Clip toenails more. (My own.)

21. Apply for the position of RBI governor.
22. Be more supportive of LGBTQ people.
23. Find out what LGBTQ stands for.
24. Stop pretending to finish a book by either a) stopping or b) finishing.
25. Speak to aunties more often.
26. Conduct cautious experiments with cow urine.
27. Become fully e-compliant.

As you can see, this is a wonderful list, adroitly blending the sociological, the cultural, and the personal. In case you want to steal from it, please go ahead. You can leave out the bits which don't apply. For example, your toenails could be normal, and you may have fewer aunties. But self-improvement is the need of the hour. As the government has pointed out repeatedly, the main problem with this country is us. Our country is dirty because we are dirty, not because of lack of water or plumbing. Our economy is black because of the darkness in our souls. The problem is us. We are thwarting the governance. If we improve, the nation will improve. So please use this useful list to do the needful. And remember, even if you have no currency, it's not a problem. This process is absolutely free.

Hindu Business Line, 6 January 2017

WILL PROTECT COWS FROM ROMEOS, SAYS UP POLICE!

My investigations begin in front of a meat shop. The crowd is throwing stones. I am caught in the crossfire. I duck to avoid one. A policeman shakes his head. 'These people make it very difficult.'

'To arrest them?' I ask, clutching my notepad as another stone whizzes by.

'No, to arrest the shopkeeper,' says the policeman. 'All the problems are because of him. Luckily, there are only a few of them, so it won't take much time. Then we will shift to our top priority.'

'Our top priority is cows,' explains another officer, standing nearby. His belly is gigantic. He must be very senior. He picks up a stone, which has been dropped by a rioter. He dusts it off on his khakis and hands it back.

And then he turns to me. I step back hastily, but his expression is benign.

'Cow is like our mother. For non-Hindus, cow is like their auntie. Whoever you may be, she is your close relative. She deserves our respect and protection. So far we have been distracted by other crimes. But now every thana has special squads devoted to cows. We had to leave out some constables who were lactose intolerant, but the rest are eager to serve. Please inform concerned members of the public that we are fully committed to keeping unaccompanied cows safe from the attention of Romeos.'

This sets me thinking. As I walk around Lucknow, I interview some cows. I talk to Chameli, who is chewing cud under a lamp post on MG Road. She supports the administration. 'It's a good initiative. We are always on the street, exposed and vulnerable,' she says, 'Meanwhile, the number of Romeos is increasing.'

Other cows are more liberal, especially the younger lot. 'I have no objection to going out with a Romeo,' says Premlata, a pleasantly plump three-year-old, 'so long as they take prior permission from the *angrakshak* of the *gaushala*.'

There has been a visible upsurge of confidence in the bovine community. 'I can roam in the park without fear now,' says Meena Devi, a senior cow whom I meet near a statue of Mayawati. 'Plus my owner is now much more polite. Earlier, when he wanted to move me, he poked me with a stick. Now he requests politely. Sometimes he folds his hands.'

She nuzzles me fondly. I pet her head. In the distance, I see a nervous buffalo, hiding behind a tree. 'Don't worry,' I whisper, 'Your time will also come.'

Hindu Business Line, 31 March 2017

BJP TO HOLD PRAYER SESSION FOR RAGA!

In developments referred to as 'richly deserved and long overdue' by *Monarchy Digest*, the Bharatiya Janata Party has announced a massive religious event in Rae Bareli district, where thousands of party workers will conduct a 16-hour prayer session for the long life, good health, and continued well-being of Congress vice-president Rahul Gandhi. 'People accuse us of not tolerating opposition, but this is not true,' says a BJP leader, 'We believe that the opposition space is very important in any democracy, and we will go to any lengths to ensure that it is filled by Rahul Gandhi. Thanksgiving prayers are not common in Hindu culture, but in his case, we will be offering them.'

Beyond the prayer session, the BJP has announced a wide variety of measures designed to support the veteran youth leader. 'Volunteer squads from the BJP will attend his speeches and clap a lot. Our IT Cell will retweet him regularly. In case Congress party funds are running low, the BJP will provide him with a special plane for election rallies, so that the public is never deprived of the chance to see him in person. Our only request is that no non-veg food should be served on the plane. The puja itself will be a lavish affair, funded anonymously by leading industrial houses. The ceremony will be followed by a buffet, in which high-quality vegetarian food will be served. The menu will include paneer pizza and pasta with brinjal, in honour of Rahul-*ji*'s heritage, as well as elaichi-flavoured cow urine, which everyone is expected to enjoy.'

Hindu Business Line, 31 March 2017

NEW ACRONYM LAUNCHED
TO FIGHT MAOISTS!

The map of Chhattisgarh on the wall is upside down, but I hate to point this out. I am very polite to policemen, especially in Chhattisgarh. Currently he is patting his stomach and looking quite happy, but you never know. He hands me a small piece of paper with the word 'SAMADHAN' on it. 'See!' he says, 'here is your answer.'

'Is it some kind of chit fund?' I ask, cautiously.

'No no,' he says, 'It's the solution to the Maoist problem. We just received this from New Delhi.'

'Will you be giving loans to the Maoists at concessional rates,' I ask, 'thereby bringing them back into the mainstream of society?'

'That's also a good idea,' says the officer, 'we could help with the disbursal. But this is much bigger. Each letter of SAMADHAN is loaded with meaning. It stands for Smart Leadership, Aggressive Strategy, Motivation and Training, Actionable Intelligence, Dashboard-based Key Performance Indicators, Harnessing Technology, Action Plan for each Theatre, and No Access to Financing.'

I am impressed. 'It looks like there's going to be a lot of action on the Maoist front,' I say.

'There has already been a lot of action,' he confirms. 'A task force of senior officers spent eight weeks creating this acronym. In fact, much of it was the brainchild of a colleague from Chhattisgarh. Unfortunately he is no longer with us, because when they asked him how he could be rewarded, he said, "Please transfer me out of Chhattisgarh".'

'Would you say that the absence of strategy has hampered anti-Maoist efforts?' I ask.

'No, that was because officers in the field were forgetting to follow Standard Operating Procedure. This was the problem.'

'What are these SOPs?' I ask, shrewdly slipping in an acronym of my own.

'I don't have a copy,' he says, 'so I have no idea. Nobody does. But not following them is the main problem. Also the men are unable to follow clear-cut instructions. We tell them go out and get the Maoists, but the CRPF boys keep asking questions, like where are they, how many are they, and so on. Meanwhile, our own boys keep running away, saying things like there are 100 of them and only 1,500 of us, like during that unfortunate incident in Burkapal. Things were bad. The lack of an acronym was really hurting us. Now, thanks to SAMADHAN everything will be fine. Usually such words have four–five letters, but this one has eight. Our success is guaranteed.'

One thing is puzzling me. 'What does Dashboard-based Key Performance Indicators mean?'

He smiles. 'It was late at night, and they couldn't come up with anything else that starts with D,' he says.

Hindu Business Line, 26 May 2017

MAN WITHOUT AADHAAR REFUSED TOILET FACILITY!

New Delhi native Jatinder Bagga, 46, a resident of Karol Bagh, was arrested yesterday evening in Kalkaji for failing to provide Aadhaar card details while entering a public toilet. 'We stopped him in the nick of time,' said constable S. P. Singh of Delhi Police. 'He was about to unzip. He pleaded that the matter was urgent, but we ignored him. He managed to make a break for it, but we apprehended him near a lamp post. My uniform is now slightly damp, but I feel proud that I upheld the law.'

The culprit is currently being held at the Kalkaji police station, where FIRs have been lodged against him for 'public urination', 'wetting an officer' and 'non-possession of Aadhaar card despite repeated reminders'. The case raises a number of questions. Does this mean that all toilet facilities will now be connected to Aadhaar cards? When contacted, a senior member of the government confirmed this. 'In keeping with the "more governance, less government" policy, we are minimising government by combining functionalities. As a first step in this initiative, the Swachh Bharat scheme and the Aadhaar card are being combined to create one seamless programme, in which citizens remain identifiable, urination is minimised, and wear-and-tear on toilet facilities is reduced.'

Meanwhile, Bagga remains in police custody. On being asked whether he had learnt a lesson, he said, 'Definitely. In future, I will avoid Kalkaji.'

Hindu Business Line, 23 June 2017

GROUSE OF CARDS

On the night before Diwali, people in the nicer parts of Delhi play cards and lose large sums of money, in the hope that this will bring them good fortune in the coming year. Given that most of them come back and play again, it's a plan that seems to be working. This is not as surprising as you'd think. There are huge amounts of gravy in Delhi, and so long as they can keep the outsiders out, there's more than enough for everyone.

These Diwali card parties also serve as a useful social yardstick. Cars can be hired. Homes can be rented. The diamonds could be fake. But a Diwali party pegs you in cash. Your status is defined by how much you lose. If you lose ₹5 lakh per move, you are at the high end of the market. You are a major loser. Your invitation will come with a mason jar of gold-leafed chocolate-covered coffee beans. You get your choice of single malts. Well-known musicians play softly in the background. They serve you poached scallops and baked beetroot purée accompanied by puffed rice, with caramelised garlic as appetiser.

The ₹20,000 to ₹1 lakh range makes you a mid-level loser. You get vegetable momos and regulated quantities of cashews, with Black Label. At the ₹10,000–20,000 range, you get papad and mid-level sweets, and Blender's Pride, which will run out early. Ice will have to be picked out with fingers.

This may sound very rigid and hierarchical, but over time, the system has evolved. For example, credit is no longer provided, and all settlement is up front, after a former cricket star and a late hotelier[1] came to blows in a bar, over an unsettled gambling debt of ₹1 crore. This was when a crore was considered a large sum. The father of the star settled the matter amicably, and the payment was made in instalments. However, settlement in kind is still accepted, which is why cars and farmhouses sometimes unexpectedly change hands. I was

---

[1] He was alive at that time.

personally very moved by the story of young Pritish, a 19-year-old BBA student, who gambled away his Zippo, his iPhone and his BMW, as well as ₹45,000 in cash, but promised to come back the next day, determined to win everything back. With youth like this, there is hope. It's important to note that all this gambling is done mostly by men, since women can't be trusted with money. The women gamble with much smaller sums, trying to win back some taxi fare in case their husband loses the car.

Luckily I have never been in this position, despite spending years in Delhi. I do not play cards at Diwali parties. It's a result of psychological programming by aunties. In middle-class Bengali circles, gambling is frowned upon, especially by aunties. This is because our literature, films and recent family history are full of debauchees who blew up their fortunes on gambling and loose women, and, in some cases, pigeons, leaving their children to fight over one small residence in Kalighat. I had more aunties than most. So whenever anyone invited me to play cards, or tried to teach me how, their faces would float in front of my eyes, all 14 of them, shaking their heads and pursing their lips. 'We knew it,' they would say, 'What else could we expect from you?' As a result, I still don't know how to play.

At parties, I sit in a corner, out in the garden, under a mid-sized tree, with the two or three other non-players and a deaf uncle. Most parties have a special place for those who don't play cards. The lighting is dim. The snacks do not reach us. The last time I was in such a position, I was with three middle-aged men with big noses who talked only about Lahore. 'The roads in Lahore, so smooth,' said one of them. 'The kebabs in Lahore, so tasty,' said the second. The third just said 'Lahore' once in a while and sighed, misty-eyed.

They discussed the roads and the kebabs, and, lowering their voices, the women. They were three adult Punjabi men, sitting right next to Outer Ring Road in Delhi, longing for Lahore. There was a poetic element to their sadness that was completely unexpected.

Ever since, whenever I go to a Diwali party in Delhi, I'm reminded of Pakistan, and how people sometimes celebrate what they have, because of what they've lost. Some of it might be fake, but the celebrations are real enough.

A very Delhi Diwali to all of you!

Hindu Business Line, 13 October 2017

LAW MIN TO LAUNCH SELF-SERVICE APP!

The officer from the law ministry looks relaxed and happy.

'The Digital India initiative is going very well,' he says, 'As per internal data, almost all targets have been met. A group of us from different ministries was sitting in the Delhi Gymkhana, enjoying Darjeeling tea, when a joint secretary asked, "What else can we digitize?" and another said, "Why not the courts also?" and we all agreed that this would be a good thing.

Due to unforeseen circumstances, average pendency of cases in court is now approximately 37 years. Citizens are suffering. Something needed to be done. Our fundamental principle of governance has always been self-help is the best help, so we felt that the time had come to empower citizens in the legal arena. Judges and government officers have already adopted the self-help principle. In cases involving them, they are investigating themselves, thus saving time and effort on the part of others. It also makes sense because they are the most familiar with the case, since they are the accused. We now want to extend this principle to the public. We were guided by the example of Uber, which allows anyone to be a taxi driver. In the same way, we will democratise justice. After downloading our Self-Service Courtroom Application, customers can examine the evidence against themselves, judge their case on merits, and sentence themselves accordingly. In this way, pendency will be reduced, and justice will be freely available. The Android version is ready. The iOS version is coming shortly.'

Hindu Business Line, 8 December 2017

A BRIEF HISTORY OF R-DAY FLOATS

For me, the best part of Republic Day are the floats. Every year, thousands of man-hours go into constructing things that are seen briefly on TV and then dismantled and sold for scrap at the army cantonment less than a week later. Before they can reach that stage, they have to be approved by the officials of the defence ministry. Various States and government departments submit their proposals, and the ministry selects the best ones. You would imagine that the defence would be too busy to judge floats, considering that in the case of a war, according to last year's CAG report, the armed forces would run out of ammunition in 10 days, but true patriots will always find a way. It used to be a much simpler process.

The first Republic Day Parade started at Red Fort and marched through the city, witnessed by huge crowds at Connaught Place. The floats were simple and homespun, Dr Rajendra Prasad was humble and dignified, and the celebrations were genuine and heartfelt. The first proper parade at Rajpath was held in 1955, with the Governor General of Pakistan as chief guest. As the pageant evolved, so did the floats. A float is a product of many elements, limited only by human imagination. Over time, designers began to realise this.

By 1959, just five years later, featured floats included a dam, a giant onion, and a tableau in which labourers labour away while a supervisor in a black waistcoat menaces them. In 1963, just after the war with China, the NEFA (now Arunachal Pradesh) float was themed 'Tawang back to normal' and both the Kashmir and Himachal Pradesh floats featured soldiers guarding the border. From the late '60s to the early '70s, the energy seemed to flag a bit. In 1969, for example, the Haryana float, entitled 'Wheel of Progress', consisted of a large wheel with three or four people standing behind it, trying to look progressive. But this was just a phase.

As the nation has grown in confidence, so have the float-makers.

The year 2004 was a watershed. That year, Madhya Pradesh celebrated *The Jungle Book*, with a large animatronic Baloo threatening to devour a surprisingly calm Mowgli. The Supreme Court float was another highlight, featuring a live three-judge bench, providing a rare opportunity for many Indians to actually see a judge. This was also the year in which the Indian Railways, for the first time, but not the last, featured a railway compartment with passengers getting in and out.

After the riches of 2004, 2005 was a bit of a letdown, except for a surprisingly truthful float from the ministry of parliamentary affairs, depicting dozens of disembodied hands, crushed under the weight of parliament, reaching out in despair. Other than this, the Manmohan Singh era was largely dull; except for the 2011 float from the National Disaster Management Agency, with the theme 'Plan to manage chemical disaster'. It featured a bright, shiny chemical factory and did not mention Warren Anderson.

Also deserving honourable mention is the effort of the ministry of agriculture in 2014, involving a model 'Common Service Centre', two chickens in a glass case, and half a gigantic woman speaking on her mobile. This trend towards featuring giant half-people on floats has been growing in recent years. In 2015, the same year that thousands of children were terrified by the giant crab on the Goa float, Uttar Pradesh featured a giant half Wajid Ali Shah. In 2016, Bihar gave us a giant half-Gandhi. At least they put in more work than Chandigarh, whose float consisted of four young people doing stretches, and two senior citizens reading newspapers. In 2017, Lakshadweep presented a large turtle stuck on a small hill, flapping its flippers hopelessly. The same year, Maharashtra brought us a giant half-Tilak, with an expression of deep sadness, with two young men wrestling just behind him. Also notable in 2017—the GST float, consisting of a large bowling ball with 'GST' written on it, knocking over pins labelled 'Excise' and 'Octroi'.

As the floats have improved, our interest has increased. Social media has been enriching the Republic Day float experience in recent years, with accusations of the Haryana float trying to overtake the other floats from the left, for example, and of too many Biharis trying to get on

Columns

the Maharashtra float.

At the time of going to press, I am looking forward to the 2018 floats, and so should every Indian. Float-watching is a great hobby. There's so much to learn, such as, how many people can do bhangra on the back of one truck, and what the government babus running different schemes really think about us.

Hindu Business Line, 26 January 2018

DIRECTOR OF NIRAV MODI BIOPIC REVEALS ALL!

We bring you an exclusive interview with the director of Niru, *biopic of international gem fancier Nirav Modi. The interview was conducted at an undisclosed location in the Cayman Islands, due to a misunderstanding with the Indian tax authorities. I was blindfolded throughout, and found it very hard to read my notes afterwards.*

WHAT'S THE STORYLINE?
It's the story of a boy from a relatively underprivileged family. We see his early struggles, when he could only afford very small diamonds.

DO WE LEARN ANYTHING NEW?
We debunk a lot of vile rumours. For example, it's not true that he wears high heels and a diamond tiara when he's relaxing at home. Nor did he start eating tandoori chicken as a mark of gratitude to Punjab National Bank.

SO IT WAS PALAK PANEER THEN?
That he was already having. It's also not true that he installed a statue of the PNB chairman in his ancestral village. Only a small photo in his pooja room. Anybody who spreads such rumours will be prosecuted to the fullest extent of the law.

IS THERE A VILLAIN?
Yes, Nehru. For unnecessarily encouraging the public sector. Plus, he smoked.

DOES IT HAVE A HAPPY ENDING? DO HIS EMPLOYEES GET PAID?
Please. This is not a fantasy. We are trying to keep it as realistic as possible.

Hindu Business Line, 20 July 2018

PATRIOTIC CHANNEL LAUNCHES
WIDE RANGE OF MERCHANDISE!

As soon as I walk under the metal detector, the national anthem starts playing. I stand to attention, inside the frame. The guard stands to attention too. My guide, who is already inside, beams at me encouragingly, standing to attention. The anthem ends and I step out. 'This is our anti-anti-national security system,' explains the guide. 'If you do not stand to attention immediately, we eject you from the building. It's simple and elegant. We love it.'

Not the guard so much, I think, looking back at him. He is standing to attention again as the anthem starts playing. He has to do it every time a visitor steps through. He must be the most patriotic person in the building. I walk past a gigantic portrait of Arnab Goswami, wearing a gorgeous navy blue suit, beaming down at us benignly. I am shocked. This is not the Arnab that I know. 'How did you get him to smile like that?' I ask. 'It was very difficult,' admits the guide. 'So much betrayal of the nation is going on. Finally someone suggested that we should shoot him immediately after his bowel movement. Of course, this meant he had to visit the washroom in full make-up, wearing his suit, but he was quite cooperative in that regard. Come let me show you the merchandise.'

I am here to review their merchandise. This is a channel that enjoys a deep and enduring bond with its viewers, constantly urging them to take action against evildoers. Now, they are strengthening that bond, by selling useful items at moderately marked-up prices. I am standing in front of a long table covered in objects, large and small, such as a giant finger, suitable for pointing, and a life-size Arnab hug pillow.

I pick up what appears to be a jigsaw puzzle of the PM. 'What's this?' I ask. 'This is a tukde-tukde puzzle. By putting these pieces together, children can be trained to undo the damage caused by the tukde-tukde gang. Along similar lines, we have the Find the Urban Naxal video game, in which you have to locate the Naxal in a variety of hiding places, such as shopping malls, railways stations, college campuses and upmarket wine stores. Over here you can see our Pakistani detector,' he says, picking up what looks like an umbrella. 'Many of them look like us. It's easy to get fooled. Using this device, with a quick jab you can take a DNA sample. Results will be shown in the small display on the handle. We also have vacuum packed hot air, collected at source, and, for the select few, a very limited quantity of our signature fragrance, Insanity.'

Hindu Business Line, 24 August 2018

TATKAL SCHEME ANNOUNCED
FOR ABSCONDING PROMOTERS!

When I enter the joint secretary's office, he is waterboarding a junior CBI Officer, except they don't seem to have the budget for a board. A bearer is dunking his head in a bucket. He comes up for air, gasping. 'Next time I suggest that you lose a file, will you ask for written instructions?' asks the joint secretary, standing nearby. His tone is very civil. The officer shakes his head, spluttering. The bearer drags him away. 'These young people, I tell you,' says the joint secretary, wiping his hands on his grimy hand towel. 'It takes so much longer to train them these days. But the traditions of the Service have to be maintained. How can I help you?'

I sit down, eyeing the bucket nervously, until the bearer comes back and removes it. 'What's this about a Tatkal scheme?' I ask. 'It was long overdue,' says the officer. 'It's a matter of India's prestige. Some of our leading industrialists have been forced to leave the country in an undignified manner, due to misunderstandings with the banking system. International papers are commenting regularly. The impression is being created that they are criminals. Just the other day, Mr Mallya was featured in *The Guardian*. The cabinet secretary was very upset. Many of his friends read *The Guardian*. Accordingly, a wide range of measures has been announced to smoothen the process. All escapees will now receive priority customs clearance, unlimited baggage allowance, and one free ticket to the Cayman Islands. The Airports Authority will assign six attendants to carry their baggage. Each escapee will receive a complimentary departure drink. If they choose a local drink, such as feni or Old Monk, they will receive one extra. If the default level with banks crosses a particular threshold, the escapee will receive a guard of honour, and be personally seen off by a minister of state and three joint secretaries. Obviously this level of service comes at a price. This is why political donations are now anonymous, and foreigners are also welcome. We have formalised the process, in the interests of greater transparency.

Each donation must now be accompanied by an anonymous letter, which declares that all donations have been made voluntarily. Candidates will receive either the Bharat Ratna or seven years' rigorous imprisonment, depending on which party they donate to.'

'Isn't this a little unfair to the banks, though?' I ask. 'We are not at all worried about the banking sector,' says the bureaucrat, smiling. 'After all, LIC is always there. Plus we are charging a wide variety of cow taxes. You don't actually think it's all going to cows, do you?'

Hindu Business Line, 12 October 2018

TRANSPARENCY OFFICER SELECTED IN SECRET!

In news welcomed as 'one more step in the right direction' by the Kremlin, the government has appointed India's Chief Information Commissioner, responsible for ensuring transparency, in an atmosphere of complete secrecy.

'Free speech is under threat, and our enemies are everywhere,' said an officer attached to the Commission, in an exclusive interview from an undisclosed location. He chose to remain anonymous. 'We cannot allow our secrecy to be compromised. We were hesitant to even reveal his name, but reluctantly, we agreed. As a result, the public has been informed of his identity, but we were careful to avoid revealing unnecessary information, such as the criteria for selection, the process followed to select him and even who it was exactly who did the selecting. He will not be assigned a telephone, so that there will be no way to contact him. This allows him to stay focused on his task, free of unnecessary questioning regarding his bona fides. Suffice it to say that there were four eligible candidates, in the form of the existing commissioners, all of whom are retired bureaucrats. One of them has been elevated. This is right and proper.' Were there no other suitable candidates available apart from retired bureaucrats? 'The serving officers are all very busy,' he explained.

Hindu Business Line, 4 January 2019

JUDGE RECEIVES GLOBAL SPEED READING AWARD!

The United Association of Speed Readers, a global body designed to recognise extreme acts of speed-reading, has awarded a judge with its Lifetime Achievement Award for Speed Reading Excellence, a rare honour conferred only once every decade.

This was after a heroic act of speed-reading, unfairly ignored by the main-line media. 'It's as if speed-reading is completely irrelevant,' groused a member of the Association. In a matter regarding the dismissal of a senior police official, the concerned judge read and analysed a 1,000-page report in less than 24 hours, before providing a decision. In doing so, it is estimated that he read 40.2 pages per hour, with no sleep and no bathroom breaks. The amount of coffee he consumed has not been revealed. 'His colleagues are not normally known for high speed,' said the President of the Association, 'but this man has absolutely outdone himself.' A sour note was struck by a prominent American judge, who lashed out at 'unreasonable benchmarks being set by judges from third world countries, whose standards of living are much lower, as a result of which they have much less to live for.' The winner will be awarded in a glittering ceremony aboard a Japanese bullet train, where the award will be personally handed over by noted sprinter Usain Bolt.

In related news, the government has categorically denied that the decision was reached quickly because it was written on the cover page of the report.

Hindu Business Line, 1 February 2019

BOLLYWOOD IN PERIL DUE TO DECLINING BIRTH RATE!

While Bollywood continues to bask in the success of *Gully Boy*, certain sections of the industry are not so sanguine. 'I foresee dark clouds ahead, darling,' said an eminent director, from an undisclosed closet somewhere in South Mumbai. 'For the next 10 years or so, things will be fine. But what happens after?

Where will our heroes and heroines come from? No one is having any babies. It's becoming a crisis. When his time comes, around 2035, how much can one Taimur do? I keep asking Kareena to have more children, but she refuses to. The other day at their house, I raised the subject again, but after Saif went to get his hunting rifle, I left quickly. Alia and Ranbir are refusing to get married. Deepika has married, but is still not doing her duty. Our only hope is Priyanka. Now that Meghan is expecting, maybe she will follow suit. But there's no guarantee. It's a pity. Her children would be gorgeous, and probably sing well. Artificial insemination looks like the only option, but it seems so pointless. Half the fun is in imagining beautiful bodies from good families coupling and uncoupling, and producing more beautiful people. But it looks like we won't have a choice. Otherwise the industry will grind to a halt. Plus I worry about Tiger. Too much exercise can lower the sperm count, and if there's one thing we need more of, it's him.'

Hindu Business Line, 1 March 2019

REVEALED! POLLUTION IN DELHI DUE TO SMOKING BY NEHRU!

In news that has led to 'WhenWillHeLetUsGo' and 'WhatAboutShahRukhKhan' becoming the top trends on Twitter, government experts have determined that the current pollution levels in the National Capital Region are directly attributable to Jawaharlal Nehru, former prime minister and notorious smoker. 'We had our suspicions from the beginning,' said a senior member of the Pollution Control Board. 'People have been blaming farmers from Punjab, but how is this plausible? In order for the smoke to reach Delhi, it would have to cross over Punjab. This means they would be poisoning all Punjabis first, including the chief minister, who owns significant amounts of farmland. They would have to be complete idiots to do such a thing. Instead, we have discovered that the bulk of the pollution in Delhi is emerging from areas near the former residence of Nehru. This is supported by eyewitness accounts stating that he used to smoke on the lawns every evening, and sometimes in the bathroom also. We even have photographs. The evidence is irrefutable. This means that apart from engineering poverty, misguiding the youth, and causing India's recent defeat against Bangladesh, he has also been destroying our lungs,' he said. In order to get the other side of the story, we interviewed a statue of Nehru, currently stored in a godown near Badarpur. The statue has expressed regret. 'I was already feeling guilty about the Chandrayaan thing,' said the statue. 'Now I wish I had smoked a pipe instead. It spreads less smoke, and looks much more distinguished.'

In related news, citizens of Delhi have expressed dissatisfaction with the advice given by government officials on fighting pollution. 'I left the house chewing carrots,' said Santokh Singh, a resident of Majnu ka Tila, 'and by evening I was suffering from acute bronchitis. Subsequently, I listened to music and prayed to Lord Indra, but still there was no improvement. When I raised this with my local councillor, he said that I was listening to the wrong kind of music. In addition, he has suggested buying a cow, which he says will convert carbon dioxide into oxygen, but I remain doubtful.' Meanwhile, government teams are leaving no stone unturned in tackling the issue, and are monitoring the situation very closely. 'We will continue to monitor until the problem solves itself,' said an official.

Other government sources have recently suggested that the pollution problem may have been caused by poisonous gas released by Pakistan. Does this not contradict the earlier stand on Nehru? 'Not at all,' said a government spokesperson, 'we cannot rule out the possibility that they were working together.'

Hindu Business Line, 8 November 2019

PUBLIC SHOCKED AFTER DELHI
POLICE ARRESTS CRIMINAL!

In news that has been widely condemned by members of the Criminal Welfare Association (CWA), the Delhi Police has been caught live on camera apprehending a criminal. The mishap occurred in Patparganj, a locality notorious for tandoori chicken. This has led to widespread surprise, especially in Patparganj. 'Is this new approach by the police only going to apply to Patparganj or the rest of Delhi? If it is only us, then why are we being singled out in this manner?' asked Pyarelal Munshi, a local resident. Other localities are not taking this lightly. Neighbourhood committees are up in arms. 'Why have they started in Patparganj?' asked Bhim Bahadur Sharma, a resident of Trilokpuri, 'Crime is much higher in our area. Are we any less deserving?' The unprecedented act by Delhi Police has raised a variety of questions in the minds of Delhi-ites. 'How often will they be doing this,' asked Srinivas Nagappa, a resident of Sarita Vihar. 'Will it be once a week or once a month, or only on national holidays? How will they select the locality? Will there be some kind of lottery? Will preference be given to Hindu, Buddhist, Christian, Jain, Parsi, and Sikh localities? Is there some kind of *tatkal* scheme we can avail of? We need clarity on these issues.'

Senior officers of the police have been extremely apologetic. 'This was a careless mistake by a junior officer,' said one of them. 'The culprit has been severely reprimanded. Exemplary punishment is being administered to prevent its recurrence in the future. The guilty officer will no longer be provided biscuits with his tea for the next two weeks, although he may appeal against this after one week.'

The culprit has expressed remorse. 'I acted impulsively and I deeply regret it,' he said. 'The crime was happening right in front of me, but as my commanding officer pointed out, this is no excuse.' The commanding officer has also been subjected to internal discipline and will now be allowed only Marie biscuits with his tea, instead of Digestive. This has led to general unrest amongst commanding officers. 'This is completely unacceptable,' said one of them. 'If senior officers are held responsible for the actions of their juniors, where does it end?'

Meanwhile, members of the CWA will be taking out a protest march that will end at Jantar Mantar, with a brief detour for some chain snatching at Connaught Place. 'This betrayal cannot go unanswered,' said Pulkeshwar Dhingra, secretary of the association and a gunrunner from Meerut. 'The worst part is, the whole thing happened in broad daylight. This never used to be a problem before.'

Hindu Business Line, 7 February 2020

BIHAR LEADER TO BE SECULAR ON
TUESDAYS, THURSDAYS AND SATURDAYS!

In a move described as 'yet another display of flexibility that is very impressive for a man his age' by the Olympic Gymnastics Weekly, a tall leader of Bihar, who has steered the ship of governance with a steady hand for many years, has announced that if he is re-elected, he will be secular on Tuesdays, Thursdays and Saturdays. 'This has the potential to be a game changer,' said Dr Paltu Kishan Parekh, an eminent former editor who now heads a think tank occupying premises on Pusa Road in New Delhi. 'For several decades now, this was a dilemma faced by many politicians. By constantly playing Hindu–Muslim kabaddi, they were able to consolidate the support of 35 to 40 per cent of the potential voters throughout the year, with a slight increase on festive occasions. But during elections, there is a need to reach out to others also. The gentlemen in question had earlier solved this problem by spending a year or two as secular, and then, subsequently, a year or two as non-secular, and so on and so forth, thus appealing to both segments during the same electoral cycle.'

'It worked very well with me,' said Deen Dayal Chaurasia, a secular voter from Begusarai. 'When election time came, it was hard for me to remember whether he was secular or not. Usually, I assumed he was on my side and voted for him anyway. In any case, I knew that even if he was not on my side at that particular point in time, at some point he would switch sides and then he would be. So, everything would work out for the best.' Why then, is this radical new approach being adopted by the veteran leader? 'It was inevitable,' said Dr Paltu. 'Firstly, the example you have cited is not common. Deen Dayal is an example of what we in the psephological profession refer to as the Slightly Confused Optimist. Over time, as voters have become smarter, this segment has diminished in size, and may no longer be relevant. In addition, voter attention spans have become shorter. It is no longer possible to appeal to secular voters in 2020 just because someone was secular in 2017. People simply cannot remember that far back. Instead, being a rabid fundamentalist on Monday and mildly secular on Tuesday is a much more coherent strategy.'

Assuming that he will be rabid on Mondays, Wednesdays and Fridays, what type of person will he be on Sundays? And will this not upset the balance in one direction or the other? 'Not at all,' said Dr Paltu. 'Such a lot of gymnastics is naturally very strenuous, and he is not getting any younger. Sunday will therefore be a rest day. On this day, he will have no ideology at all.'

Hindu Business Line, 6 November 2020

WE THE PEOPLE

To brand Shovon's writings on current affairs as 'political columns' would be a disservice to him. He wrote as a citizen of India, who believed in certain fundamental rights, and often reacted with anger and horror at how India's politicians betrayed their people.

The framework of his arguments was built of an unwavering rationality—a structure that gave him the ability to look at events from a distance, but filtered by a deep empathy for the powerless. He discarded ism-s to get to the basics.

Passion guided by clear logic. It does seem paradoxical. Yet, it was true.

EXCUSE ME, BUT WHAT IS RIGHT WING?

Apart from being opposed to left-wing people, who or what is a right-wing person? In judging this, we usually go by instinct. Very often they have lots of money. Sometimes they wear khaki shorts. Like Paul McCartney, they long for yesterday. All these are clues. But such a burning issue can no longer be left to guesswork, not when whole magazines are being put together on the subject.

In India, it could be anyone who hates Sagarika Ghosh. While this can be deeply satisfying, it seems rather fragile, ideologically speaking. What happens if she actually does immigrate to Pakistan? How do we fill the empty space in our lives? We could replace her with Arundhati Roy, but the emotions she evokes are so strong that sometimes people end up frothing too much at the mouth to form coherent sentences. This is not conducive to debate.

Until the 18th century, there were no wings, only kings. The principles of governance were simple. You obeyed the king, or he chopped off your head. If he was a bad king, he chopped off the heads of your family too, and in some cases, the rest of your village. If he was a good king, he settled for an arm or a leg. Even though kings were divine, and much greater than the rest of us, it was hard for them to do everything. So they surrounded themselves with a small group of well-armed and well-funded people. This became the aristocracy. They became rich and powerful because of their proximity to the ruler. As a result, life was very good for the king and his friends, but not so good for the rest of us.

The French are well-known troublemakers. They changed this. They had a novel thought. 'Why don't we cut off the king's head instead?' they thought. 'Maybe things will be better then.' This was called the French Revolution. It was this Revolution that gave us the term 'right wing'. Members of the French National Assembly in 1789, who supported the king, sat on the right. They supported the *ancien regime*, which is French for 'this is the hotel of my father'. Outside the Assembly, the French people were busy killing clergymen and burning the homes of the rich. The right wing hurriedly gave away as many of their privileges as they could. Soon after, the people burst in and hauled most of them off to the guillotine. From this, the right wing learnt, at the very moment of its birth, that giving things away is never a solution.

The next 100 years were full of action, as people in other countries thought, if it worked for the French, then why not us? The Russians rose repeatedly. The British were far more gradual. They did kill their king, but they brought back his son, and they let most of the aristocracy live. These aristocrats became the Tories, whose philosophy was best summed up by the Duke of Cambridge. 'There is a time for everything,' he said, 'And the time for reform is when it can no longer be resisted.' The French right wing continued to thrive, inspired by Edmund Burke, and represented by people like Joseph de Maistre, who thought the most important employee of the State was the executioner, the ultimate guarantor of order. Meanwhile, Ferdinand of Naples, another notable conservative, dressed up as a woman and had himself sculpted as Minerva, Goddess of Wisdom, by Canova. This shows that, even at this early stage, right wing politicians were willing to embrace diversity.

As usual, what used to be a simple matter was unnecessarily complicated by the Americans. In the early 19th century, Andrew Jackson, an angry man who massacred many Native Americans, invented producerism. Producerism rallied hard-working producers against evil parasites. The middle class, the honest farmer, and factory-owners were the producers. The poor, the bankers, and people who had immigrated more recently than them were the parasites. This is a rich and powerful tradition, which lives on in America. Even today, elements of the Tea Party attack big business for supporting immigration, which is an evil plot to get themselves cheap labour.

In fact, America was where economics was first introduced into the right wing thought process. At the turn of the 20th century, economic liberals and social conservatives joined hands, and the infernal brew that resulted was known as modern conservatism. They formed a union which has lasted for over a century, and has two guiding principles, 'Don't touch my money!' and 'Why aren't you reading the Bible?'

This thought process has been very influential, and today most countries have at least one party which hates gay people and loves bankers. But there are wide variations across societies and cultures. For example, in America, 'liberal' is a swear word. In the UK, it's a political party. In India, it's a girl of loose character, as in 'she is very liberal'. Most fundamentally, what differentiates the right wing from the left wing is their attitude towards change. The right wing believes nothing should change. The left wing believes everything should change until they can take charge.

How has it worked out in India? We see everything through the lens of secularism. Broadly, we have two types of people: people devoted to cows, and anti-national pseudo-sickular Porkistani sluts. I'm no expert, but it's probably not that simple. Why view everything through the lens of religion? A toilet has no religion, and neither does a roti. Many people in India need both. This doesn't mean that faith isn't important. Just that it's not all-important.

In India, like everywhere else, the right wing is a force of reaction. Reaction to one man, and his theories, economic and social. I'm not naming him because I'm not sure that's allowed here. Let's call him the Evil One. But maybe it's time to move on. Maybe we should just thank him that we're not Pakistan, and get on with our lives. Because there's more to life than secularism. It's a good thing we're remembering Rajaji again. His views on caste are a bit worrying, but he was also the man who coined the phrase 'License Permit Raj'. Instead of spending all our time cursing the Evil One and his socialism, maybe we can think about this.

Who issues the licenses? Who produces the permits? Under whose Raj do we live? Why are they answerable to no one, and immune from any form of prosecution, unless they give permission, which they rarely ever do, even if we ask nicely? Adam Smith talked about the Invisible Hand. Whose hand is it that we feel on our necks, governing everything, from where we can put our penises to what we can make money from, and how much? Whose hand builds the schools without toilets, and the hospitals without doctors, and the irrigation systems for wineries, while farmers save up money for poison? Whose hand takes away 85 paise out of every rupee that's supposed to reach the poor? Whose hand arrests the victims, and pats defense lawyers on the back, saying there, there, don't worry, the file will be misplaced shortly?

Whose hand steals the homes of war widows, and jeopardizes our international relations because of a nanny, and keeps our brave soldiers on glaciers, with same-size-fits-all boots and no oxygen, and the nearest medical facility hundreds of miles away? Whose hand signs the vouchers for millions of phantom cleaners, while the garbage piles up on our streets? Could it conceivably be a hand nourished on salaries that come out of our pockets? Are we actually paying them to do this to us?

Pappus will come and Fekus will go. Even AK49 will one day leave us wondering whether he was a CIA agent or a Maoist, or just a man in a muffler with delusions of grandeur. The Evil One will become a distant memory. Maybe it's time we stopped fighting each other, and saw who our real enemy is. Maybe we should pause, just for a while, in our battle on behalf of labour, or against it, and stop arguing about what our fiscal policy should be, and what exactly a Hindu Muslim is, and whether bikinis are good or evil. Maybe we should get together, as citizens, joined by a common cause, and push through new laws that will get that dead hand off our necks, once and for all. If some of those hands break stones in Tihar, so much the better.

That's when we'll really be free. That's when we'll have genuine *swarajya*.

Swarajya, 27 September 2014

WHY MODI'S US TRIP IS LIKE 'AMAR AKBAR ANTHONY'

America is very far away, and until the discovery of flight, we rarely met. Swami Vivekananda was one of the first, visiting by boat in 1893, which is one more reason to admire him. Mark Twain came in 1896, as part of a world tour he made to settle his debts. He collected around Rs 2,600 per night, doing shows at the Novelty Theatre in Bombay. He was sympathetic to India. So was President Roosevelt, who pushed hard for independence during World War II, but stopped when Churchill threatened to hold his breath.

Our prime ministers started visiting the US early on in our history. Nehru visited in 1949, leaving the women misty-eyed, but President Truman unimpressed. During a banquet at the White House, he and his Chief Justice mostly discussed whisky. It was during this visit that Indira Gandhi, accompanying her father, formed her first impression of America, and realised that her right profile was better than her left profile. The visit was a flop. Nehru was too proud to beg for aid, and too aristocratic to talk to businessmen, so he came back with nothing. No agreements were signed, and no business deals were made. M. N. Roy described his trip as an attempt to 'increase his popularity with the vocal middle class at home by appealing to nationalist conceit'. This was long ago, so things were very different.

The situation improved slightly in the sixties. The US provided over $2 billion worth of aid, double what the Russians gave. Nehru was too tired to talk to Kennedy, or flirt with his wife, during his visit in 1961. Kennedy forgave him, and sailed an aircraft carrier into the Bay of Bengal during the 1962 war. Had he not done so, people in Assam would probably be speaking Chinese today.

A BITCH AND A WITCH
Then Indira Gandhi visited in 1971. Nixon and she did not get on well.

She lectured him like a schoolboy. Nixon later referred to her as 'that goddam woman' and 'a bitch and a witch'. Being a diplomat, Kissinger only referred to her as a bitch. Shortly afterwards, the US declared full support for Pakistan in the Indo-Pak war, and sailed an aircraft carrier into the Bay of Bengal, this time to threaten us. We then became part of the Soviet bloc, thereby ensuring that we would have a lifelong supply of defective weapons.

The truth is, Indian prime ministers and American presidents have never gotten along. George W. Bush was the only exception. He loved Manmohan Singh without reservation. When you look at their pictures, you can see the love in his eyes. While it's hard to tell anything with MMS, in most of them, he looks mildly pleased. This upset Prakash Karat so much that he destroyed the CPI (M).

Why have our relations been so poor, even though we repeat the phrase 'natural allies' three to four times a week? It's because our PM selection was wrong. In early twentieth century America, religious conservatives and economic liberals joined hands and evolved modern conservatism, a strange cocktail of Bible bashing and profit stashing. This means that every US president since then has had to hug businessmen, pose with flags, and go to church every Sunday. Black or white, left or right, they have to follow these rules. A socialist or a Sikh has as much chance of being US president as Lady Gaga.

IT'S OUR OWN FAULT

Our own choices show no such consistency. We've had godless commies with English accents, like Nehru, and worshippers of foreign goddesses, like Manmohan Singh. Vajpayee rarely prayed, and spoke in mysterious couplets. Even an atheist like Jyoti Basu almost got a chance to turn India into West Bengal. There was a brief ray of hope in the '70s, when the US had Jimmy Carter, a peanut farmer, and we had Morarji Desai, a pee nut. But he banned Coca Cola, which was a terrible mistake. Coca Cola had him replaced by Indira Gandhi soon after.

Now, finally, with Modi, we've got it right. He's the perfect candidate for success in America. Like Nixon, he keeps tabs on everyone. Like

Reagan, he's a Great Communicator. Like Clinton, he plays musical instruments. Most crucially, he supports business, but he also fasts for Navratra. Americans understand this mixture better than they ever understood Hindi poets, urine therapists, and scary women with Soviet friends. America and India are now like *Amar Akbar Anthony* without Akbar. We are brothers separated at birth, finally reuniting. Much love will be in the air.

Poor Akbar may be a little worried, but just like the movie, which you must see if you haven't, I believe that everything will work out fine in the end.

Scroll.in, 28 September 2014

HOW THE SEDITION LAW MAKES INDIA A MORE LOVING NATION

Throughout history, rulers across the world have faced a fundamental problem. Their citizens do not love them enough. The sedition law is a powerful tool against this menace. Most recently, it was used against a gentleman from Kerala, who faces the possibility of life imprisonment for not standing up during the national anthem. The police are currently investigating his disloyalty.

The British like ruling people, so they were the first to think of this law, in 1648. Early offenders had their ears cut off, but, as society evolved, this was modified to life imprisonment. This law was the backbone of the British Empire. As the empire dwindled, so did its use. The last time people were charged with sedition in the United Kingdom was in 1972. Predictably, they were Irish. After this, a process was started to repeal it. Once the British were absolutely sure there was no further chance of empire, they did so, in 2010.

Most Commonwealth countries no longer use this law, except in the specific case of kidnapping or assaulting the queen. Malaysia is a notable exception. There the government arrests people for sedition quite often. The United Nations Humans Right Commission has protested. In reply, the Malaysian foreign minister has said that 'the mould of Malaysia is different'. The United States has a very active sedition law. People are picked up for it frequently, making America the land of the brave and the somewhat free.

A QUESTION OF LOYALTY

How loyal have we been in India? Until 1857 things were fine. In 1857, there was a lot of disloyalty. As a result, the period between 1860 and 1870 witnessed hectic activity on the legal front. The Indian Penal Code was put together in 1861. It was designed to ensure the suppression of natives. But the British felt that something was missing. Hence, in

1870, they introduced Section 124A.

Section 124A, popularly known as the sedition law, makes it a crime to 'promote, through word or deed, disaffection against the government'. This law legislates affection. It means that if you do not love the government, you could go to jail. In the nineteenth century, the British made a lot of rules about love, because Queen Victoria was against it. For example, Section 377 tells you where you can or cannot put your penis. It regulates this activity, not in public, where children could be watching, but in the privacy of your own home. It enables policemen to pick you up, at any time of day and night, and ask you about your sex life. Sometimes they take pictures.

Initially, Section 124A was used against newspapers who were not loving the government sufficiently. Subsequently it was used against Bal Gangadhar Tilak and Mohanlal Gandhi. Tilak was found guilty in 1916, despite a strong defense by Mohammad Ali Jinnah. During the trial, Jinnah asked a question which has puzzled many. What is this 'disaffection', he asked. 'Absence of affection,' the judge said promptly. Gandhi was arrested a few years later. His opinion on sedition was very clear. He called it 'the prince among the political sections of the Indian Penal code designed to suppress the liberty of the citizen'.

What happened after we gained freedom? Since Gandhi had such a high opinion of it, we decided to keep Section 124A, along with the rest of the Indian Penal Code. Soon after, the Indian Penal Code faced a strong challenge from a new document called the Constitution. As early as 1949, judges across the nation had started hampering the government, using Fundamental Rights as an excuse. At which point, enter Jawaharlal Nehru, stage left.

MAGAZINE BANS

Jawaharlal Nehru was the architect of modern India. Yet there were many who did not love him enough. One of them was a left-wing magazine called *Cross Roads*, which was banned for criticising him. The Madras High Court overturned this. It ruled that the rights given to citizens through article 19(1)(a) of the Constitution could only be suspended when there was a clear danger to security. One of these rights was the freedom of speech. Soon after, an attempt to censor the Rashtriya Swayamsevak Sangh mouthpiece, *The Organiser*, was also overturned. In both these cases, the courts took the revolutionary view that loving the government was not compulsory.

This left Nehru in an awkward position. He wanted to suppress left-wing opinion. The judges said no. He wanted to suppress right wing opinion, the judges said no. It was as if he was not allowed to suppress anything. 'Where is the love?' he demanded of the bureaucrats, 'And why are we not enforcing it?' 'What can we do?' said the babus, 'The Constitution is blocking the governance.' Nehru then repaired the Constitution, in 1951, through the First Amendment. Post this amendment; the Constitution continues to guarantee every citizen a wide variety of fundamental rights, unless the government thinks that 'public order' is in jeopardy. It does not specify what 'public order' is, or how it can be jeopardised. Constables and magistrates decide this, with the help of local bigwigs.

Despite this clear guideline, judges have continued to create difficulties. In the 1950s, the Punjab and the Allahabad High courts ruled that Section 124A was rendered void by the Constitution. Luckily, the Supreme Court stepped in. In 1962, in the Kedar Nath Case, it upheld Section 124A. But it also diluted it. It ruled that it could be applied only in cases where 'incitement to violence' was involved. This was a big setback for love.

UPHOLDING TRADITION

Fortunately, our lower courts and local officials have not been misled. They have chosen to stick to old traditions. It also helps that most of our legal system is yet to discover computers. As a result, messages take time to reach the grassroots. Constables and magistrates have continued to fight for love. People have been picked up for a wide variety of crimes, including singing, reciting poetry, cheering for the Pakistan cricket team, not standing up for the national anthem, possessing paint brushes, and resembling a Maoist. It's true that the accused are always freed once they reach the Supreme Court. But by that time, they are much, much older. Knowing this, most citizens continue to love their government, as per the law.

Unfortunately, the march of progress cannot be stopped, although this is no excuse for not trying. The government has recently announced that they will be repealing many old laws, including the Oudh Taluqdars Relief Act, 1870, and the Indian Treasure Trove Act, 1878. Does this mean that the sedition law is in peril? Prime Minister Modi is a cause for concern. Currently, he is feeling a lot of love. As a result, he may not see the need to enforce it legally. Therein lies the danger.

On the other hand, if the government respects our traditions, and retains the sedition law, we can heave a sigh of relief, knowing that love of government, an idea essential to stable governance, will remain enshrined in our hearts forever.

Scroll.in, 16 October 2014

AN ARDENT PLEA TO A PUBLISHER TO CONSIDER AN ORIGINAL SERIES ON YOUTHFUL LOVE IN INDIA

Re: Proposal for Romance Novel Series

Dear Sir,

I have read many of the books published by your esteemed publishing house, and I have enjoyed all of them. I must compliment you for quality of selection. Today, I am presenting you a proposal through which nation will also benefit, and revenue will also increase.

Due to persecution of Valentine Day and increasing restriction on clothing, romance in India is suffering. As it is, our supply is very limited. Many young men are not getting any romance. As a result they are frustrated. They are feeling jealousy. Misguided by political leaders, they are assaulting those who are kissing, and protesting against coupling in parks. Consequently, the supply of romance is reducing even more, thus further reducing the chances of the frustrated young men for finding love. This is not logical. If they are suffering from lack of romance, should they not be encouraging it? If romance flowers across nation, will their chances also not increase?

We must not be impatient with young people. Sometimes they carry weapons, and law and order situation is bad. Instead, we should try to improve society. We can achieve this by spreading a culture of romance. Therefore I am suggesting a romantic novel series, which is in the national interest, and also will entertain the youth. Chetan Bhagat cannot write everything, as he is only one person. In addition to novels, he has to provide advice and guidance to youth through national newspapers, as also twittering. It is not fair to put all the burden on him. Others must also contribute.

Therefore I am proposing a romance series. I have carefully studied this field. Most romance writers in foreign countries are ladies, but here big ones are gents. They are young and slightly plump. I am also young and slightly plump. They have had bad experiences in the past involving death and rejection. I have come close to death on many occasions, and suffered a lot of rejection. This makes me a very suitable candidate.

Now coming to other technicalities. My study has revealed that successful romance novels summarize the plot in the title. In this way, public clearly knows what it is purchasing. First book in my series will be called *My Love Ran Away*^{TM}, in which the girl I love will run away.

In the first part of the book, I fall in love. In the second part of the book, she runs away. This is not because of body odour, or any crude statement made by me, but because of Destiny.

We are both students in a management institute, giving the story a contemporary feeling. She is rich girl. I am poor boy. She has bodyguards with guns.

Early on in first volume, I stalk her in a romantic and playful way, sometimes pulling her dupatta, and at other times kissing her from the back side, until subsequently, I am beaten up by her bodyguards, who are large men from interior of Bihar. She is quite used to this, but there is something in the way I am beaten up that touches her heart. Unable to help herself, she comes to nursing home.

Despite dizziness due to medication, on the spot, I compose a poem for her. She falls in love with me. In this way, we promote, not just romance, but also poetry. Subsequently, there is humour section, where we as a young couple use many tips and tricks to avoid her guards and do romance. I am not sure how much doing there should be. Kindly provide guidance. If you like, I will add more masala.

Other characters will also be there, such as one sympathetic professor of marketing, and one CBI agent. CBI agent is mysterious, and his reasons for investigation are never revealed. In this way, we maintain suspense for volume two. Volume one ends when, mysteriously, with no explanation, she runs away, and my heart is broken.

Volume two will be called *My Love Came Back*^{TM}, in which she returns. At this time, I am working for Pepsi^{TM}. Only now do we realise that she had earlier run away because her father is mafia don from Dhanbad, who will brutally kill any person who spoils her daughter. Hence she was trying to protect me.

Situation is very unique. Because she loves me, she cannot love me. In the movie version, girl could be Sonakshi Sinha, and father could be Shatrughan, mixing reality and fiction in a unique and memorable way. But despite risk to my life, she cannot resist me, particularly after I handle Ranbir Kapoor very tactfully during shooting of Pepsi™ TV commercial.

Rest of book is full of light humour and hot romance, until the news is received that khap panchayat has given adverse ruling, and girl's father is coming to Delhi with shotgun. Book ends on note of suspense. Faced with this danger, what will we do?

Third book is called, *My Love Ran Away....Again!*™ In this volume, once more she runs away, but because I love her, I do not get irritated. Plus, I am getting used to it. Instead I try to find solution.

Her father comes, and initially I am tied to chair and beaten severely, although some of the bodyguards are saddened by this, because by now they are my friends. Unfortunately for them, it's a question of duty.

Nevertheless, I apply my mind and I am able to convince father, using my intelligence. I point out that his daughter has run away, and at this point in time, unknown third parties could be getting fresh with her. Is it not better, I point out, that known third party such as myself should indulge in such activities?

Inside, the don is actually a very warm-hearted person, and he is convinced by this. We become very close, and decide that together we will search for this girl, whom we both love in a very obsessive and intimate way, and who has mysteriously run away, giving no reason or explanation.

The fourth book in the series will be called *Has Anyone Seen My Love?*™ in which story will come to conclusion, with many heart-touching scenes and small amount of sex and violence. Amount can vary, depending on your requirement.

This can be a highly original and successful series, contrasting the rich and the poor, the truth and the fiction, and the bold and the beautiful. In addition, it will feature popular elements such as management institutes, Pepsi™, and Shatrughan Sinha.

Success is practically guaranteed. All I require is huge advance money, so that I feel happy and inspired before writing. The nation will also benefit. We will be fighting the enemies of romance, and ensuring the victory of love. Because at the end of the day, without love, who are we?

I am sure my proposal will see a positive response. Please let me know who to send my bank details, in order for you to do the needful.

Yours Affectionately,

Shovon Chowdhury

Scroll.in, 21 December 2014

WE NEED MORE TRANSPARENCY IN CORRUPTION

The other day I was watching some corruption on TV and I was completely confused. According to a piece of paper in Arnab Goswami's hand, something was rotten in the state of Himachal. M. J. Akbar spoke at length about apples. #applegate kept flashing on the screen. Details flew thick and fast. It was hard to keep track. Did cash turn into cheques, or were cheques turned into cash? Who gave an unsecured loan to whom? And where did all the apples go?

Without resolving these issues, the channel then moved on to the Vyapam scam, where many statistics were quoted. What bothered me was the lack of precision. Were medical seats going for Rs 15 lakhs or Rs 50 lakhs? Was it 40 dead, or 22? When they were selling government posts, did they include the police or not? All these things are essential to the math, and without math, there is no proper understanding. Nevertheless, everyone else was angry, so I started getting angry too. But how angry was I supposed to be, vis-à-vis the earlier exposé?

To make matters worse, soon after this they switched to Goa, where a former chief minister was being accused of stealing Rs 1 crore, while his minister allegedly took Rs 70 lakhs. They were looking pretty sheepish and I don't blame them. Who gets fingered for 70 lakhs? Are we supposed to get mad about this? I was confused. I had no guidelines. That's when it struck me. Our perspective on this is flawed. What we need is a more analytical approach.

THE NEED FOR STANDARDS
The problem with corruption is, we have no standards. Even earthquakes have standards. When we register 7.0 on the Richter scale, we feel a modest sense of pride. Our approach requires more professionalism. It's why the Japanese are so far ahead. What we want are solid numbers, preferably audited by CAG. We want balance sheets, and profit and loss statements, and net asset values. We need facts that we can trust. Wipro

and Infosys are compared this way. Why should scams be different? Proper quantitative tools lead to better understanding.

The Goa case provides an illustration. The sums of money were small, but then, so is the state. Logically speaking, we should factor in population. Hence one useful measure of scams would be a Scam Outlay Per Capita or SOPC Index. Let us apply this to Goa. Goa has a population of 14.6 lakhs. Dividing rupees in crores by people in crores, a scam involving Rs 1.7 crores yields an SOPC Index of 11.6. Now, look at Madhya Pradesh. MP has a population of 7.27 crores. A scam of Rs 40,000 crores gives us an SOPC Index of 5502. This means that compared to Goa, we should be 500 times more upset about MP.

Next, let us take the Spectrum scam. Assume it was worth Rs 120,000 crores. Dividing this by the population of India in crores, we arrive at an SOPC Index of 991.7. According to this calculation, we should be approximately 90 times more upset about this than we would be about Goa. Individual state-wise scams can also be added up to help us arrive at a state-wise ranking. This could be an annual event, with sponsors.

NUMBERS, NUMBERS, NUMBERS

There are other ways to use the power of math. Swiss banks often feature in discussions on corruption. Why just discuss them, when we can apply the power of math? *The Economist* has a Big Mac Index. For corruption, we could have a Swiss Franc Index, which answers the question, how many Swiss Francs could I buy today with this sum? This would take care of both inflation and currency fluctuation in an elegant and mathematically precise way.

We also need to distinguish between Recurring Value scams and Fixed Value scams. A fixed value scam is a one-time transaction, as in 'I like your face. Keep a bunch of spectrum.' These are rare and happy occasions. A recurring value scam flows like a mighty river. Take the case of Madhya Pradesh. It's safe to assume that the battle to provide better medical services in MP will continue, especially since most of the whistleblowers are dead, and our brand new Whistleblower Act makes it highly inadvisable to complain against a government officer. This means that this scam has recurring value. It also means that it's best to avoid medical emergencies in Madhya Pradesh.

Once such tools have been developed, and vetted by CAG, corruption will become much more transparent. We will be able to measure the relative value of scams, and adjust our response accordingly. There is no doubt that this is an area, which needs further exploration. It's virgin territory. For a trained economist, there could even be a Nobel Prize in it. All I ask is that they acknowledge me during their acceptance speech.

Scroll.in, 5 October 2015

OBITUARY FOR INDIAN NATIONAL CONGRESS (1885–2016): 'DEATH WAS SLOW IN COMING'

On the afternoon of May 19, 2016, the Indian National Congress, sole surviving issue of Allan Octavian Hume and Dadabhai Naoroji, passed away peacefully, in its sleep, at the age of 131.

Death was slow in coming. After an extended period of illness, injuries inflicted by Rahul Gandhi, son of the current owner, proved to be fatal.

Born in 1885, the Indian National Congress was designed to be irrelevant. After over one hundred years of involuntary fund transfer to Britain, the natives were restless. The Raj was in peril. Sensing the danger, British civil servant Allan Octavian Hume created the Indian National Congress, whose task was to mumble inarticulately. This it did until 1920, when it was acquired by M. K. Gandhi. Historians refer to this as the pre-imperial phase of the Congress.

PROPRIETARY CONCERN

Ignoring the will of the founding fathers, M. K. Gandhi connected the Indian National Congress to the masses. As a result, India became independent in 1947. In 1948, the Congress was acquired by J. L. Nehru, at which point it became a proprietary concern. He did not dissolve the Congress, as suggested by Gandhi, as it was required for future elections, focusing instead on transfer of power.

The handover process was smooth. As a party founded by a civil servant, the Indian National Congress supported the British Raj. Its only objection was that it was run by the British. Once an Indian head was installed, tranquillity was restored. The system of involuntary fund transfer from the population to the Raj resumed. Over time, it grew and flourished. The party prospered.

In the following decades, the Indian National Congress witnessed several changes in management. During the tenure of Indira, daughter of JL, all her opponents were removed.

Meanwhile, poor people had begun to notice that they were still very poor. As a result, once more, the natives were restless. In response to this, under the leadership of Indira, the Congress declared war on poverty—24 years after coming to power. From this point onwards, it mentioned poverty more frequently.

THE LAST STRAW

An attribute that always distinguished the Congress was its love for children. The party believed that the children are our future, and that they should be cherished. Initially implemented at the central level, recent years saw the application of this principle at the state level. Fearing its extension to the district, block and panchayat levels, many Congress workers, unwilling to support the children of others, chose to leave the party instead.

Meanwhile, despite strong endorsements from the comedy community, youth leader Rahul Gandhi was unable to inspire the youth. In the battlefield of ideas, too, the Congress was unable to compete. The Congress ideologies of 'Would you like some spectrum?' and 'Please help my son, Rahul', were thoroughly defeated by the opposing ideologies of 'Development!' and 'Yes! Hindu!'

Towards the end, many Congress leaders sensed impending doom. They supplied Rahul Gandhi with travel brochures, highlighting the benefits of various holiday destinations, such as Switzerland ('Chocolate!') and Mount Kilimanjaro ('Provides a clear view of Jupiter'), but these efforts were in vain.

A small but tasteful memorial service will be held for the Indian National Congress on Sunday, May 22. All attendees will receive a small bag of money, plus the chance to win great prizes, such as coal mines, pizza, and autographed volumes of the poetry of Kapil Sibal.

Scroll.in, 22 May 2016

NOBODY IS ON THE RAMPAGE IN INDIA AND IT'S HIGH TIME HE IS BROUGHT TO JUSTICE

Ever since Independence, a menace has stalked the land, and his name is Nobody. We know he's a he because thousands of crimes are committed against women every month, and after due investigation, the culprit is usually Nobody. This would suggest that Nobody is a man. Throughout history, Nobody, like the Phantom, has been in many places at once. In 1984, he was all over Delhi, and single handedly massacred thousands of Sikhs. In Gujarat, in 2002, he was not alone. Around 40 other people were convicted. But even if they killed around 10 people each, this would add up to 400 or 500. The rest were victims of Nobody.

The Congress regime was a circus of scams. Mind-boggling figures were bandied about. Names were taken in vain. Now, after three years of a change in regime, we've found the culprit. It was Nobody, once again.

In the area of governance, which costs more every year, Nobody is extremely active. When buildings collapse, killing dozens, Nobody is to blame. When little children fall down wells, and potholes kill bikers, it's Nobody's fault. When money meant for irrigation vanishes without a trace, Nobody knows where it went. When children die without oxygen in hospitals, or learn nothing in school, Nobody is responsible. During the recent floods in Chennai, Nobody opened the floodgates. When a foot overbridge collapsed in Mumbai, Nobody was to blame.

NOBODY'S FAULT

Nobody has a close relationship with the police. He travels from thana to thana. Whenever people die in their custody, Nobody is responsible. When they refuse to register crimes, Nobody is at fault. Nobody is responsible when cases drag on for years. When the CBI falsifies evidence, Nobody deserves to be punished.

Nobody also causes destruction on a scale seldom seen before.

During the recent Jat agitation in Haryana, he caused over Rs 20,000 crores worth of damage.

Nobody is deep into finance and farming. Nobody knows how the money reached Panama. When farmers commit suicide, it's Nobody's fault. When food grains rot, it's Nobody's doing.

Nobody is only human. He has his likes and dislikes. Nobody hates writers and journalists. Nobody fired three bullets into Gauri Lankesh. Nobody shot Kalburgi in the head and the chest. Nobody killed Pansare. Nobody killed Dabholkar. Shantanu Bhaumik from Tripura was stabbed to death. He was a young boy trying to cover the news. Nobody killed him. He was covered in blood.

As the years go by, Nobody is becoming bolder. Whenever criminals go scot free, they expand the scope of their work. Nobody is no exception. Nowadays, Nobody is acquiring a taste for Muslims. Nobody killed Pehlu Khan. Nobody killed Mohammed Akhlaq. Who knows which profession or community Nobody will dislike next? The rest of us are naturally anxious. His activities are expanding at an alarming rate. The forces of law and order need to look into this urgently, and ensure that Nobody is brought to justice. Once they apply their minds, we can rest assured that they will do the needful, and Nobody will pay the price.

Scroll.in, 23 October 2017

THE 4-MINUTE MANAGER™

Having received the best management education that India had to offer and spent a quarter of a century in advertising and marketing, Shovon decided that as an upright citizen, he needed to do his bit for the nation and give something back to the children, nephews, nieces, and cousins of the taxpayers who had heavily subsidized his two years on a sylvan campus on the outskirts of Kolkata. And what better way than to reveal the secrets that the business schools keep hidden from their students, to make dry marketing theories come alive through examples ranging from Narendra Modi to Chetan Bhagat, and distill 456-page management tomes down to 117 words?

The 4-Minute Manager™ lessons, along with their open-book student tests, were an effort to make management gurus out of even those unfortunates who believe that a 'market' is just a collection of shops.

THE 4-MINUTE MANAGER™

'There is no try, only do.'

—*Yoda*

I have spent twenty-five years as an advertising and marketing professional. Over the years, I have moulded many minds. Recently it occurred to me that if I do this on the internet, I can mould many more minds at the same time. Also it was time to start giving back to society.

Thus was born THE 4-MINUTE MANAGER™.

OUR PHILOSOPHY

Our philosophy is that everyone has the capacity to win, including chickens. There is no reason why they should be left behind. Sometimes the thorns can be painful, but eventually the diamond in you will shine. If you dare to dream, no one can ever drink your chicken soup.

OUR MOTTO

0% effort. 0% money. 100% success.

CUSTOMER ORIENTATION

This management course was itself designed using management principles. Extensive consumer research was conducted amongst existing consumers of management courses, in order to identify lacunae, shortcomings, or gaps, which will be plugged by us, thereby creating a superior product.

These were some of the issues thrown up by the respondents:

1. Could we have more case studies about real people, like Priyanka Chopra?
2. Also some more pictures?
3. Strictly speaking, are exams necessary?
4. Can we do the course after we get the job?

5. Can we avoid paying any money for it?
6. Could the course be done in a charming and cheerful way, so that we learn many things while also enjoying? Preferably on the sofa?
7. Can some experienced professional tell us little stories about real-life experiences, introducing us to the different types of characters we will meet in our corporate career? Preferably he should wear spectacles.
8. Can we have more jargon?
9. What are the Dos and Don'ts of sexual harassment?
10. Could the course kindly provide summaries of popular management bestsellers, such as *Who Moved My Cheese?* and its sequel 'Touch My Cheese and You Die, Bitch!'

Thanks to a special software purchased in Noida, a huge staff of qualified people at THE 4-MINUTE MANAGER™ have been able to specifically design this course to fulfil all the above requirements, except point number 1. Mr Abhinandan Sekri has assumed responsibility for this, and is currently involved in negotiations. Any day now there should be a breakthrough.

FLEXI-COURSE APPROACH

In business, as in yoga, flexibility is critical. Recognising this, we at THE 4-MINUTE MANAGER™ have adopted the Flexi-Course Approach.

Our course consists of Core Elements and Flexi Elements. Core Elements will be fixed elements of the course, covering traditional areas of management such as Working Capital Management, Marketing Management, Operations Management, Boss Management, Minor Fraud Management and Strategic Sabotage. Subjects will be brought alive through heartwarming true stories and, in some cases, simple physical games that usually cause no injuries.

The Flexi Elements will reflect ongoing events in the world of business. We will analyse trends and identify hot-button issues. We will also be ~~making up~~ focusing on revolutionary new thought processes in the field of management. This will ensure that even in the case of a paradigm shift, you will continue to leverage synergies. It's what highly effective people do.

LOCALISED CONTENT

At THE 4-MINUTE MANAGER™, we are proud Indians. Hence most management principles will be illustrated through case studies using familiar faces, such as Vijay Mallya and Asaram Bapu, and familiar products—such as wine made by Pune people.

MYTHOLOGICAL CONTENT

In recent years, some people have been unnecessarily dragging beloved epics such as the Ramayana and the Mahabharata into the field of management studies. We plan to continue this grand tradition. In case your sentiments are hurt at any point, kindly do let us know. We will immediately take steps to ensure that the sentiments of other communities are hurt also. In this way, balance will be maintained. In management parlance, this is known as the Circle of Life.

PSYCHOLOGICAL CONTENT

Psychological warfare is an essential ingredient of management success. It is important to thoroughly understand your enemies, many of whom will be working with you. At the beginning of your career, most of them will be older than you, giving them an unfair advantage. A proper understanding of their psychology will equip you for the battles ahead.

ELIGIBILITY CRITERIA

All readers of *Newslaundry* will be eligible, along with all gazetted officers of the rank of under-secretary and above.

GRADUATION

Students will be allowed to graduate as soon as they feel sufficiently managerial. At THE 4-MINUTE MANAGER™, we do not believe in pressurising students, which is why there will be no examinations. However, marks will be awarded on graduation. These marks will be based on an index, factoring in the number of comments made by the individual, as well as a completely arbitrary assessment of the quality of comments. Marks once assigned will not be subject to review, unless VIPs are involved.

Students who donate money to *Newslaundry* will graduate instantly.

One lucky donor each month will win a jewellery voucher from D'damas for an unspecified amount, along with an autographed picture of Sonakshi Sinha.

YOUR CAMPUS

Based in the sunny environment of your living room, this course provides you all the comforts of home, in addition to a wide variety of student facilities. (See 'Student Facilities')

STUDENT FACILITIES

At THE 4-MINUTE MANAGER™, we do not have a building. But luckily you do. We provide a wide variety of in-home facilities to regular students, including foot massages and pizza delivery. Members of the *Newslaundry* team will be providing these facilities as and when required. A list of these facilities will be uploaded shortly.

In case you have ideas for other ways in which we can make your period of study more comfortable, please send us an e-mail. Remember to use 'We want further facilities' in the title.

SURVEY

At THE 4-MINUTE MANAGER™, we are always interested in your feedback. Here is the first in a series of questions designed to help us know you better.

How long would you like this course to continue?
a) 6 weeks
b) 6 months
c) 6 years
d) Until retirement
e) Stop now or I'll shoot you!

Newslaundry, 16 January 2014

BLANKET MARKETING

FUNDAMENTALS OF MARKET SEGMENTATION: I
(There has been some criticism that this course is not 'entertaining' enough. Please note that the purpose of this course is education, although small amounts of low quality entertainment may also be there. In order to benefit, you must learn, absorb, imbibe, and respond. Why should this be so difficult? Look at Rahul Gandhi. Even at his age, he is studying. Surely you are capable of doing something Rahul Gandhi can do? You cannot become a Management Guru™ just like that. It requires effort from your side. Whatever you give to the course, the course will give to you. In case you are not completely satisfied, Newslaundry will re-fund every paisa of your fee.)

WHY IS MARKET SEGMENTATION IMPORTANT?
If you use the term 'market segmentation' in any conversation, people get very impressed. This is because it combines two very powerful words in a unique way. A 'market' is a place where customers come and give away money, in the hope of getting something in return. Most companies are very interested in markets, except for the ones that make gas. They are more interested in ministers. 'Segmentation' is a very big word which not many people clearly understand. It helps if you make a sharp chopping gesture with your hand when you utter the word 'segmentation'. This makes you look confident, and also hints that you may know karate. People disagree less with people who know karate.

The next step is understanding what 'market segmentation' means.

WHAT IS A MARKET?
To you and me, a market is simply a collection of shops. This is lower class thinking. To more evolved people, a market is a theoretical construct. The market for a product is the sum total of all the people who are going to buy it. For example, the market for blankets would be the sum total of all those who want or need a blanket. Where these people live

is irrelevant. What they do with the blankets is also irrelevant. Some could be in bed. Some could be in front of Rail Bhavan. This does not concern us. What concerns us is that they need blankets. In this thrilling episode of The 4-Minute Manager™, we will be using blankets to understand market segmentation better. Later we will be using Indian English fiction.

WHAT IS SEGMENTATION?
Segmentation is the key to marketing success. Remember this sentence. If you repeat this enough, you too could become a Marketing Guru™. Whatever guidance you may be providing, if you say 'Segmentation is the key to marketing success' in the beginning, you will get more money.

Segmentation involves chopping and slicing, but in a non-lethal way. By slicing the market in different ways, you can understand the market better. In order to do this, you must decide what the key drivers of the market are.

For example, in the blanket market, you could decide that 'style' and 'comfort' are the two main factors. This will enable you to put the market players in a map, which will help you in market analysis. At the very least, it will teach you how to draw a map. However, if you introduce a new parameter into the blanket market, such as 'scaring policemen', the whole picture can become different. New opportunities arise. New customers emerge. New marketing techniques may be required.

Let us understand this better through a case study.

CASE STUDY I: PEEPWELL INDUSTRIES
Blankets have traditionally been a seasonal product, used only in winter. Many customers use the same blanket for years, leading to low re-purchase. Because of the lower potential for making money, blanket manufacturers are usually depressed, and make little effort to promote their products. Some of them actively hate their customers, and make their blankets rough so that they cannot sleep easily. All this, along with global warming, has made the blanket market very unattractive.

But lately, there have been dramatic developments in this market.

One Mr K, who is also Chief Minister of Delhi, has spent two nights in front of Rail Bhavan, wrapped in a blanket. Many policemen tried to remove him and his blanket, but he refused. As a result, the blanket has received widespread publicity on Facebook, Twitter and national television, where it has been repeatedly abused by Arnab.

You are the eldest son of Lala Maal Pakar, patriarch of Peepwell Industries, an old and reputed blanket manufacturer. In fact, the company is so old that very few people remember its name. Your father expects you to now take over the company, as he wishes to retire to Scotland, in order to be closer to whiskey. He also wants you to marry the daughter of KP Jewellers, as he sees more of a future in jewellery. Plus it ensures that the bride's jewellery will be genuine. You, on the other hand, want to marry Abhisarika, a girl who makes candles, because your gratitude when she agreed to do it with you is something you simply cannot forget. Unfortunately, her father's business is too small to justify a merger between you and her.

If you take up the challenge, and demonstrate success at Peepwell, your father may allow you to marry Abhisharika. Now that blankets are part of the national ethos again, this could be your big opportunity.

How will this event change the blanket market? What new market segments could emerge? What is the significance of the floral pattern on the Chief Minister's blanket? Is this the beginning of a bold new India, where gender stereotypes are a thing of the past?

Can you re-define the market in such a way that Peepwell gains huge market share and becomes an iconic Indian brand?

The best answers will find special mention in the next lesson of The 4-Minute Manager™.

HOW TO BECOME A MANAGEMENT GURU

FUNDAMENTALS OF MARKET SEGMENTATION: II
Now that you know the basics of Market Segmentation, let us learn how to use tools. The first tool created by mankind looked like this.

It was known as the stick. After a brief amount of practice, mankind found that it could use this to bash animals, and, when necessary, each other. Archival footage of this discovery can be viewed.

In the cow belt, this is still the primary tool used by mankind, leading to the popular saying, 'Who has the stick, he has the buffalo'. Policemen in India also continue to use this as their primary tool, partly because their revolvers don't work and partly because it helps them to round up buffaloes.

The next quantum leap in tool-making happened a few thousand years later, when a management professor thought, why use one stick when we can use two? He created a tool which looks like this.

He called the vertical stick the Y-axis, and the horizontal stick the X-axis. In this way, he created a richer and far more complex tool called the Market Segmentation Map. This is the beauty of management. We managers take simple tools and convert them into something people have to pay money for. Sometimes, merely mentioning the Market Segmention Map is enough—but it helps if you know how to use it. The Map enables us to do something called Market Modeling, which is a more robust and enduring source of income than ordinary modeling, where even a pimple can lead to losses.

What is the purpose of a Market Segmentation Map? The purpose is to understand markets better. Markets are very complex. Sometimes, like Rahul Gandhi, they are hard to understand. We can simplify this complexity by asking ourselves, what are the two key factors that drive this market? Once we decide what they are, we can use one as the X-axis and the other as the Y-axis.

Now all you have to do is place the major players in the map, and voila! You have a market segmentation map. Voila is a French word meaning '*dekho kya kamaal ki cheez hai*' or 'come see the beauty'. It is not essential to use French in management, but nowadays so many people have learnt English that this is no longer an advantage, unless you can speak it with an accent like Montek Singh Ahluwahlia. I once heard him on television from an adjacent room and thought he was Queen Elizabeth.

Let us use an example to understand how this works.

Consider the Vote Market. In the Vote Market, various politicians are positioning themselves in various ways in order to get your vote. Traditionally, the key factor in politics has been the wing. Some politicians are right-wing, while others are left-wing. They often fight to prove their leftness or rightness. For example, Communists are very mad at the Aam Aadmi Party for trying to occupy their space, which is why they have accused them of everything except child molestation. The case on the right is very similar. This constant battle on one narrow axis limits the scope for new entrants in the market.

But suppose we introduce a second factor? Traditionally, appearance has been an asset for politicians. In the US, the handsomeness of John F. Kennedy was a plus point for him. Even today, this principle would apply, and many fear that Priyanka Gandhi could get a lot of votes because look at her complexion, no? In order to level the playing field, let us look at overall appearance, not just God-given looks. This makes clothing very critical.

A market defined on this basis would look like this.

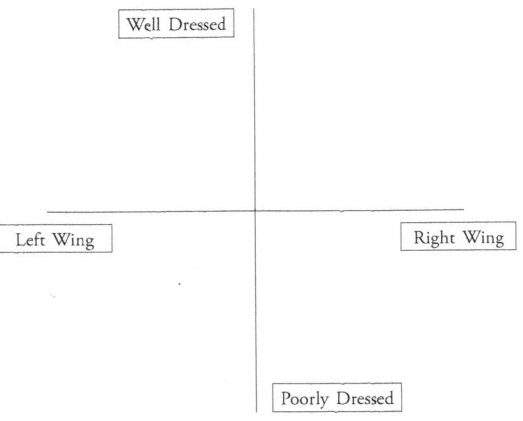

Now let us place some of the existing players on this map.

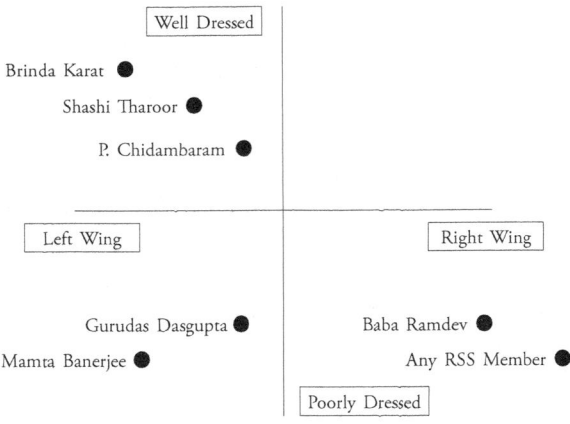

Voila! (Do you remember what this means?) Immediately you have a much clearer picture of this market. It also indicates what different brands can do to change their brand positioning. For example, Mamata Banerjee could dress better, and move up towards Brinda Karat. She would then get invited to more parties.

For a new brand, or an old brand that wants to re-position itself, this map also indicates gaps that could be occupied, like this one.

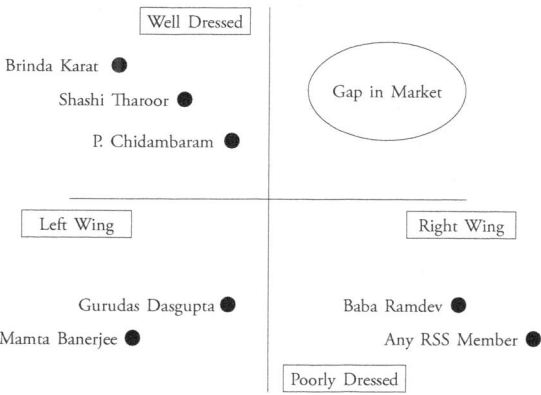

One man has seen this opportunity and moved swiftly to occupy it. Seeing that the other segments were crowded, he has defined a niche of his own for himself.

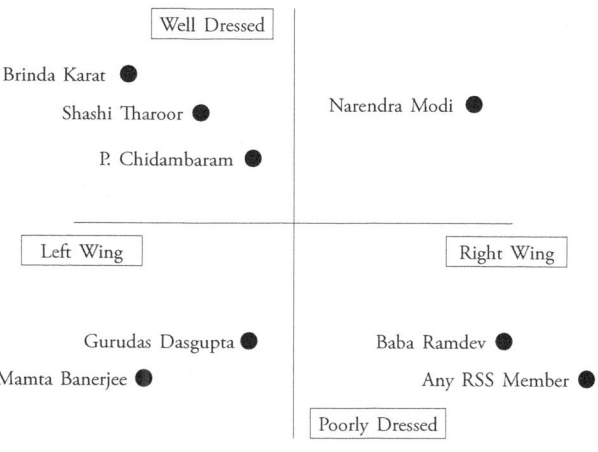

Columns

This is an example of successful use of market segmentation. As you can see, Mr Modi is unchallenged. His only potential challenger is Mr Chidambaran, who is gradually shifting right, but someone is constantly tugging on his *veshti* pulling him back.

Let us look at another case, which is of Indian novels written in English. Since you are reading this, you must know English. Since you know English, at some point you must have thought, if an idiot like XYZ can be a novelist, then I can be one too. This is quite true, but application of the Market Segmentation Model can help make your effort more successful.

We can define the X-axis and Y-axis for this market in many different ways, but here is one way to do it.

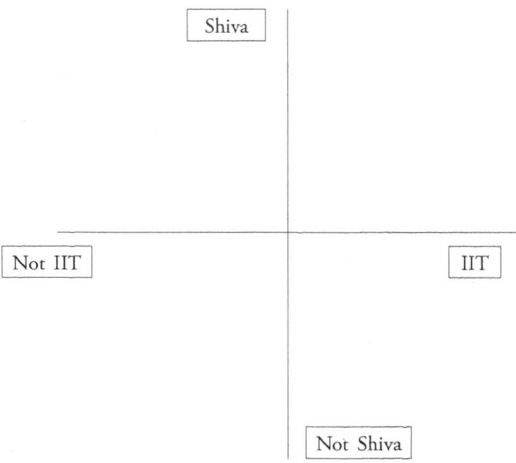

Current English novels in India occupy two broad areas on this map.

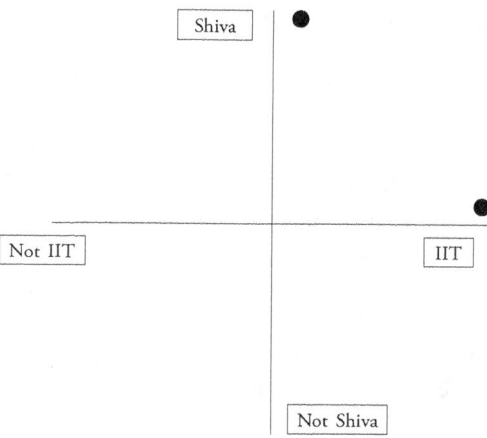

Authors are gaining great success, and they will continue to do so. As the crowd increases, however, it is becoming harder. But because we are management experts and know how to use advanced tools, we can easily see a way out of this trap, which will combine successful techniques used by others in a scientific way.

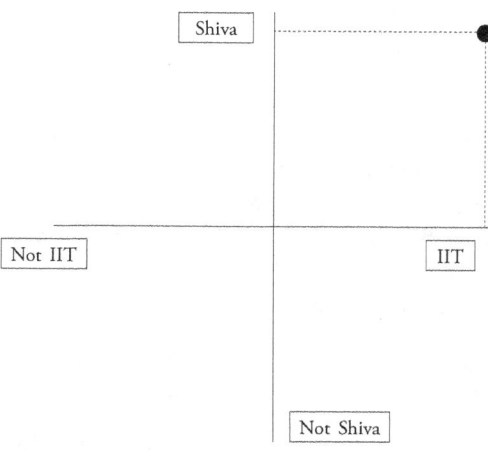

Thus the ideal product for this market would be a novel in which Lord Shiva goes to IIT. However, is this enough? Can blind reliance on tools, however advanced, truly bring stupendous success?

The answer is NO. Sometimes you have to think out of the box. One must not be rigid, as Asaram Bapu said during his potency test. Ravinder Singh's *I Too Had a Love Story* is an example of another great success, which our current map does not recognise. If we factor this in, then the ideal bestselling novel could be described as follows:

'In which Lord Shiva goes to IIT and falls in love...again'.

As you can see, this powerful tool that I have just given you can help you succeed in almost any field. As a management person, you have great power. Use it wisely, because with great power comes great responsibility.

PEEPWELL CASE: STUDENT FEEDBACK

As we had hoped, several potential stars are already emerging. *Vigilant Indian* in particular looks like a future CEO of Microsoft. He gave us some good points:

RFM Analysis: I have no idea what this means, but if you say it with conviction, I have no doubt that the audience will be impressed. Don't forget to mention that you will soon be arriving at independent scores for R, F and M.

Blanket as Medium: Blankets have large surface areas, and there is no reason why this cannot be used to communicate something. Peepwell could practice political market segmentation. Blankets with a lotus motif could appeal to BJP supporters, while cute khaki shorts could appeal to RSS sympathisers. The principle can be extended to a Jupiter motif for Congress supporters, buffaloes for the Samajvadi Party, etc., etc.

Purposive Segmentation: The blanket market can also be segmented as per purpose e.g. making children soundproof.

Student *Human* has suggested a Cross-Marketing initiative, whereby Peepwell ties up with the AAP and launches a scheme of one floral blanket free with every membership ('As worn by CM on TV!')

Student *N Jayaram* has suggested treating Madhu Kishwar as a market segment. I am too scared of Madhu Kishwar to respond to this.

Newslaundry, 12 February 2014

MANAGEMENT CLASSICS MADE EASY

Airport bookshops are full of management books, because top corporate bosses have a lot of free time. Typically, once the boss has read a management book, the employees have to read it too. Thus, everybody gets sucked into its vortex—and the book becomes a bestseller. In management parlance, this is known as the Downward Spiral of Doom.

The good news is that most management books can be summed up in a paragraph. However, most people do not like to pay money for a paragraph. Hence, they are turned into books. As a public service, *Newslaundry* is providing you a selection of these paragraphs, free of cost.

The 7 Habits of Highly Effective People: Prof Stephen R. Covey

Over 15 million people have become more effective after reading this book, including former US President Bill Clinton. They used techniques such as 'Being Proactive', 'Encouraging Win-Win Scenarios' and 'Synergising'.

The seven habits mentioned in the title are actually a process with three stages. In Stage I, we make ourselves independent. In Stage II, we learn how to become dependent. In Stage III, having thoroughly confused everybody, we draw ahead of the pack by improving continuously. After this comes death, which is not covered.

A sequel to the book, called *The 8th Habit: From Effectiveness to Greatness* was released recently. This has led to widespread demands for refunds from buyers of the previous book, who had thought there were only 7.

Who Moved My Cheese?: Prof Spencer Johnson

Sometimes bosses communicate through books. Imagine one day you are standing in the corridor with your coffee, fantasizing about the girl in the accounts department, harming no one, when the boss comes and gifts you a book. If your boss gifts you *Who Moved My Cheese?*, it could mean one of three things:

a) You are about to be fired.
b) Your company has been purchased by Google.
c) The office is shifting to Badarpur.

Through this gift, the message your boss is trying to convey is, 'Embrace change, so I can get more money. Or I will hurt you.'

The boss smiles, pats you on the back and walks away. You will not stand outside with your coffee in future. But today it is too late. You look at the book in your hand. Your head is reeling. You fear the worst. But the worst is yet to come. The worst is when you open the book and realise that the main characters in this book are two talking mice and two tiny people. Which means that through this gift, your boss is also telling you that you have the intellectual capacity of a four-year-old. You suppress your anguish and read on. You discover that the mice and the little people, all of whom speak English, are eating cheese at a Cheese Station, until one day the cheese runs out. The mice bravely venture out to look for more cheese. The little men blame each other for moving the cheese that they already had, which has now vanished, not realising that they have consumed it. Subsequently, driven by severe cheese withdrawal, they too go out and search for cheese, and eventually they find it. On the way, they write each other encouraging messages with the word 'cheese' in them, such as 'The quicker you get rid of old cheese, the sooner you can enjoy new cheese' and 'Smell the cheese often'.

The key message we get from this book is that mice are smarter than humans.

Competitive Advantage: **Prof Michael S. Porter**

Over 456 pages, this management classic explains that in order to succeed against competitors, we need to have something they do not have. In the pre-management era, this was known as an advantage. Now it is known as Competitive Advantage. Many slides have been created with this title. In fact, a recent worldwide survey has revealed it to be Number 4 in terms of popularity as a slide title, closely following 'SWOT Analysis', 'Way Forward' and 'Thank You'.

Competitive Advantage has given birth to another powerful term, Barrier to Entry. This is something that companies erect to maintain their Competitive Advantage. For example, if other companies are unable to manufacture swimsuit calendars because Kingfisher has signed up all the models, this is known as a Barrier to Entry. If you use these two phrases often, people will be convinced that you have read this book. Thanks to your knowledge of advantages, you will be seen as a person who can give thorns to competition. Which brings us to....

Discover the Diamond in You: **Prof Arindam Chaudhuri**

This book was written by Professor Arindam Chaudhuri, whose tailor was recently executed for 'crimes against humanity'. According to the author's website, the book has extraordinary remarks from Shahrukh Khan, and admiration from Amitabh Bachchan. The purpose of this book is to help you shine, through application of the nine Ps, which are very similar to the 4 Cs used to measure diamonds, except that they are Ps instead of Cs, and the number is different. The Nine Ps are Passion, Positive Energy, Personality, People Skills, Performance, Perseverance, Principles, Perspective and Patriotism. A Tenth P—Prawns, is rumored to have been dropped at the last minute.

The book is designed to be completed in 59 minutes, leaving you one minute to reflect on the hour of your life which will never come back.

The Dilbert Principle: **Prof Scott Adams**

This book uses simple logic to make us feel better as corporate employees.
   Everyone is an idiot.

1. However, some people are bigger idiots than others.
2. Recognising this, modern organisations automatically promote the most ineffective workers to the place where they can do the least harm—management.

This is known as the Dilbert Principle.

This book provides a philosophy designed to help us survive corporate life. It tells us that everything we do as corporate employees is pointless, so we might as well make fun of the boss. A vast majority of the corporate employees worldwide subscribe to this philosophy, making *The Dilbert Principle* the single most influential management textbook ever written.

STUDENT EXERCISE

1. What is the difference between Cheddar cheese and Gouda cheese?
2. Apart from your boss and Manmohan Singh, which other Indian examples illustrate the Dilbert Principle?
3. What other words beginning with P can help bring out the diamond in you?

Newslaundry, 25 February 2014

WHAT IF

Shovon was a history buff, and like many such enthusiasts, was interested in 'alternate histories'—what if a certain event had not happened, or had turned out differently? Among his favourite novels were Philip K. Dick's *The Man in the High Castle* (President Roosevelt is assassinated in 1933, the Great Depression continues, and by the 1960s, half of the United States is ruled by Nazi Germany and the other half by Imperial Japan) and Len Deighton's *SS-GB* (Britain has lost the Second World War and is now occupied by Germany).

Swarajya magazine had commissioned a 'What If' series of articles by Shovon. The questions were asked by the editor, and Shovon thought through the consequences. The premises were wide-ranging, from Mohandas Karamchand Gandhi not being ejected from the train in South Africa, to the Marathas winning the Third Battle of Panipat, to the horrifying possibility that Madhuri Dixit did not perform the 'Ek Do Teen' dance in *Tezaab*.

WHAT IF GANDHI HADN'T BEEN THROWN OFF THE TRAIN?

On June 7th, 1893, at a little station called Pietermaritzburg, Mohandas Gandhi was thrown off the train. His baggage was thrown off separately. This was a big mistake. For over 25 years, he was a thorough nuisance to the South African regime. He avoided violence. He talked of virtue. He made them gifts. He refused to play fair. They were very relieved when he left for India in 1915. His parting gift to Prime Minister Jan Smuts was a pair of slippers, which he had made himself.

But what if this had never happened?

Supposing his fellow passenger had said, 'Hullo, you look quite decent for a brown chap. Fancy a spot of tea?'

Gandhi was not a born revolutionary. He was conservative by nature. His family had hoped that he would earn some money and experience in South Africa, and then come back and take over from his father as the Dewan of Porbander. Perhaps that's what he would have done, and remained a lifelong loyal servant of the Empire, and built Porbander into a model state, with good roads, full adult literacy, clean toilets, and many goats. Life would have been happy there. Once India became independent, they would have become an example for the rest of us.

But was Gandhi not the engine of the freedom struggle? Without him, would we be free? We probably would, because the British were running out of things to steal. They could have kept us as a captive market for their products, but unfortunately they had already taken all our money, so we were not in a position to buy anything. So there were reasons for them to leave.

Nevertheless, if you visit any Governor's house anywhere in the country, you can see why they might want to stay. Check out the chandeliers and the sofas, and the number of salutes. Who would want to leave such comfort, unless someone broke in through the window and set fire to the curtains?

So we would definitely have needed the freedom struggle. Who could have led us to freedom? Would it have been Nehru, or Bose, or Patel? Or even Jinnah? We could empty a bar discussing that one, but still, let's give it a shot.

At first glance, it looks like Nehru is ruled out, because of uncles. 'Gandhi was always febharing Nehru,' my uncles would say, 'He was doing partiality.' But even without the partiality, Nehru was no pushover. He was a patriot from an early age. He joined the Indian National Congress long before Gandhi. He was the son of Motilal Nehru, a respected leader. He was an excellent speaker. He would have been a player in the Congress, through the 20s and the 30s, and been pointed out as a leftie at tea parties.

Like Nehru, Subhash Bose turned nationalist early, punching out professors in college, and resigning from the Indian Civil Service, because he didn't want to serve the British. He was a disciple of C. R. Das, who achieved the remarkable feat of uniting Bengali Muslims with Bengali Hindus. No one else has managed that before or since. Bose joined the Congress in 1921. He admired Gandhi as a great man, but his thinking was very different.

There might never have been a Sardar Patel, though. For the first 42 years of his life, Vallabhbhai Patel took no interest in politics. He was a good citizen and a good family man, practicing law and building his fortune. Of all our great men, he was the one who was inspired into action by Gandhi, suddenly, in his middle age. The attraction must have been strong. Without it, maybe he would have remained a respected member of the local community, known for his clear thinking, the right man to go to with any problem, never in his wildest dreams imagining that one day he would become a statue.

Which leaves a Congress with Nehru and Bose as key leaders, along with one Mr Jinnah. A fine mind, but a cold fish. Both Nehru and Bose are impatient men. With them in charge, the Congress pushes for freedom sooner. With no Gandhi to hold them back, they are more militant. They avoid large-scale violence, but the British are getting nervous. Meanwhile, the Indian Army is getting restless. The British raise salaries, which they can ill afford to do.

In both 1938 and 1939, Bose becomes the President of the Congress. People notice that some of the Congress volunteers are wearing khaki, and marching. Jinnah and Azad are both part of the team, and no one has ever mentioned the word 'partition'. Jinnah finds Bose's costumes funny, but he can deal with him.

Nehru and Bose part company when World War 2 breaks out. Nehru's heart is with Britain. He sees Hitler as evil. Bose sees him as opportunity. He has always been interested in the army. At this crucial moment, he is in India, surrounded by Indian soldiers. Many historians believe the Indian Naval Mutiny of 1946 was the final nail in the British coffin. In this scenario, with Bose to inspire them, things happen faster.

By 1942, the Indian Army is disintegrating, fatally weakening the British war effort. Some have broken away and formed units of the Indian National Army. Others stay true to their salt, but they will not fight. The Japanese win the Battle of Kohima, supported by overseas elements of the Indian National Army, whose ranks swell as they advance. They beat the British in a series of battles, till they break through to the plains of Bengal, where the Japanese are thrilled to find so much fish. Netaji gives the order to rise, and New Delhi falls in a military coup. Garrisons across Western and Southern India rally to his name. It's worth remembering that in the Congress elections of 1938, every single Congress delegate from the South voted for him.

Netaji is declared Supreme Leader of India, with Nehru as his Foreign Minister. Nehru is not sure where this is going, but he is happy that the country is free. Netaji's first priority is to launch elements of the Indian National Army into Hyderabad, which crumbles after some initial resistance. His troops march into several other princely states. He has to be quick. He wants to take them before the advancing Japanese. They are his allies, but he has trust issues. Then the Americans drop the bomb on Japan, and the war is over.

The Japanese surrender and give up their possessions. These include Burma, the whole of the North-East and Bengal Province. But who do they give it back to? To the British, or to Bose? The British are exhausted.

The remnants of the British Army are itching to go back to England and kick Winston Churchill in the pants. They are happy to let go.

But Subhash Chandra Bose is a notorious leftie. The first thing he has done after becoming Supreme Commander is request Stalin for support. Stalin is busy taking over Europe. He is distracted, but sympathetic. Nehru flies down to Moscow, and their meeting is a great success. As usual, he floors all the women.

The Americans cannot allow this. They make the British take back the Japanese possessions. A much smaller British India is re-established, right next to the freshly independent Republic of India, where boots echo in the corridors, and Nehru and Jinnah are whispering to each other about forming a resistance movement.

An iron curtain falls over the subcontinent. Soon enough, a wall goes up, somewhere in the region of Patna.

Swarajya, 14 November 2014

WHAT IF RAMAYANA HAD NEVER BEEN TELECAST?

Back in the 1980s, the only television we had was Doordarshan, which mostly showed documentaries on the Gandhi family and fertilizer. Sometimes we would go over to a nearby auntie's house to watch Chitrahaar, or Hindi Feature Film. The film was irrelevant. The main thing was that it was free. Alok Nath was unavoidable. We thought impure thoughts about female newscasters. Our world was very small. Arnab was still in school, and the nation was far less curious.

Until someone called the Information and Broadcasting Minister in 1986, and told him that Doordarshan should broadcast serials that depict the values enshrined in our ancient texts and philosophy, the kind of values that were contained in the Mahabharata and the Ramayana.

This was not part of an RSS plot. This was a suggestion by Rajiv Gandhi, who was PM at the time, and in the middle of his term. The first flush of public affection was beginning to fade. He had just altered the constitution to prevent poor Shah Bano from getting alimony, and the Hindus were angry. It was time to do something nice for the Hindus.

Eager to please, the babus at Mandi House moved with lightning speed, and commissioned the production of both the Ramayana and the Mahabharata. Given the rush, there were no tenders. One project was given to Ramanand Sagar, and the other to B. R. Chopra. Several episodes of both were produced, after which Doordarshan decided to run Ramayana first.

It started in the third week of January, 1987. Soon after, Rajiv Gandhi opened up the site of the Ram Janmabhoomi in Ayodhya for worship. In this way, he became a founding father of the BJP. Years later, his son Rahul played a big role in helping Narendra Modi become the PM. From this, we can see that no other family has contributed more to the rise of the BJP than the Nehru–Gandhis. While the original Nehru was clearly an enemy, his descendants have done their best to make up for it.

Once Ramayana started, our lives were never the same. For two years, at 9:30 every Sunday morning, the nation came to a stop. Trains were delayed at stations while passengers finished watching. People bathed early, and applied tilaks to themselves and their TVs. Cinema halls across the country cancelled morning shows. The nation watched, transfixed, as the actors spoke very slowly, and arrows fired by combatants took up to 15 minutes to hit their targets.

How could such a programme shape the nation? It's because the Hindu religion is defective. Christians have to go to church every Sunday. Muslims have to pray five times a day. Hindus are under no such compulsion. Even on those few festive days in every year, our God is not the only focus. There's food, and friends, and family. Plus we have too many gods. As any brand consultant will tell you, it's better to focus on one or two brands. For hundreds of years, we Hindus have been loose and shaggy, worshipping our different gods once or twice a year. We also had a wide variety of idols, instead of one clear picture in every heart. The whole thing was fuzzy.

Ramayana changed all this. Our God was no longer an abstract figure who varied from person to person. He was a tall man with kind eyes, nice shoulders and a heavenly smile. He was real. He was human. When we were deprived of his temple, we felt it personally. We rose up when Lal Krishna Advani called. We emerged from the shadow of Nehru and realized that faith could play a role in politics.

But what if there was no Ramayana on Doordarshan?

Until 1987, for 40 years, public broadcasters in India had avoided religious programming.

According to legend, on that fateful day in 1986, Rajiv Gandhi switched on the TV, thought Doordarshan was boring, and then called the minister. Supposing Hindi Feature Film had been running at the time, showing *Amar Akbar Anthony*, or *Chalti Ka Naam Gaadi?* Rajiv Gandhi would have been richly entertained. He would never have made that call. Secretary Gill would not have called Ramanand Sagar, and asked him to make Ramayana.

Without a government guarantee, Sagar might never have attempted such an ambitious project, moving smoothly instead from Vikram Aur Betal to Jataka Tales, or Akbar–Birbal.

How would our history have been different? It would probably have been slower. Unlike church, or the muezzin's call, Ramayana did not go on forever. It was just a two-year run. It must have awakened something that was already there.

So in this new world, when the time comes, Advani still sets off on his rath yatra. He gathers followers, although perhaps not as many. Vajpayee never comes to power, but the BJP grows in strength. Without the prestige of the PM's chair, Vajpayee is eclipsed by Advani, leading to a purer, stronger, surer BJP. Advani fights his last election in 2014. The country is still not ready to trust him, but it cannot stomach Pappu. A motley coalition led by Mulayam Singh Yadav comes to power. The country is in for a rough six years.

The BJP is strong, and sitting in the opposition. Advani passes the flame to Narendra Modi, who has risen through the ranks. The BJP gets ready for the electoral battle of 2019, with new inspiration, and a new slogan.

Agli Baar, Modi Sarkar.

Swarajya, 27 Novemeber 2014

WHAT IF THE MARATHAS HAD WON AT PANIPAT?

For nearly 250 years, Panipat has seen no conquests or victories, unless you count McDonalds. It's the place on the way to the hills where you stop the car, so that the ladies can look for bathrooms. If you're a gentleman, you help them find one. The city produces power, fuel and fertilizer, and you can smell it in the air.

Since October 2014, Panipat City has been represented in the Haryana state assembly by Ms Rohita Rewri, whose Facebook page has 2,741 likes. She has been photographed with a broom. One of the posts on her page features a quote from Guru Nanak: 'Before becoming a Sikh, a Muslim, a Hindu, or a Christian, let's become human first.' Industry flourishes in Panipat, and a working man can hope to get paid a little more than elsewhere. Many come here looking for a living.

But for centuries, Panipat has served a different purpose. It was the last stop on the road to Delhi, and after Aurangzeb went to heaven, this road became a hotbed of activity. Ahmed Shah Abdali, the great Afghan chieftain, travelled to it regularly, because ATMs were yet to be invented, and he had little chieftains of his own to pay off. He would drop in whenever funds were getting low. United by cash flow, the Afghans were enjoying one of their rare periods of unity, to the detriment of all their neighbours.

It is now 1761. The British have made some progress. They have talent for spotting traitors, and this has served them well at Plassey. They control the rich province of Bengal, from where they can see as far as Burma. On the other hand, Hyder Ali will soon be in charge of Mysore, and the Nizam can never be trusted. Madras is looking vulnerable. Bombay is surrounded by well-armed Marathas. The French are everywhere, hatching plots and putting garlic in everything.

The British presence is fragile. They are not yet confident enough to bring over their women. As a result, India is safe from the memsahibs, the most deadly invasion of all. Once they take charge, there is no looking back. In 1761, this point has not yet been reached.

The Maratha Confederacy is at its height. So is their squabbling. The leading chiefs all hate each other, and are united only in their resentment of the Peshwa, who is the medieval equivalent of an HR Manager. He handles bonuses and promotions, and he tells them where to improve, but he does not seem to be doing much work himself.

Peshwa Balaji Baji Rao has kept them busy invading other people. His plan has worked well. Their empire stretches from Bhubaneshwar to Baroda, and from Bijapur to Lahore. Here too, cash flows are good. Family fortunes are being made. A bandit with a flair for leadership could once dream of rising high amongst the Marathas. But now, bit by bit, these positions are becoming hereditary.

Much blood is being spilled in Punjab, as usual. Ahmed Shah Abdali rampages through it in 1756, and captures Delhi. He loots the place and leaves a token force. The Marathas rampage through it in 1757, after recapturing Delhi, and drive off the Afghans.

By 1758, the Marathas reach Peshawar, where they defeat the Afghans again. They collect tribute from everyone, and satisfied with collections, return to the plains, leaving behind a token force. Ahmad Shah Abdali storms back in 1759, sweeping past the token force, and recaptures Delhi.

The mood is grim. Collections have been thin, as everyone in Delhi is largely penniless by now. Ahmad Shah allies with local leaders, including Shujauddaulah, Nawab of Avadh, and the Mughal Emperor, who by this time is being passed around like a rubber stamp.

Led by Sadashivrao Bhau, a Maratha army of 60,000 marches to Delhi. The march is slow, as they are accompanied by over 100,000 pilgrims, keen to see various pilgrimage centres in North India. They feel safer in the company of troops. The pilgrims do not stop to consider that these troops are about to fight one of the biggest battles of the 18th century. Their faith is strong, but their brains are weak.

The march to Delhi is delayed as the pilgrims stop at all the important pilgrimage centres on the way, giving Ahmad Shah Abdali enough time to organize his forces. Thanks to his alliances, he has nearly 100,000 men. After a series of skirmishes, the Maratha army, pilgrims and all, are trapped at Panipat, and besieged for two months, with their food and water running out. Due to the need to feed the pilgrims, their situation is desperate. The soldiers are weak and starving. They beg to die in battle, rather than hiding behind walls.

Sadashivrao Bhau leads his men out, against a superior foe. The force of their first charge is so great that the enemy is driven back. The Maratha infantry, supported by the Gardis, are cutting the Afghans to pieces. The Afghans and their allies begin to flee. Disobeying orders, the Maratha cavalry gives chase, scenting victory, and charges right into the Afghan artillery, which blows them up.

The Marathas fight bravely, but the tide is turning. Ahmad Shah throws in his reserve troops. The Marathas are hungry and exhausted. They have no reserves. Ahmad Shah sweeps the field. Out of a Maratha army of 60,000, only 17,000 make it back home. An entire generation of military talent is destroyed.

Ahmad Shah Abdali is unnerved by this battle. If he ever had any plans of hanging around, he shelves them. Instead, he keeps commuting, ending his career with a total of nine invasions. Punjab suffers the most. He massacres the Sikhs and desecrates the Golden Temple. His criminal spree is ended by his death, in 1769.

Meanwhile, by winning the Battle of Buxar, the British gain control of UP, Bihar, Bengal, Orissa and Assam. They crush the French and repulse the Dutch. They grow rich and powerful. When the time is right, they divide up the Maratha chiefs, and defeat them one by one. By 1818, they rule most of India. Soon after, the first memsahib steps ashore.

But supposing the Marathas had won?

Supposing Vinchurkar and Gaikwad had held back their cavalry till afternoon, and attacked when Ahmed Shah brought in his reserves? Supposing Peshwa had appointed Holkar or Narayan Rao as general, both of whom had begged Sadashivrao to make more allies, and knew North India much better than him? Supposing, at the height of the battle, Sadashivrao had stayed on his elephant, instead of getting off to fight on foot, leaving his soldiers unable to see him, and thinking their general was dead?

The Afghan line breaks. Ahmad Shah Abdali flees with the remnants of his army. On his way through Punjab, he is attacked by the Sikhs, and dies in the Battle of Lahore. The Marathas celebrate their great escape, and forever after, Sankranti is a time of great joy in Maharashtra.

The prestige of the Peshwa is at an all-time high. A slightly confused Shah Alam II is put back on the Mughal throne, with Scindia as his local guardian. Riding high on victory, the Marathas crush the Nizam, and discover that he was not as poor as he pretended to be. They force Hyder Ali to become their vassal. Madras is now completely surrounded by the Marathas and their allies.

Meanwhile, in Bengal, the British realize that Mir Qasim, Nawab of Bengal, is not a very good puppet. He is building his own army, and grumbling about British greed. Mir Qasim decides to revolt, and asks Nawab Shujauddaulah of Awadh for help. Shujauddaulah, former supporter of Ahmad Shah Abdali, has quickly switched sides after Panipat. He's nimble that way. He asks his overlord the Peshwa for advice.

Bengal was always the next step for Peshwa Balaji Baji Rao. He blesses the enterprise, and sends Scindia to support them. With the Maratha hand on their necks, there are no betrayals at Buxar. The British are pounded by Maratha artillery, and this time, the cavalry charges at the right time. Mir Qasim becomes Nawab of Bengal once more, and resumes paying tribute to the Marathas.

The Marathas want him to drive out the British, but he keeps them. They are useful for making money. Calcutta grows and flourishes. After the British lose America, many of the troops are transferred to Calcutta, along with units of the Royal Navy.

Balaji Baji Rao is succeeded by his son, Vishwas Rao, one of the heroes of Panipat. The Maratha Empire prospers, except that it is gradually becoming a confederacy, as Scindia, Holkar and other Maratha princes build their kingdoms. Rivalry is fierce. By early 19th century, each one of them is growing impatient.

The death of Vishwas Rao triggers a struggle for succession. Over in Madras, Arthur Wellesley, the man who will one day defeat Napoleon at Waterloo as the 1st Duke of Wellington, is getting bored. He had hoped to advance his career in India, but there's been very little action. Now, at last, he hears rumours from Calcutta about a campaign against the Marathas. British forces in Madras will be supported by Tipu Sultan, son of Hyder Ali, who is itching for freedom from Maratha rule.

Meanwhile, across the Sutlej river, Maharaja Ranjit Singh is expanding his power. Punjab will be united soon, and much stronger than before. By 1802, he is master of Amritsar. When he looks across the border, he does not see the British Empire. He sees the quarrelling Marathas, and he hears a voice whispering in his ear.

To Delhi, it whispers. To Delhi.

Swarajya, 6 December 2014

WHAT IF THE CHINESE HAD STAYED ON IN 1962?

The imperial British loved making maps, because of the fresh air, and the loyal native bearers. As a result, the borders of India were redrawn repeatedly, by Henry Strachey in 1847, H. W. Johnson in 1865, G. W. Hayward in 1868, T. D. Forsyth in 1874, and many more in the years to come.

Inevitably, this led to a lot of lines. They produced Johnson Lines and McCartney–MacDonald Lines and McMahon Lines. Many of the culprits were Scottish. The map of India was redrawn 11 times between 1847 and 1947. Generations grew up not knowing which country they lived in. Confusion was widespread. Some would say that this was the root cause of the Sino–Indian war of 1962.

Another explanation is that war broke out because big men were in peril. The Chinese people were very annoyed with Mao, because of the Great Leap Forward, which started in 1959. Things were not going according to plan, mainly because no one knew what the plan was. Subsequent historical study has revealed that the plan was to keep shooting people until China became an industrial powerhouse.

Casualties were high. Many people also starved to death, because their kitchen utensils and agricultural implements had been melted down to meet steel production quotas. Local officials reported the quotas, but not the deaths, because they were afraid that Mao might shoot them.

Nevertheless, by 1962, too many people had died. In January, Mao was publicly criticized, and lost much of his clout. However, his fellow leaders neglected to put him in a mental institution, something that they would come to regret. Mao went into hiding, and began planning his next move. He needed to recover his position.

Meanwhile, the Indian public was beginning to have doubts about Nehru's manliness. This was after an incident at Kong Ka, in 1959, where nine CRPF men lost their lives. In a sign of things to come, the jawans were poorly equipped and heavily outnumbered, and the Chinese occupied the high ground. Our boys fought bravely. The nation was outraged. Will we not have revenge, bellowed the critics of Nehru, who included eminent men like Acharya Kripalani, Dr Lohia, Atal Behari Vajpayee and Rajaji.

They were upset with Nehru because he kept winning elections. They were loud, eloquent, and astonished at his spinelessness. Editors roared and thundered. The government was roundly denounced for inaction. To any man who had drunk his mother's milk, it was obvious that we had to go to war.

The nation demanded action, and Nehru gave it to them, against military advice. When Nehru found his generals reluctant, he did the only thing that he could under the circumstances. He changed his generals. He found new generals, who confirmed that pushing forward was a good idea, and that the Chinese were cowards. 'Experience in Ladakh has shown,' said one of them, 'that a few rounds fired at the Chinese would cause them to run away.'

The truth was, the Chinese had just fought the Korean War, where they had not run away, and they had learnt a thing or two about mountain warfare. During the 1962 war, the Indian Army assumed that the Chinese would stick to the roads, and deployed forces accordingly.

But the Chinese kept cheating by using mountain trails, and wading across rivers. This, along with the fact that our generals forgot to stock up on ammunition, winter clothing and food, proved to be a major handicap. They also discovered, as the Americans did in Vietnam, that each of their own boys was not the equivalent of 10 Chinese soldiers, although the boys never asked questions, and did the best they could.

All this makes Nehru look like a fool, which is exactly how Neville Maxwell would have wanted it. Neville Maxwell is the source for almost everything we know about the 1962 war. In every interview he has given, he calls Nehru a fool. Sometimes, for variety, he calls him an ass.

He does not seem to be very fond of India. In 1967, he predicted that India's fourth general election would be its last. In 1972, in *The New York Review of Books*, he quoted the old Raj saying—'there is not, and never was, an India'. His glee at the thought is hard to miss. He lived in India in the 60s, as correspondent of *The Times*. The climate must not have suited him.

A less prejudiced person might draw a different conclusion. It can be argued that Chinese perceptions of borders depend on Chinese perceptions of strength. In Haryana, this is known as 'who has the lathi, he has the buffalo'. For example, throughout the 50s, the Chinese seemed to accept the MacMahon Line.

Suddenly, in 1956, once they were confident about Tibet, they started publishing maps in which large chunks of India were shown as part of China. When Nehru asked Chinese premier Zhou Enlai about this, he said the maps 'had little meaning', much like his response.

Their strange behaviour bloomed into full-blown paranoia after the Lhasa Uprising of 1959, during which they blew up many Tibetans, and burnt down the Dalai Lama's house. In this way they proved, in the words of the loyalist Panchen Lama, that 'the Tibetan people are patriotic, support the Central People's Government, ardently love the People's Liberation Army, and oppose the imperialists and traitors'.

Once Nehru gave refuge to the Dalai Lama, the Chinese were convinced, contrary to all evidence, that India wanted Tibet. The details of politburo meetings in Beijing between 1959 and 1962 show this quite clearly.

They believed that Nehru would not rest until the whole of Tibet was his. Mao repeatedly says so, and everyone agrees with him. It's also possible that Mao was jealous of Nehru, who was much better looking, and was getting girls without threatening them.

Nevertheless, until mid-1962, as the Indian troops move forward, the Chinese do retreat. This was because in early 1962, they were facing a challenge from Taiwan, where the nationalists had smoked too much opium, and were threatening to attack the mainland. By June, this threat is over, once the Americans make it clear that they do not favour this plan.

But the Chinese still have a problem. Both the Americans and the Soviets prefer Nehru over Mao, mainly because he seems more normal.

If China attacks India, will they step in? The Chinese hesitate. Until October 1962, when the Cuban Missile Crisis begins.

Suddenly, it looks like war between America and Russia. American schoolchildren are being taught to hide under their desks in the event of a nuclear attack. Suburban families are reinforcing their basements. Bearded men carry placards which say 'Repent!' Mao seizes the moment. On October 20, he orders a 'self-defensive counter-attack' against India, because of its actions in Tibet, and Nehru's 'dark mentality'.

The Indian Army stands no chance. Our boys are always outnumbered, and often outflanked. By October 24, the Chinese are 15 km beyond the MacMahon line. At this point, there is a break, in the hope that better sense will prevail. It does not.

The Lok Sabha vows to throw the invader off the sacred soil of India, although how the army is supposed to do this without ammunition is not adequately explained. The war resumes on November 14, Nehru's birthday. Within a week, the Chinese are on the outskirts of Tezpur. Assam lies open before them.

In the real world, this is the point where Mao gives the order to withdraw, back behind the MacMahon line. But supposing they had kept moving? Mao was a murderous madman, responsible for not one, but two of the great calamities of the 20th century—the Great Leap Forward and the Cultural Revolution. If there truly is a Hell, he is the centerpiece in the lobby.

People often wonder why he ordered his troops to withdraw, but this is pointless. Trying to apply logic to the actions of such a person is futile. But it's worth remembering that he was the man who once said, 'The way to world conquest lies through Havana, Accra, and Calcutta.'

Perhaps this seems far-fetched, or too dependent on the whims of one person. Let's review some facts. In the 50s, India lobbied hard to get China a seat on the UN Security Council. China has always opposed the same for us. India recognized Tibet as Chinese, while Chinese maps change every few months. China helped Pakistan go nuclear, through their wholly owned subsidiary North Korea.

China is surrounding us with naval bases. Just a few months ago,

Chinese troops were causing border incidents, while we were feeding their President dinner. The food was vegetarian, and there was no alcohol, but that is no excuse. Since the mid-50s, every action of China towards us has been the action of an enemy. The only surprise about the 1962 war is, why were we so surprised?

Mao looks at the map. Assam lies before him. Greater the victory, greater his glory, and more thoroughly he can crush his enemies. The two nations have just fought bitterly over barren rocks. Assam is rich in resources.

And was Assam not the Kingdom of Ahom for 600 years? Was this kingdom not founded by the Mong Mao, originally from Yunan province, and sworn vassals of the Yuan emperor? The first Ahom king was Chao Lung Siu-Ka-Pha, a fine Chinese name. What could be more Chinese than Assam? Their claim on it is stronger than their claim on Tibet. But the action has to be quick. American ships have sailed.

The PLA storms into Assam. Guwahati falls quickly. In four days, they reach the border of East Pakistan. By this time, the US Seventh Fleet is in the Bay of Bengal, in response to frantic calls for assistance from Nehru.

Defense Secretary Robert McNamara advises President Kennedy that a nuclear strike on China is the only viable option. Kennedy hesitates, because he has already listened to his advice on Vietnam, and this is not working out well. Mao declares a unilateral ceasefire, and a new line-of-control. There will be no debate or discussion. Assam becomes the Autonomous Republic of Ahom. The Americans advise India to accept the status quo.

Nehru resigns, and dies soon after. Lal Bahadur Shastri takes charge. Pakistan attacks in 1965, but this time, India is better prepared. The Chinese do not interfere. They have their hands full with the Autonomous Republic of Ahom, where the rebels are receiving arms from India, and the Nagas and Mizos are proving to be quite a handful.

Once more, Calcutta is the hotbed of revolution, home to rebels of every description. In 1966, the Cultural Revolution begins. In China, the lunatics take over the asylum.

By 1971, Indira Gandhi is Prime Minister, and things are heating up in the east. India supports freedom for Bangladesh. Pakistan sees this as a conspiracy. Across Pakistan, stickers appear on cars, with the words 'Crush India'. Pakistani politicians march with the same demand.

On December 3, 1971, the Pakistan Air Force launches air strikes on India, using a grand total of 50 planes. They have underestimated the requirements for crushing India, and India responds swiftly, and with force. Indira Gandhi is not fighting for Bangladesh. She is fighting for revenge. She will establish a puppet state in Bangladesh, and she will use it as a base to liberate Assam, and undo the betrayal of her father.

She has 11 mountain divisions equipped and ready to strike. On the other side of the border, the Cultural Revolution is in full swing, and the Chinese are busy hunting class enemies and revisionists. She can count on support from the Americans. After the annexation of Assam, they are terrified of Commie expansion. Her will is strong, and her plan looks good.

But as her troops enter the outskirts of Dhaka, she has forgotten one thing. Thanks to lavish assistance from the Soviet Union, the Chinese have been a nuclear power since 1964. On December 13, Pakistan begs China for help.

Meanwhile, Mao has been having problems of his own. With no one left to persecute, the Cultural Revolution is running out of steam. In September, his deputy Lin Biao died mysteriously. There are whispers of a military coup.

The PLA is growing stronger. Mao needs to turn the PLA against an external enemy, to keep their hands from his throat. He orders his marshals to prepare for a nuclear strike on India, which does not have nuclear weapons of its own.

By December 15, the Bay of Bengal is getting crowded. The US Seventh Fleet is there, along with a Soviet Task Force from Vladivostok, including a nuclear-armed submarine. The Americans are staunch allies. The Soviet position is unclear. If the Chinese launch a nuclear attack, will the Americans respond? Or will the Americans pre-empt them and strike first? And if they do, will the Soviets respond as well?

It is the evening of December 16, 1971. In Washington DC, a ferret-faced little man is poised, his sweaty finger on the nuclear button. He may not be going to China any time soon, but it's time to send them a message. The Russkies won't do anything, says Kissinger, because this is what his boss wants to hear. Still, he hesitates. It's his name that will go down in history.

The fate of the world is in the hands of Richard Milhous Nixon.

Swarajya, 8 February 2015

WHAT IF MADHURI HAD
NOT DONE 'EK DO TEEN'?

In 1988, Rajiv Gandhi was Prime Minister of the country. I was a trainee in an advertising agency now named after a dead, white person, in the city formerly known as Bombay.

We were in Nariman Point, surrounded by vada pao. We had a small audio-visual department. They occupied a tiny room just big enough to fit three people. It was filled with state-of-the-art equipment, which allowed us to transfer things from Beta to VHS. On the morning in question, I was supposed to transfer a copy of the latest Liril commercial and take it to our lords and masters at Levers. They were our lords and masters because they were over 50 per cent of our business.

I was in charge of Liril. I had a cupboard full of green bikinis. I was in a cruel and inhuman situation. They never took me for any of the shoots, but I had to keep track of the bikinis. I was also in charge of Lifebuoy, and something called Lifebuoy Personal, for which Ravi Shastri was the brand ambassador. This was at a time when Shastri was having chairs thrown at him at Wankhede Stadium (I'm not making this up). As a result, sales were not encouraging. Our boss was nervous. He was smoking like a chimney and swearing like a sailor. Getting this tape to Levers was critical. When it came to seeing Liril films, they did not like to be kept waiting. They fixed times and invited friends.

I pushed open the door of the tiny room to find all three members of the AV department sitting inside. Their mouths were slack. Their eyes were glazed. On the small monitor, they were watching a cute girl in pink shaking it like no one had ever shaken it before. As I watched, she finished, and started again. They had taken a 90-minute Beta tape and looped the clip so that it ran continuously. I humbly requested for the transfer. I told them that the Vice President (Marketing) of Levers, also known as God, was waiting, so if they could kindly, maybe? They waved me away. None of them spoke to me. None of them looked at me. Their eyes were glued to the screen. Their attention was completely focused. The atmosphere in that little room was the holiest that I have ever experienced, and I have sat in the front row with Mithun fans and watched Disco Dancer. I crept out, closing the door quietly behind me.

The very next day, the girl in pink cropped up in Vikhroli, in the evening, at the modest company accommodation of my college friend Venky. His full name was MP Venky. The 'MP' stood for 'middle-parting'. On campus, it helped to distinguish him from HB Venky. The 'HB' stood for 'Hiking Biking', of which he was the secretary. MP Venky was quiet, thoughtful, and extremely smart. He now does clever things in Silicon Valley. I've never spent much time in Tamil Nadu. What little I know is mostly due to him. Venky shared with me his love for the author Sujatha, and the music of Ilayaraja, and educated me about Kamal Haasan. Rajinikanth I was already aware of.

On this particular evening, he had other things on his mind. 'You have to see this film *Tezaab*,' he said. 'You have to.' I'm not much of a moviegoer, so I asked him why. His eyes lit up. He leaped to his feet. I had never seen him so excited. 'There's this dance number, "Ek Do Teen", with this girl called Madhuri,' he said, 'You can't believe what she does! First she goes like this.' He demonstrated. 'Then she goes like this!' He demonstrated. He may have hopped a little. 'Then she throws her breasts on the floor, to the right side, then immediately again on the left side, like this!' He demonstrated, heaving his torso. 'And again! And again!' For a while he was unable to speak, due to lack of breath. The next day I went and watched *Tezaab*.

Like the Christian calendar, Indian cinema can be broadly divided into two phases—Before 'Ek Do Teen' and After 'Ek Do Teen'. These phases were defined by the answer to a simple question: Who's going to shake it? Before Madhuri Dixit ripped apart the fabric of reality as we know it, nice girls did not shake it. Such entertainment was provided by bad girls. Bad girls in Hindi films were of broadly two types—vamps and tawaifs. Vamps were westernised. They smoked and drank. Tawaifs were more traditional. They poured drinks and held the hookah. There were also a few subroutines or sidebars, such as snake dance movies, in which the women danced like snakes, and the men were usually Amrish Puri.

But these things are matters of historical detail. The overall trend was towards itemization. Itemization, originally known as cabaret, was started by a lady called Cuckoo, in the 1940s. It was clearly an idea whose time had come. At one point, she did 17 films in one year. She was followed by Bindu and Padma Khanna and Aruna Irani, and of course, the Queen of the Cabaret, the hostess with the mostest, the undisputed champion, the one and only Helen. The fact that there is not a single statue of her anywhere in India shows how ungrateful we are.

While all this was happening, were heroines sitting idle? Not entirely. Vyjayanthimala invented the reverse buttock flip, in 'Hothon Mein Aisi Baat' from *Jewel Thief*. Parveen Babi gave Amitabh something to think about in 'Jawaani Jaaneman' from *Namak Halaal*. Like Rahul Dravid, Zeenat Aman batted steadily in a variety of conditions. Sridevi frequently found herself without an umbrella when she needed it most. As usual, injustice was done to Jaya Prada, and her contributions in films such as *Tohfa* have largely been forgotten.

But examples of heroines shaking it remained few and far between. Until Madhuri came along, the working girls still had a chance. They could earn an honest day's pay for an honest day's work. She was the one who single-handedly blew them away. She was so obviously a nice girl that the old distinctions between nice girls and bad girls dissolved away into nothingness. Madhuri gave birth to the 'item number'. It's called an item number because in Bombay slang, a hot girl is called an item, and because maal would have sounded too vulgar.

This has made working conditions much harder for heroines. Not only do they have to be slim, gorgeous, and shorter than Aamir Khan, they have to be expert shakers of booty. Sometimes they have to put up with other heroines intruding into their films, for the sole purpose of shaking booty. To make matters worse, nowadays, even the men are doing item numbers. Hrithik is frequently better than the heroines. This makes everyone fitter, but adds a whole new level of stress. It has also wiped out an entire profession. A simple girl from a small town, with modest talent but good flexibility, can no longer rise to fame and fortune through the simple act of a buttock flick. The heroine is already doing it for her.

What if there had been no 'Ek Do Teen'? What if the art of cabaret had not been killed in 1988, by some, well, killer moves and a million-watt smile? A noble profession would have survived. The definition of good girls and bad girls would have been clearer, leading to less confusion amongst Indian youth, who, as everyone knows, form 53 per cent or something of the population. As the economy boomed, the films would have been bigger, just like today. The competition for better dance numbers would have increased.

Foreign infiltration would begin. Girls would come from Brazil and Russia, and Kazakhstan. Today Kareena and Katrina and Priyanka are fighting back on behalf of local industry, but what if they were all playing good girls?

With our finest items restricted by goodness, how could we have resisted foreign domination? It all starts with one Amy. It looks harmless. We enjoy the Amy. But the Amys multiply. The East India Company too started in exactly the same way, with one Englishman earning small amounts of money in the court of Jehangir. Thanks to Madhuri, in the area of items, India has nothing to fear. Inspired by her, our best and brightest are defending the nation from foreign influence, and holding the flag high, to such an extent that an 18-year-old English boy visiting our house took one look at the TV and said, 'Ah, Kareena.' Such pride I felt that day. There is no doubt that we owe Madhuri a lot.

If she had found Dr Nene sooner, our lives would have been very different. I would have been able to get that tape transferred, for one thing, which I maintain is the main reason why they did not promote me, although the fact that I never wore socks may also have played a role. We would have gone on with our lives, all of us, not knowing what might have been.

Without Madhuri, there would have been an empty space in our hearts, a phantom ache with no reason why.

Swarajya, 7 May 2015

ASK UNCLE

In the early 2010s, Shovon started his blog *India Update*. It had several regular features, among which was the advisory column 'Ask Uncle'.

Here, he answered a range of queries, from issues that concern all of us—for instance, what you should do if your grandmother is talking to the furniture (depends on whether the furniture is talking back to her), or whether you should emigrate if you don't like any of the prime ministerial candidates in the upcoming elections, and if so, what's a good country to go to (Sweden is very nice, although the cuisine may not suit you. In France, the cuisine is very good, but the people may not suit you).

20 June 2012

Dear Uncle,

I was planning to pursue further studies in Australia, but my tout ran away. What should I do?

Regards,
Raman, Coimbatore

Dear Raman,

It all depends on whether you can swim. If you can, New Zealand is a good option. They are currently facing a problem whereby the number of sheep is exceeding the number of people, and the sheep are getting restless. Consequently, their immigration policy is very liberal. If you look at Google Maps, you will see that the distance between Australia and New Zealand is very little. So go to New Zealand and just swim across. Visa regulations may require you to swim back occasionally.

Regards,
Uncle

22 June 2012

Dear Uncle,

The other day I heard a public announcement saying that if I am being followed by a suspicious person, I should inform the police.

But what do I do if I'm being followed by the police?

Yusuf, Baroda

Dear Yusuf,

Try to walk faster. Due to their large stomachs, policemen cannot do this. After a while, he will give up and follow someone else. If I were you, I would start thirty minutes of power walking from tomorrow morning. You never know when such a situation could arise.

Love,
Uncle

27 June 2012

Respected Uncle-Sir,

How much butter is enough?

Venky, Madurai

Beloved Venky,

It all depends on to who you are applying it to. Senior people usually require large quantities. You can also differentiate your offering based on the kind of butter you use, such as:
Hand-churned Butter: Churning it yourself adds the personal touch.
Holy Butter: This is butter produced by a particularly holy cow.
Imported Butter: This shows you have access to foreign cows.
Whatever you chose, its probably best to keep a small drum handy at all times. You never know when a requirement may arise.

With many blessings,
Uncle

4 July 2012

Dear Uncle,

I love this girl, but her father wants to kill me. What should I do?

Ranjeet, Jaipur

Dear Ranjeet,

In order for me to help you, you must provide me full information. Is the girl of a different caste? In that case, her father may be justified. Is she of the same sub-caste? In this case, also, the police are likely to take a sympathetic view. In either case, it is probably best for both of you to convert to Islam and shift to Moradabad. Historically, this has been a tried and tested method for solving caste-related problems.

In case he just dislikes you, that's a different case. Then I am afraid there is nothing I can suggest, except maybe try to improve your personality. Sometimes you can avoid death this way.

Your Loving Uncle

27 July 2012

Dear Uncle,

Nobody in our office wants to bell the cat. What should we do?

Shekhar, Chennai

Dear Shekhar,

First, you need to creep up on the cat with chloroform. Reach out gently and cover its nose. Be careful of dosage. Remember, you have to bell the cat, not eliminate it. Once the cat is unconscious, fix the bell to its collar. Your promotion is practically guaranteed.

Regards,
Uncle

16 August 2012

Dear Uncle,

My neighbour has purchased a Harley-Davidson. I am apprehensive. Can you give any suggestion?

Sashi Kant, Ghaziabad

Dear Sashi,

You have forgotten to mention whether your neighbour is married or unmarried. If he is married, then there is no need to worry. Within seven to ten days, the vehicle will disappear. If he is unmarried, then the matter is more complex. Perhaps he is seeking a woman. Do you know any? You should urgently introduce them. He may also be planning to go off on long holidays. In that case, you should borrow his household appliances.

I prefer to see such things in a positive light. He sounds like a large-hearted fellow. Perhaps he will give you his car.

Love,
Uncle

9 September 2012

Dear Uncle,

Our grandmother has started talking to furniture. Is this a cause for concern?

Javed, Bangalore

Respected Javed-bhai,

The key question is, is the furniture talking back? If so, you have poltergeists. You will have to call either a Catholic priest or Steven Spielberg. If you have small children in the house, it's better to call Mr Spielberg. Don't worry if the furniture appears to be moving. They are simply trying to escape your grandmother. I'm guessing they learnt this from watching you.

If the furniture is neither speaking nor moving, then I suggest you try talking to her. It's quite possible she may prefer talking to you, although I cannot judge, since I have never talked to you myself. All I have as evidence is the question you asked me. The question is concise, but not particularly entertaining. She may be chatting with chairs in order to avoid talking to you. If this is the case, buy more furniture. You could also put her in touch with Mr Clint Eastwood, who does the same thing in front of large audiences. Perhaps they can form a club.

Love,
Uncle

1 October 2012

Dear Uncle,

Nowadays I am unable to lift Pinky. Can you suggest any solution?

Regards,

Rocky, Chandigarh

Dear Rocky,

You could go to the gym more. Or she could eat less. Alternately, she could go to the gym more, and you could switch positions. Don't be misled by gender bias. At a more philosophical level, you have to ask yourself, do I really need to lift Pinky? In the first flush of your marriage, it may have been pleasurable. But now health is also a factor.

In case you are not married, I urge you to stop lifting her immediately. She sounds like a healthy girl. Her parents are probably the hefty type.

Love,
Uncle

29 October 2012

Dear Uncle,

Should I vote for Barack Obama or Mitt Romney?

Sunita, Bengaluru

Dear Sunita,

Seeing the massive media coverage, I had anticipated that this problem would arise. Please note that Indian citizens are not eligible to vote in the US elections. Consuming large quantities of food from McDonald's does not automatically qualify you for US citizenship. Certain unscrupulous local employees may be spreading such rumours. Do not fall for their tricks. Your location in Bengaluru is also a cause for concern. Are you working in a call centre? Do you pretend to be American on a regular basis? This can cause a wide variety of mental disorders.

In case you are actually American, the answer is much simpler. Successful American presidents are always very handsome. Less attractive people, such as Richard Nixon and Jimmy Carter, faced a variety of problems. Luckily, both Barack Obama and Mitt Romney are particularly fine specimens of manhood, so you cannot really go wrong. Such things are subjective, so simply do what your heart tells you to do. I always do, with good results.

Love,
Uncle

24 January 2013

Dear Uncle,

My son wants to grow up to be like Rahul Gandhi. How can I help him?

Nita, Mumbai

Dearest Nita,

He needs help from a trained professional. My cousin in Lajpat Nagar is a psychiatrist. He can help you. I can sms his details. His rates are very reasonable, although you should avoid the electro-shock therapy, as there is a lot of voltage fluctuation in that area.

In case I have misunderstood your requirement, here is a simple three-point program that will meet your needs.

1) Set up a blood donation camp on Rajiv Gandhi's birthday
2) Invite Rahul Gandhi to participate. If you allow Kapil Sibal to read his poetry to you, he will make the necessary arrangements
3) Once you have procured Rahul Gandhi's blood, transfer this blood to your son.

After this, tell everyone that the blood of the Nehru–Gandhis is flowing in his veins. The rest should be simple.

Love,
Uncle

10 April 2013

Dear Uncle,

The candidates for prime minister are not to my liking. Is emigration a good option?

Regards,
Charandas Chaurasia, Varanasi

Dear Mr Chaurasia,

There have been very few times in the history of India when emigration has not been a good option. This is why there are so many Indians all over world. Reception has been mixed. Generally we get beaten up a lot. If you are married, avoid Saudi Arabia. Your wife will be upset, and your marriage may suffer. Of course, recently they have allowed women to ride bicycles, but overall, the situation is not good. I believe Sweden is very nice, although the cuisine may not suit you. In France, the cuisine is very good, but the people may not suit you.

USA is always a good choice, but their preference is for scientists and comedians. In case you are a man of science with a sense of humour, you should apply for a visa immediately. Make sure they do not mistake you for a Pakistani. We are totally different, but they do not seem to understand that.

I, too, am finding both choices for prime minister unpleasant. Once you reach your destination, if the outlook is favourable, kindly do inform me. I may join you. Other countries also need Uncles.

Bon Voyage!
Uncle

HEALTH IS WEALTH

Editors move in mysterious ways. Those at *The Hindu* decided that Shovon was the perfect person to write a health and wellness column. Thus was born 'The Creaking Tree'.

Over time, this turned out to be the essential advisory for the rest of us, those who would run (or rather walk, with periodic rests) a mile at the prospect of running a mile, and prefer bars to barbells. Many important issues were addressed, such as Karan Johar as a potential health hazard, how CEOs keep fit (spoiler: by shouting at subordinates), the tough choice between cow milk and cow urine, and whether the invention of the gymnasium had something to do with the collapse of the Greek civilization.

IN PURSUIT OF WELLNESS

The pursuit of wellness leads to an increase in human happiness, especially for those who provide it. Deepak Chopra is worth over $80 million. Baba Ramdev will soon be bigger than Procter & Gamble. Maharishi Mahesh Yogi's attempts to promote yogic flying never rose beyond six to nine inches above the mattresses on which his yogis bounced, optimistically, in the lotus position, but the value of his real estate holdings has skyrocketed. This is commendable. The first thing purveyors of wellness have to do is achieve wellness themselves, because otherwise, how will they help other people? Currently, those at the top of this profession feel a deep and abiding sense of well-being.

What about the rest of us? Our search for wellness begins at birth, when we realise that amniotic fluid is no longer available, and we will have to find things to eat. In India, many of us are still doing this. On the other hand, many others have achieved this goal, which is why close to 5% of our population can be classified as morbidly obese. According to the National Family Health Survey, Delhi has taken the lead in this matter, with 49% of the women and 45% of the men falling in this category. This has placed a lot of pressure on the transport system, leading to breakdowns of buses and overcrowding in the metro. Flights leaving from Indira Gandhi International Airport may soon be unable to take off. The runner-up is Punjab, where 37.5% of the men and 30% of the women are obese. This once-proud state is being brought to its knees by a combination of drugs and butter chicken. Kerala, Goa, and Tamil Nadu round out the top five.

I was a little surprised by this. I was brought up to believe that South Indian eating habits are healthier than ours, but this appears to be a canard spread by the Udupi mafia. What this data tells us is that, in India, our preliminary pursuit of wellness involves large amounts of ghee. In Amritsar and Ludhiana, which have always been more open to Western influences, butter is preferred. However, there is no escaping evolution, and over time, our needs have begun to evolve. We order Diet Cokes with our Maharaja Macs. We have an extra spoon of dahi with our aloo parathas. These urges go beyond the physical. We have come to realise that carbohydrates cannot fill the yawning emptiness in our souls. It is at this point that our true pursuit of wellness begins. In the coming months, we will explore ways and means of achieving this, including inner engineering, quantum health and bananas.

The Hindu, 20 February 2017

THE HIGH WAY TO HEALTH

Today, we will discuss alcohol, one of the most popular techniques for achieving wellness. For as long as I can remember, people have been telling me that I'm not well. My teachers in school were particularly vocal on the subject. Conscious of this flaw, I have spent a lifetime trying to get better.

After a certain amount of trial-and-error, I found that alcohol works best. When consumed in moderation, it fills me with a deep sense of peace and well-being. I laugh a lot. Sometimes I fall down, causing minor injury. I'm just lucky that way. I'm not one of those drunks who beats up his wife. Besides, my wife would probably beat me right back, and her reflexes are better than mine.

You could be one of the lucky ones too. You could be a happy drunk. So if you're seeking wellness, one of the first things you should do is try pouring yourself a couple of stiff ones. Millions of people are doing this every day, and you know millions of people can't be wrong. It's the essence of democracy.

Once you've had a couple, probe your brain to see how you're feeling. Are you feeling the urge to commit acts of violence? This could make you feel better afterwards—improving your mental wellness—but it can be risky, especially if you're in a bar. You will have noticed that the bouncers are getting bigger. It's human evolution. As we speak, entire villages across India are feeding their sons protein supplements from a very young age so that they can grow up to become bouncers. It's a growing market. People need people to beat up other people. As a result, once you wake up in the hospital and see your bill, both your physical and mental wellness will decline considerably.

One other result of alcohol could be that you start feeling depressed. Is the face of your boss floating in front of your eyes? Did you just realise that most of your classmates are earning much more than you? Is it becoming clear how flawed you are as a parent? Are you feeling lasting regret that you did not learn Gujarati? You should stop drinking immediately. Alcohol is not for you. What you need is drugs. We will share the guidelines for this in a later issue.

The Hindu, 6 March 2017

EVIDENCE THAT GYMS ARE UNNATURAL

In medieval times, your average upscale residence came equipped with a dungeon, where beastly instruments were kept, which inflicted unspeakable tortures on the flesh of humans. Over time, as humanity evolved, they have been replaced by gyms. Most now have air conditioning, so that people can suffer in comfort. Some of the instruments have touch screens.

My own experiences with gyms have been mixed. I come from Bengali gentry, where sudden movement is frowned upon. When I was young, my culture protected me. But we all have to leave the nurturing bosom of our family at some point, and eventually, I had to come to Delhi, where this unholy practice is quite widespread.

I first realised my peril sitting at a bar on New Year's Eve. It dawned on me that I was sitting in between two young men in sleeveless tees, with arms the size of my thighs. They were drinking moodily, no doubt reflecting on the fact that while their bodies were temples, they still didn't have girlfriends. I knew that after a few more drinks, I would be making humorous remarks about this. I finished my drink and slunk away quickly.

Subsequently, I faced challenges from the corporate sector. In Kolkata, the corporate sector was mainly about leather armchairs and gin, with some light noodling on the golf course thrown in. Delhi was more active. I realised this in Janakpuri. During a period of financial trouble, our boss shifted us from Vasant Vihar to Janakpuri. Vasant Vihar is a posh part of town, full of expats, cafés, and shoppes. Janakpuri was more of a work in progress.

This social downfall affected us deeply. Morale plummeted. We mumbled when asked where we worked. Despite being a bit of a penny pincher, and somewhat lacking in human qualities, our boss was not immune to our sorrow. He thought of ways to cheer us up. He was willing to spend money, as long as the budget was reasonable. He created a lavishly appointed gym in the basement, with several treadmills, a shiny bondage rig, and hooks to hang our towels on.

Once it was set up, I remember a group of us going down to see it. We tiptoed around and touched the instruments gingerly. We spoke to each other in whispers. We trooped back up in silence, determined never to come back again. By and large, we kept this promise. I went down once, a few months later, just to see how it was doing. The place was covered in dust, and the security guards were using the treadmills to dry their socks and underwear.

This gym in Janakpuri revealed to me a basic truth. Gyms are an unnatural construct, forced upon us by supermodels and Photoshop. Under actual laboratory conditions, when left together in the middle of nowhere, our natural inclination is to avoid them.

The Hindu, 17 April 2017

THIS SLIMNESS FETISH MUST STOP!

As a society, we need to stop harassing fat people. There are many reasons for doing so. If one of them sits on you, you will regret it. But it goes beyond self-preservation. It's morally wrong.

Fat people have illuminated human history. Winston Churchill, Alfred Hitchcock and Queen Victoria were all pleasantly plump. Their silhouettes were distinctive. American president William Howard Taft had a waist size of 54 inches and bathed in a specially-constructed bathtub. He looked out on the Atlantic Ocean one morning and said, 'I'll get a piece of that fenced in some day, and then when I venture in, there will be no overflow.' Hemingway was no gazelle, and neither is Bhappi Lahiri. Adnan Sami did his best work when he was well fed. Elvis Presley's favourite snack was a peanut butter, jelly and bacon sandwich. Farah Khan has shown Shakira how to shake it.

Across the ages, well-rounded individuals have filled the world with joy and inspiration. And how do we repay them? By telling them they're not good enough. All these dieting tips and fitness routines are just ways of humiliating them. We are singling them out as defective. Why do we need to write about such things, that too in national newspapers? What you do to your body in the privacy of your home is your business, but this type of public flaunting is just hurtful and cruel.

I am also disturbed on a personal level. Quite a few of my relatives are full-figured, and I have never held it against them. They serve the best meals. For Bengalis, meals are very important. We discuss what to have for dinner while eating lunch. At dinnertime, breakfast is a popular topic, along with some light strategizing on lunch again. In Calcutta, we call this the circle of life. 'Health food' is an oxymoron. When we call a man healthy, we mean that he has some flesh on him, with curves in all the right places. My dietary requirements are rich and diverse. Why should I open newspapers and keep seeing pictures of salads? Who are you to push salad in my face? Everyone is trying to tell me what to eat. People complain about Gau Rakshaks, but what about Salad Fanciers? How are they any better?

And why must I keep looking at abs? This is what the Greeks used to do, and see how their civilisation has fallen. This type of malpractice must stop immediately. If you want to get thinner, go get a room. And if you think you're better than fat people, try belting out one song like Bhappi-da; then we'll see.

The Hindu, 1 May 2017

CAN YOU HANDLE THE DIET OF THE GODS?

Wrestling is a subject that has to be approached very carefully, especially if wrestlers are present. The Great Gama once lifted a stone which weighed 1,200 kilos. You can go see it in a museum in Baroda. In his youth, ladies in Khali's village used to ask him to pick up cows and buffaloes, which were refusing to move as instructed. Many men in India like to take liberties with women, but it's unlikely that young Sakshi Malik is facing this problem.

I would never argue with a wrestler, and neither should you. But their connection to health and wellness needs to be explored, because there is scope for confusion. Take diet, for example. The search for the perfect diet is one of the cornerstones of wellness. It can take a lot of time because there are so many of them. There are high-carb diets and low-fat diets and all-meat diets and Kareena Kapoor diets and my own personal favourite, the popcorn diet. So why not consider the wrestler's diet? It seems to be working. They're rich, famous, and look good in leotards. Why not eat like them?

Let us examine this, starting at the top. Most wrestlers will tell you that India's greatest wrestler was The Great Gama, who was outwrestling men twice his size at the age of 10. In his prime, this was his daily diet: 20 litres of milk, half a kilogram of pure butter, 4 kilograms of fruits and lots of yakhni.

The Great Khali was a superstar in the US for a decade. Originally known as Giant Singh, he changed his name in honour of the great goddess Kali, making him one more person with whom you should not mess. His dinner consists of cheese, legumes, vegetables, 10 wheat breads, brown rice, chicken, six eggs, and two litres of milk and ice after dinner. He also loves coffee, curd and candy.

This all sounds great, but before you rush out to buy candy, consider this. The Great Gama used to do 5,000 squats and 3,000 push-ups every day. Bruce Lee followed his methods. Or look at Gobar Guha, the pride of Bengal. In the 19th century, the Brits were very contemptuous of Bengalis. Macaulay called us effeminate, sedentary and languid. Journalist G. W. Stevens spent a lot of time examining our legs. 'By his leg you shall know a Bengali,' he said. 'The leg of a Bengali is either skin and bones... or else it is very fat and globular, also turning at the knee, with round thighs like a woman. The Bengali's leg is the leg of a slave.'

Bengalis were mortally insulted, and took to wrestling with a vengeance, inspired by Swami Vivekananda, amongst others. The end result of this was Gobar Guha, who was 6 foot 1, had a 48-inch chest and became the first Asian to win a world title. He was known for his appetite, and his diet was full of goodies. But he also did 2,500 push-ups a day, and wore a collar around his neck that weighed 70 kilos. All of which tells us a fundamental truth about wellness and diets. You can eat what you like, and enjoy it, so long as you remember—some amount of movement is also required.

The Hindu, 29 May 2017

WHY I WILL AVOID BOSU WORKOUTS

When I first heard that *The Hindu* was doing an article on Bosu workouts, I was nonplussed. There has only been one Bosu in my life, and his name was Jyoti. You can anglicise his surname as much as you like, with your Tagores and Mitters and Sinhas, and the corruption of innocent Bandopadhyayas into Banerjees, but he will always be Bosu to me.

I was shocked because the words 'Bosu' and 'work' have rarely been used in the same sentence before. It seems unnatural. Despite being a legendary leader, he was very democratic. He never did any work, and he didn't expect us to do any either. We were receptive and eager. We too felt that work was inherently wrong. It was a long, slow process. I spent 20 years in Calcutta. I grew up, got a job, and had children, and throughout this period, two things were constant. He was always the Chief Minister, and the Calcutta Metro was always under construction. His influence was all-pervasive. I have two nephews, who used to beat each other up when they were small. They've stopped now, because they're in their 40s. Their father was a dedicated communist. In between the punches and the hair pulling, they would call each other terrible names, such as 'petit bourgeois' and 'capitalist roader', while their mother wept in a corner, dabbing her eyes with her pallu. In this way, he inspired the youth.

I never quite understood the secret of his appeal. He was largely inert, and spoke very little. Perhaps, he just seemed like the type of person who ought to be a leader. He came from a good family, and his English was good. His dhotis were always spotless. His taste in whisky was refined. His sarcasm was withering. It never occurred to any of us to ask him to actually do anything. In hindsight, this was a mistake. Economically and socially, he left us with nothing but chit funds and cultural activities. Politically, many of us automatically reach for a rock whenever we hear the word 'communist'.

What about health? How did he affect us, health-wise? Our mental health was good. We were spared the trauma of work stress, because we didn't have any work. Wealth can also be a source of stress, but this too was never a problem. Physically, we faced certain drawbacks. We were beaten savagely by party cadres, leading to a rise in medical expenses. Due to frequent power cuts, we had to study by candlelight, which is why so many Bengalis wear spectacles.

Personally, I live in fear that he might come back, a decaying corpse in an excellent dhoti, reaching out blindly to switch off the lights. Whenever I see his picture, or hear his name, a shiver goes down my spine. So I'm sure the Bosu Workout is excellent, but I'll give it a miss.

The Hindu, 7 August 2017

MY EXPERIENCE AS A FIRST-TIME RUNNER

I have vivid memories of the first time I ran. I was four years old and in a pyramid in Egypt.

I was on holiday with my parents, the first holiday that I can remember. We had just entered the pyramid, and I found myself in a long, dark, narrow corridor, dimly lit by flickering torches. 'Don't run, you might fall down,' said my mother, so I immediately started running. I did not feel like listening to her. I was disgruntled.

Things had not been as per my liking. There was no Scooby Doo on TV in the hotel. My mother had refused to buy me chocolate-covered nuts, even though I had shouted a lot. She said she could make them at home, yet another promise that she did not keep. I wanted to see Snow White and the Seven Dwarfs at the local cinema, but my parents refused because it was dubbed in Egyptian. Without proper audio, we would not get full value for money. The sun was scorching. The heat was unbearable. There was sand everywhere and the people looked funny. My small souvenir sphinx had broken in two when I dropped it. My packet of potato chips was empty. I was thirsty, but the Fanta here tasted wrong.

Just a few minutes earlier, my parents had taken a camel ride, but relegated me to a donkey, because I might fall off. It was a very small donkey, and my feet almost reached the ground. Its head was drooping. It walked very slowly. It was embarrassed too. Local boys had pointed and sniggered.

Standing there inside the pyramid, I was still feeling keenly humiliated. I needed to break free. I ran down the corridor as fast as I could, leaving my parents far, far behind, my mother's cries growing fainter, a vague notion of escape blooming in my mind, into a future where the chocolate-covered nuts ran wild and free, until I fell down and injured my knee, twisted and scraped on the ancient stone.

It took a while for the others to reach me. There was blood

everywhere and it was very dark. One of the guides helped carry me back out into the sun. I never saw a single mummy. The bleeding stopped once we reached the hotel room, which had no AC. Eventually, I recovered and we left Egypt. This was my experience as a first-time runner. I must have run before, but this is the first case that I can remember. It prejudiced me against running from a very early age, and I have never visited Egypt again.

The Hindu, 18 September 2017

IS SOCIAL MEDIA MAKING US FITTER OR FATTER?

I see many more healthy people thanks to Facebook. I also see a lot more food. It's a problem. I'm getting mixed messages from social media.

As it is, being Bengali, I am ambivalent about fitness. Hearty meals play a big role in our lives. It's not that we don't understand the importance of fitness, because we're also hypochondriacs. I have several close relatives whose medical expertise is shocking. None of them are doctors. They just want to study the human condition. In my circles, discussions about ailments are free and frank, with symptoms lavishly detailed. I have a college friend who is now a pillar of society who used to describe the consistency, colour and texture of his stool to all of us every morning, without fail. ('Today it was a rich, golden brown, very firm.') Luckily for all of us, this was in the days before phone cameras and social media.

When Arvind Kejriwal tweeted about loose motions, the nation was vastly amused. I couldn't see why. Where I came from, this was a fairly common topic at get-togethers, with people often munching on fish fries while comparing notes on the effectiveness of antacids. It was all in good spirit. The amateurs held no grudge against the professionals. If any doctors happened to be present, and made the mistake of revealing that they were doctors, they were roped into such discussions. In Calcutta, free medical consultation at public gatherings is an established social norm.

Since I left Calcutta, I have made other types of friends. Some of them run half marathons. One of them climbed Mount Kilimanjaro. Sometimes they snorkel. As a result, my social media influences are now more evenly spread between food and fitness, apart from politics, which naturally takes up a lot of space. In fact, it takes up most of the space. I would put politics in the food category, because when I see politicians, I think of food. Most of them are gruesomely overweight. Some of them are heartless, and appear in shorts. They're like the 'before' pictures in slimming ads. High-priced tailors cannot hide their love handles.

They are men of substance, and if they sit on you, you're in trouble. They're the main things we see on social media.

If you step back and think about it, you will realise that at this very moment, thousands of Indians across the country are tweeting angrily in support of some extremely fat people. So it looks like fitness is losing, because the message that we're getting from social media is clear. Stick to your chair, enjoy the gravy and don't try to run. It encourages the public to chase you.

The Hindu, 2 October 2017

POSTURE CAN MAKE YOU A WINNER!

When I was young, my mother was constantly poking me in the back and asking me to sit up straight. My aunties were pretty vigilant too, so I was poked a lot as a child. There's a small dent in my back between the third and fourth vertebrae. As a result, I leaped at the chance to explain more about posture.

During the course of the extensive research that I did for this article, I discovered that they were all wrong. According to trained orthopaedics, sitting up straight for too long puts unnecessary strain on the spine. It became popular in the Western world, thanks to Queen Victoria and Mary Poppins, but there was no scientific basis for it. It was just that Queen Victoria liked her subjects to be lined up neatly. This confused me. It seemed like science was questioning my heritage.

Personally, I blame Baba Ramdev. He was the logical person to build mass awareness about correct posture, and bring clarity to the issue, but we were too distracted by his stomach, and now he is selling toothpaste. I tried to understand the underlying science, so that I could explain it to younger readers, but I was overwhelmed by technicalities.

For example, the German orthopaedic surgeon, Hanns Schoberth, whose credentials are formidable, recommends that we should sit at a 60-degree angle, because 'this means that when moving from a standing (lordosis) to an upright sitting position, you bend the hip joints about 60 degrees and rotate the pelvis axis backwards, flattening the lumbar curve (kyphosis) of the back 30 degrees and straining the muscles of the back.' I have no idea what this means. I don't make the news, I just report it. But it did emphasise the importance of correct posture.

Another reason why we need to be careful about posture is because people are analysing our personalities based on it. *Cosmopolitan* magazine had a lot of useful information on 'How people are judging you by your posture', but I got distracted by 'Wine, pizza and the 31 sexiest movies', followed by 'I'm really insecure about my body hair and this is ruining my love life.' What I did manage to gather is that posture is a source of power. Celebrities use posture well. They hold their shoulder blades back as if there's an orange between them. They bring their heads over their shoulders and pull their belly buttons towards their spine. Posture is power. Posture is confidence. Posture also explains our political situation. Our Prime Minister's posture is superb, with his chest thrust out so beautifully, while Rahul Gandhi is constantly slouching. Posture is the key to winning.

Talking of winning, we all want a win first thing in the morning, which is why the correct toilet posture is so important. It's all about angles. The angle affects elimination. Sitting on a Western potty creates an anorectal angle, which blocks the flow, creating upward pressure on the rectum. Squatting does not involve angles, leading to easier and faster completion of No. 2, thus proving, once more, that East or West, India is the best.

The Hindu, 30 October 2017

WHY SYRINGES SHOULD NOT BE A SURPRISE

Everyone is very upset about a private hospital making 525% profit on syringes, which seems a little unfair. Fabindia makes the same on *moong* dal, and no one seems to mind. But Arnab Goswami is furious, and newspapers have been critical. We are shocked by the shadiness. I have no idea why.

The medical profession has always been shady. Until the mid-fifties, doctors were endorsing cigarettes ('Throat doctors vote Old Gold is best for your throat!'). They even suggested it as a cure for asthma. Enterprising pharma companies were selling morphine to babies, promising miraculous results, which they delivered. Their portions were generous. For example, one ounce of Mrs Winslow's Soothing Syrup contained 65 mg of morphine.

One of the first commercial applications of radium was in Radium Hand Cleaner, which promised to 'remove everything but the skin'. Electroshock therapy has been used to cure impotence. This involved machinery. A popular model was the Doctor Bell Electro Appliance, an electrified belt with a small noose to hold the organ. Dr Sanden's Electric Belt and Suspensory for Weak Men was very similar, but with some added benefits. Apart from seminal weakness and lost manhood, it also helped with poor memory.

The health industry was very active during the reign of Queen Victoria. Some Victorian doctors realised that moodiness was a serious medical condition, which afflicted women, with symptoms including nervousness, irritability, and a tendency to cause trouble. Unable to figure out that it was because of the corsets, they found a cure, which became wildly popular in both the UK and the US. This process involved vigorous manipulation by a licensed medical practitioner, which was supposed to continue until 'hysterical paroxysm' was achieved. Some doctors even advertised, with one ad from this period by Dr Swift, showing him kneeling before his patient, with one hand up her skirt, while she looks away modestly.

Defying the principle that what goes in must come out, medieval European doctors also promoted enemas. They even invented a device for it, called the clister, a metal tube that looks like a Holi pichkari, except with a small cup connected to the pointy end. The practice became very widespread. We all know about Gandhiji, but what is less well-known is that Louis XIV of France was a big fan. He had over 2,000 enemas, including some when he sat on the throne.

The conclusion is simple. Throughout history, a large chunk of the medical profession has been trying to separate us from our money, ruthlessly and without pity, just because we were having fun while they were studying for their medical exams. So there's no point getting upset about 500% mark-ups on syringes. That's normal. You're probably just jealous. What you really have to ask yourself is, what else are they up to?

The Hindu, 11 December 2017

PLEASE READ THIS BEFORE USING YOUR HANDS

The Scandi Sense diet gets its name from Scandinavia, home of Thor, and from common sense. Scandinavians have a lot of common sense, because they get very little sunlight, and sudden, impulsive actions in the dark can cause injury. Historically, Scandinavians have enjoyed a balanced diet of fish and potatoes. The Scandi Sense diet is even more balanced. The underlying principle involves the rejection of utensils. Traditionally, western societies have used utensils such as knives and forks for eating, but the Scandinavians have not allowed such biases to prejudice their thinking. They now recommend that meals should be measured in handfuls: two handfuls of vegetables, one of carbohydrate and one of protein. In addition, a spoonful of fat is permitted.

I have been trying to follow it recently, and the results have not been good. At a Chinese restaurant the other day, I measured out my portion of Chef Special Chow Mein by scooping out a handful. Driven by the need for accuracy, I carefully put back the extra noodles. Afterwards, no one else touched the noodles, and a lot of food was wasted. I got similar reactions at a wedding buffet. After I had eaten, no one else touched the *dal makhni*, or the butterscotch ice cream. Drinking has been a problem too, because the whisky keeps dribbling through my fingers.

But more than myself, I'm concerned about others. If this diet is to gain widespread acceptance, society will need to change. This is going to be an uphill task. The other day, I asked for a handful of *gulab jamuns* at Evergreen Sweet House, and things became awkward. The salesman spent a long time gazing down at the tray full of syrup, torn between his desire to sell *gulab jamuns* and the need to go and wash his hands. Eventually, I gave up and went away.

Apart from the social implications, this diet also suffers from a technical flaw. It gives an unfair advantage to people with large hands. They get to eat more, while the rest of us starve. The truth is, human hands vary widely in size, and this is not connected to height and weight. For example, the average American male is 5 feet 10 inches tall, and his hands are 7.44 inches long. However, Donald Trump is 6 feet 2, and his hands are 7.25 inches long. We know this because Madame Tussauds once took his measurements for a waxwork dummy. They retired the dummy in 2011, but they retained the hand.

How do you fare, hand-wise? Before adopting the Scandi Sense diet, it is essential for you to know. You can use the Donald Trump Scale to judge. If you Google 'Donald Trump Hand Hollywood Reporter', you will find a page which has a downloadable pdf file of his hand. Print it out and compare your hand size with his. If your hand is much larger, you may pursue the Scandi Sense diet, safe in the knowledge that you will get enough to eat. But if your hand is the same size, or much smaller, then the Scandinavian method is not for you.

The Hindu, 4 June 2018

WHICH COW PRODUCT IS BEST FOR ME?

According to newspaper reports, the price of cow's milk and the price of cow urine in Rajasthan are now approximately the same. This could soon become the norm elsewhere. This raises an important question. Assuming you have budget constraints, and cannot afford both, which should you be drinking? I am unable to guide you from personal experience, because I have never tasted cow urine. My mother only forced me to drink milk. At the time I was very resentful, but I realise now that things could have been much worse. This is where science, both foreign and domestic, can guide us. Using the scientific method, the first question we have to ask ourselves is, who will be consuming the fluid? If it is a child, milk provides some obvious benefits, such as stronger teeth and solid bones.

Besides, forcing your child to drink urine is inadvisable. Children tend to remember these things, and your chances of ending up in an old age home will climb astronomically. Young adults, typically more adventurous, can weigh their options. There are many things to consider. Youth today are often keen on bodybuilding, and cow's milk can be helpful. Cow's milk is designed to help calves grow quickly. It is rich in high-quality protein. Those looking to bulk up should therefore drink plenty of it. Those with a preference for alcohol, however, might prefer to drink cow urine. Cow urine is full of nitrogen, which is very good for the liver and kidney.

There are more points to ponder. Cow's milk is good for the skin, while cow's urine can help with depression, making it a toss-up between looking good and feeling sad. By the time we reach middle age, other factors come into play. If we are prone to high blood pressure, the potassium in cow's milk can lower it. For those with diabetic tendencies, however, urine would be a better choice.

By the time you reach your twilight years, you may not care any longer. Let's pretend you do. If so, cow's milk can help with arthritis. On the other hand, cow's urine is reported to have anti-ageing properties, but we can't tell for sure, because none of the people reporting this have lived long enough yet.

All this information may be confusing, especially if you have difficulty making choices. At a buffet, do you eat both the chow mein and the tandoori chicken? If so, there's only one thing you can do. Go fifty-fifty. Mix the two liquids, and create something light green, frothy, and brimming with health. It will make you a trendsetter. It's only a matter of time before Amul and Mother Dairy launch tetrapaks, with names like Zingy and Zest and, if they're really with the programme, Govardhan. Your skin will glow. Your teeth will shine. Your bowel movements will be magnificent. And if you cannot drink it all, don't despair. According to reliable sources, it's also a very good floor cleaner.

The Hindu, 30 July 2018

DID SOMEONE SAY 1984?

I have always been afraid of Big Brother, even before I read *Nineteen Eighty-Four*, which only confirmed my suspicions. Most of us are, to a greater or lesser extent. It's because of the circumstances of our birth. When we first come into the world, naked and wriggling, we feel like we can do anything. We are wild and free. After the initial euphoria, things go rapidly downhill.

Soon people begin to order us about. Get your hand out of the potty! Drink your milk! Don't wear your underwear on your head! Stop flushing the Lego! Stay away from the bougainvillea! Shortly afterwards, you find yourself staying in late at the office, making elaborate, meaningless diagrams for your boss' PowerPoint presentation. The fascists are all around us, making us bow to their will.

You could argue that resistance is unnecessary, and we should simply go with the flow. But if there's one thing I've learnt, it's this. Things can always get worse. We may be living and dying in subjugation, but there are times when men and women of principle have to stand up against the forces of tyranny. This is one of those times.

A new threat has arisen. The concept of Chief Wellness Officer is being floated, even in reputable publications like *The Hindu*. It's a call to arms. Action is needed. We cannot stand idly by while they proliferate. Companies have always focused on health. It's a way to pretend that they care. By and large, this involved an annual visit to the company doctor. He would feel your pulse, ask you to cough, and certify you completely fit. He never even took a blood sample, because the company was already sucking enough of it. He was pleasant, and happy to chat. He never took too much interest.

The Chief Wellness Officer, on the other hand, will be deeply interested, but have no budget, because the last thing the company wants to do is spend more money on you. He will not, therefore, be in a position to give you analgesics, or mild laxatives, or perform minor procedures. Instead, he will provide advice and instruction. He will define principles and lay out guidelines. He will examine lifestyles and regulate food choices. He will ask you to cut down on drinking. These were the few parts of your life that you could still call your own, but not anymore.

Now they will be part of your Annual Assessment, with adverse remarks such as 'tends to lose focus during meditation' and 'refuses to eat yoghurt.' Your bonus will be linked to your Body Mass Index. Meetings will end with Vedic chanting. If your company has hired a Chief Wellness Officer, there's no time to waste. Rise up now, before it's too late. Your lifestyle is all you have left. Don't let them take it away.

The Hindu, 13 August 2018

WHY DELHI CEOS ARE SUPER FIT

I have met many CEOs. Most of them keep fit by shouting a lot. They exercise parts of the body that I have never seen exercised before, like the veins in their forehead. Unlike other forms of exercise, which are predictable and regimented, shouting is very customisable. Some CEOs clench and unclench their fists. Over time, this improves their grip. Others throw things, which is great for developing hand-eye coordination. The shouting itself takes various forms. Some start low, and build to a crescendo. Others start at a crescendo and gradually run out of steam. Most notably, some can maintain a crescendo for an improbably long time. These are the ones to avoid.

I had once gone to make a client presentation with my boss. We were waiting in their reception, and the conference room was right next to it. Whenever I am near a conference room, I always try to peep in and see what's happening. In this case, the CEO, a young man in his 20s, was yelling at a bunch of depressed middle-aged men. They were one of those pyramid schemes, where the key thing for all concerned is to avoid being at the bottom of the pyramid. He shouted non-stop for half an hour, hammering the table. Spit flew as he screamed. I was awestruck. I backed away slowly, and told my boss that we were leaving. He did not argue. He had heard everything too.

A few years later, I was attending monthly review meetings in Bengaluru, for a client who worked in training and recruitment. The CEO of this company, always suave during interviews on NDTV, was already conducting morning meetings every day, where he shouted at his key people between 9 and 10, using teleconference facilities, but he felt that the human touch was missing. So he would call everyone once a month to Bengaluru in order to shout at them in person.

At my first meeting, I initially thought that things were going quite well. He seemed rather sweet, and was asking what appeared to be reasonable questions. His tone was mild. I was puzzled by the fact that everyone was sitting with very fixed smiles on their faces, like the audience at a poetry reading by Kapil Sibal. They knew what was coming. He was waiting for someone to give him the wrong answer. The moment he got one, the beast was unleashed. He paced up and down, exercising calf muscles. He glared and rolled his eyes. He shouted continuously, saying things like, 'I'm much smarter than you, so you're wrong and I'm right!' and 'Stop talking! I already know everything you're going to say!' His face went red. His blood was pumping. It was the most complete and thorough workout I have ever seen. I kept quiet and hid behind one of the larger Sales Managers. Afterwards, while we were outside smoking nervously, I felt compelled to make an observation. 'People always say how Delhi people shout so much,' I said, 'But man, you Bengaluru guys are pretty good too.' They pointed out that he was born and brought up in Delhi. This leads me to believe that this could be a Delhi thing. The implication for health seekers is clear. There are many paths to health, and this is one of them. Come to Delhi and become a CEO. Health and fitness will follow.

The Hindu, 8 October 2018

HOW TO CORRECT YOUR SLEEP CYCLE

Circadian rhythms are cycles that our bodies follow automatically over 24-hour periods, like the desire for a gin and tonic when the sun goes down.

They develop inside us, but can be influenced by external factors. Our sleep cycle is the most important of these rhythms. This handy guide identifies things that interfere with our sleep cycle, and provides advice on how to tackle them. Some of this advice is of limited value.

Anxiety about the economy: It could be that you lie awake at night thinking, 'Is the economy going to get worse?' Let us put your minds at rest. It almost certainly will. Once you accept this, there will be no need for further worry.

AC not working: Your AC may not be working, leading to sleepless nights. You have been trying to get a service engineer to come for the last three weeks, but despite occasional flashes of hope, so far you have been unsuccessful. The solution is to buy a new AC. Before buying, shortlist three companies, and make fake requests for service to each. See which one comes soonest. This is the one you should purchase.

Lack of romance: Could it be that your standards are too high? Some people who have been failing consistently are thinking of shifting to Kashmir, but we would not recommend this.

Tweets by Chetan Bhagat: You may be lying awake thinking about his tweets. Just thinking is not going to solve anything. Action is called for. Programme your Twitter feed so that it sends him a tweet every day saying; 'Read a book, Chetan!' every morning at 4 am. Eventually, success will be yours.

Annual Performance Review: There is no point worrying about this now. It's too late. In future, get your boss coffee more often, and buy small, thoughtful gifts from time to time. Show that you care.

Decline of the Left wing: The space for the Left is constricting. While this is a matter for concern, please remember that if it keeps expanding, the culmination of the process is Xi Jinping, lifetime ruler of China. Things may look bad now, but they could have been much worse. Once you realise this, sleep will come automatically.

Late night singing: Once their sins accumulate beyond a point, your neighbours will often build a *pandal* in the middle of your lane and sing to the gods for mercy. At around 2 a.m., you will also feel the need for mercy. Since their *pandal* is blocking the road, there is no way for you to escape. The best solution is to powder your face, put on a kurta, and join them. Remember, you yourself are not entirely devoid of sin.

Too many aloo parathas: Indigestion can often affect sleep cycles. The fact that you are reading the health section of *The Hindu* means that there is still hope for you. Your intentions are good. If all else fails, go easy on the pickle.

Netflix: There is no known cure for this.

The Hindu, 15 October 2019

42

42, as everyone who has read Douglas Adams' *Hitchhiker's Guide to the Galaxy* knows, is the Answer to the Ultimate Question about Life, the Universe and Everything. It was arrived at by the supercomputer Deep Thought after seven and a half million years of calculations.

In many of his newspaper columns, Shovon delved into complicated issues of the human condition, from why all that you really need is a black tee-shirt and the many reasons one should not trust men with beards to tips on avoiding burnout at work (it seems to be pure coincidence that all his bosses had nervous breakdowns).

Also included are his notes from the hospital bed as he coped with deadly disease.

WHY MEN IN BEARDS SHOULD NEVER BE TRUSTED

The only thing worse than a man in a beard is a woman in a beard, because she is pretending to be a different gender. Also, in the case of women, the beard is usually false, adding another layer of deceit to the whole enterprise. Luckily, such cases are few and far between. Bearded men are far more widespread. Therein lies the danger. We are surrounded by men who can render themselves unrecognisable simply by using a razor. Yet none of us thinks of the peril. I am, of course, leaving out those who wear beards as a matter of religious faith. I refer only to those who choose to be fuzzy, as a matter of personal taste.

This independent, unprompted impulse to be bearded is inherently shady. What type of mentality is it that leads a man to look at his face in the mirror and say, I must hide as much of this as possible? And yet society condones this. At the dawn of human history, bearded men in positions of power established social conventions that lull us into a false sense of security. We have been trained to think of them as harmless.

History is full of bearded men who have caused incalculable human misery, like Genghis Khan, Karl Marx, Fu Manchu, Hans Gruber, Osama bin Laden, Ivan the Terrible, General Zod, Tarun Tejpal and Fidel Castro. This evil comes in a wide variety of subsets, such as dictators, leftist economists and corrupt Shaolin masters. The evidence is all around us, and yet we do not use our eyes to see.

America is the most advanced nation on earth, and we should be learning from them. Kim Kardashian has never dated a man with a beard. In the last 125 years, the American public has never elected a bearded man as president. The CIA spent the better part of the Cold War trying to sabotage Fidel Castro's beard, by sneaking thalium salts into his shoes, which would 'cause his eyebrows, beard and pubic hair to fall out'. This was just one of CIA's 33 plans, which included exploding cigars, wild acid trips, poisoned fountain pens and suits with fungus. As we speak, at airports across the USA, men in beards are being treated with the utmost suspicion.

Bearded men are inherently misogynistic. Their attitude towards women is poor. They look at their life partners, smile their secret smiles and think, 'You can use all the moisturiser you like, but my beard will be scratching your cheeks on a daily basis.' Is this any way to treat the mother of their children?

Different beards tell us different things. A long flowing beard can be used to hide things, such as weapons and food items, that the bearded person does not want to share with you. A beard that covers the whole face sends a clear message—this man wants to make it as hard as possible for you to recognise him. A goatee has only one purpose—to be fingered slowly while hatching evil plots. But the French cut beard is the worst of all. The owner of a French cut beard combines evil with a sense of aesthetics. He will cause you pain and suffering in ways that are elegant and carefully art directed. Countless films in various languages have taught us this, yet we never seem to learn. Scientific studies have ranked and classified beards in order of evil, from the full beard to the soul patch, an unholy little strip on the tip of the chin.

FACIAL HAIR MAFIA

If any of your friends have become recently bearded, shave them while there is still time. The evil may not have set in yet. But for anyone who has been bearded for more than five years, it is probably too late. The only thing to do is shun them as much as possible. This yardstick should also be applied professionally. If your company has too many bearded people in senior positions, you need to leave now. Remember not to share your plans with any bearded people, even if they appear harmless. The beard mafia is everywhere. Its tentacles are in everything. Its resources are many. Its vision is long-term. Through its ownership of Gillette, which is now in a monopoly position, it is making it more and more expensive to shave.

We may not be able to do much about global conspiracies. But at least in our personal lives, we must be vigilant. The next time you meet a bearded man, ask yourself a simple question.

What does this man have to hide?

Scroll.in, 16 December 2014

WHY MY WARDROBE IS ALMOST EMPTY

My wardrobe is almost empty and this is a matter of great pride to me. It took me years to reach this position. When I was in school, my mother was constantly cleaning my room. There was never any point in hiding anything. For a while, I tried hiding things under the mattress, mainly copies of *Debonair*, which I purchased from a different store every time, to avoid looking like a pervert. They always gave it to me in a brown paper bag. My collection grew over the years. My mattress was lumpy but I didn't mind.

Until one day a friend of mine stayed the night to watch football. He is now a senior executive in a reputed multinational and a pillar of society, but at the time he was horny and desperate. I was in the bathroom when he left in the morning, and I came out to find my father sitting on my bed, studying my *Debonair* collection. They were laid all over it, like an art gallery. When I later asked Arup why he had done this, he said, 'They looked so nice that way.'

I clung to the hope that maybe my father had not opened any of them, but even the covers were problematic. It was a more innocent time, and most girlie mags pretended to be intellectual. They developed your brain while weakening your moral fibre. *Debonair* covers often featured 'Dom Moraes on Nehru' and interviews with Ashok Mitra, an angry communist, but they also featured stories such as 'A brief history of the buttock', '10 ways to increase pleasure' and 'The naughty girl next door'. I was not optimistic. I quietly slipped out through the side door and went off to college, where I spent my time lying under a tree in a more disturbed frame of mind than usual.

When I came back that evening, my collection was gone. It was a terrible blow, and it changed my thought process. Ever since, I have lost all interest in material possessions. Things come and go, I realised. All is illusion. I also got married, and it turns out that my wife, whom I love dearly, needs as much cupboard space as she can get. Marriage is a matter of adjustment, and over the years, I have tried to accommodate her by emptying my cupboards as much as possible.

What helped me was the realisation that clothes are unnecessary. They divert the intellect. Every morning, we spend time trying to figure out whether the green shirt goes with the brown pants, after which comes the question of socks. If your intellect is towering, it's a waste of time. I wear only black T-shirts, because they're cheap and they match my jeans. I was thinking of reducing it to only one, but hygiene became an issue, and my wife offered to divorce me.

I now have two pairs of jeans and eight black T-shirts. I wear the ones with no holes on special occasions. My entire wardrobe is one small pile. I can carry it with me if there's a flood or an earthquake. Of course, I still have a drawer full of socks, handkerchiefs and underwear. Handkerchiefs are an excellent invention. No gentleman should be without one. I'm in two minds about the socks and underwear. Will I be able to give them up? Only time will tell.

The Hindu, 8 January 2018

EXAM STRESS DECODED

I have been through the A-Z of exam stress. A for acute nausea, which occurred when I first checked the syllabus, three days before the exam. B for book trauma triggered by the realisation that I did not have several textbooks, and it was too late to go out and buy them. C for cruel fate, which always ensured that the three chapters I left out were the ones most prominently featured in the test paper. D for delirium, when I actually knew one of the answers. E for extremely shady, which is how I would behave when people asked me later how it went. F for fried food, which I needed in large quantities. G for Gargi, who once taught me during an exam that girls have certain inherent advantages, by flipping the book she was copying from under her skirt, leaving the invigilator nonplussed.

H for Horlicks, which my mother would make me drink, thanks to which I have a lifelong aversion to undistilled malt. I for the inevitability of failure. J for Jaba Kusum hair oil, applied liberally to cool the brain, with extra on the day of the Math exam. K for the knowledge pill, which I kept hoping someone would invent. L for the little spasms that clutched my chest, as the panic attacks came and went. M for massive optimism, which led me to believe that I could finish six chapters in the next three hours. N for Nazia Hassan, whose music my neighbour would play while I tried to memorise Organic Chemistry.

O for Organic Chemistry, then and now, a thing of horror. P for Panipat, whose battles I always mixed up. Q for Question Papers, in bound volumes larger than my head, which I would leaf through, hopelessly, as the Horlicks grew cold near my elbow. R for Rotomac, a pen that I am ashamed to admit, I used frequently. S for sympathy, which my classmates did not display when I begged them for their notes, even though there were times when I cried. T for the Tips and Tricks series, which was not as useful as I hoped, and never advised me to start studying earlier. U for unemployment, staring me in the face.

V for victory, which I had no hope of achieving. W for wedding bells, which grew fainter and fainter as my prospects for a job receded. X for xeroxing, the discovery of which seemed to make learning how to draw countries and creatures unnecessary and unjustified. Y for Yashodhara, a teacher whose beauty distracted us from geography (or was it history?) leaving us particularly unprepared for exams in that subject.

Z for zero, both the marks I expected, and what my teachers said I would amount to. We were both wrong, but just barely.

Those times were times of great suffering, but now I see them as a good thing. Whenever things look bad, and the end seems near, with neither hope nor help visible on the horizon, usually around Tuesday, I remind myself that I don't have to sit for exams any more.

The Hindu, 26 February 2018

WHY 'ACTIVE HOLIDAY' IS AN OXYMORON

'Active holiday' is an oxymoron. A holiday is a time to rest from all the hard work we avoid the rest of the year. It's a time for repose and contemplation, perhaps a few extra drinks. So many fail to see this.

People often come to me after their holidays, looking slightly worse for wear, their faces haggard and thin, to tell me how they trekked half way up to Sandakphu, and then got caught in a torrential downpour on the way down, and took shelter in a nearby forest, and spent the night in the open, eating three biscuits each for dinner, and what fun the whole thing had been. It makes me very sad.

There is such a stigma attached to mental health issues in this country, leaving so many untreated. What's worse is that it's spreading. It's becoming more and more common. I have family and friends who behave like this. Their holidays are furiously active. They go skiing and almost break their ankles, not realising that if god had meant us to ski, our feet would have been shaped differently. They pay huge sums of money to stay in a tent instead of a room, which makes no sense whatsoever. They raft down rivers. They climb up mountains. They go on horse riding expeditions, spending large periods of time on animals with large teeth and sharp hooves, who live most of their lives with people sitting on their backs, periodically kicking them in the ribs. If I was a horse, I would be kicking people in the teeth every chance I got, until I rose up one day and led my brothers and sisters to overthrow the humans, like in *Planet of the Apes*.

Active holidaymakers embrace the opportunity to bungee-jump, because everyone knows rubber bands are unbreakable. They run up hills. They snorkel in oceans. They jog on narrow mountain trails. They chase after birds. They go on safaris and get close to tigers, who see large bags of flesh hanging out of their jeeps, unarmed and defenceless. It's like Meals on Wheels in the jungle. They rappel. They sail. They hang-glide. Some of them even sky-dive. It's as if no holiday is complete without the risk of fatal injury.

Like any normal person, my idea of a holiday is room service. I need a bed with switches, excellent air conditioning, and the joy of ordering Chef Special Chow Mein whenever I feel like it. I don't mind a nice view, so long as the window is close to the bed. The sheets are fresh. The mini bar is full. There are little bottles in the bathroom, which will soon be in my bag. All is well. Sometimes, for variety, I order the Turkey Sandwich.

The Hindu, 12 March 2018

MEN OVER 40 WHO GYM

I know of several men who started doing gymnastics at 40. It's because they ditched their wives and are now dating much younger women. You don't have to be Sherlock Holmes to tell who they are. Their clothes are much sharper. Suddenly they have waistlines. Their hair is darker than you remember. But they are also gaunt and hollow-cheeked. They are extremely ripped, but slightly haggard.

I love watching them at buffets. When they spot the *lachcha parathas*, a variety of expressions flash across their faces in rapid succession. Sometimes they have to bite their lower lip to keep it from trembling. They take a few steps forward, and then they step back. It's like watching great cinema. Given the opportunity, I always load up my plate and join them for a spot of conversation. I try to help them in other ways, like asking about gym fees, and whether they've gained a kilo or two since I last saw them. They need our help.

Going around with a much younger woman must make them feel younger, but it comes with many challenges. Society has been constantly raising the bar, and these men have to live with the knowledge that right now, as we speak, their girlfriends are checking out Tiger Shroff on Twitter. Frankly, I'm very disappointed with Tiger Shroff. He seems like a nice enough boy, but he really should be thinking about the consequences of his actions. He is setting impossible standards, especially for men over 40. If some of them have heart attacks on the treadmill, or rupture their spleens, we know exactly who to blame.

In cases where the young lady works out too, the situation is even more perilous. I have a friend who has recently started seeing a yoga instructor, and I fear for his life. I understand their motivation. They want to look younger. But I'm not sure that their efforts are working that well. Some of these men were quite handsome, with an intriguing whiff of decay. One of them, a management consultant, used to be pleasantly roly poly in a very Uttam Kumar, Bengali-movie-star kind of way. Now, he is gaunt and skeletal. In Bengali movies, he would now be the fiend who tortures the hero, under instructions from the heroine's father, or the British. The director would expect him to sneer. Every time I see him, I feel like I should feed him something.

No one deserves to live like this. This is why you need to keep a close eye on your middle-aged male friends, so that you can stop them from making this mistake. It begins with the hair. If you come across one of them buying hair dye, take it away from him immediately. You may face a bit of a tussle, but eventually, he will thank you.

The Hindu, 14 January 2019

TIDINESS—THE PILING METHOD

When I was young, my mother tidied everything, including the deepest recesses of my underwear drawer. I never lifted a finger, and she learnt all my secrets, so it was a win-win. As a result, I have no sense of personal space and very limited tidying skills.

When it comes to storage, I have always taken the simple approach. I make piles. During the two years of college that I spent in a hostel, I would drop my clothes in the cupboard after use, and pick up fresh ones from the upper shelf the next morning. Over time, the stack of fresh clothes would shrink, while the pile at the bottom of the cupboard grew.

After a few weeks, I would run out of fresh clothes, so I'd do what anyone in my situation would: go home and get some more; my home was actually half an hour from the hostel.

I would return from my trip with fresh clothes, but soon enough, they would join the pile. After about a month, I would start picking up clothes from the pile. I had a system. In the evening, I would take off my clothes and shove them into the bottom of the pile, so that the next day, I picked up something relatively fresh.

Once the cupboard was overflowing, I created a second, smaller pile in the corner of the room, away from the other corner, which contained the disassembled fragments of my music system. It was in bits and pieces because late one night I had asked two of my friends, graduates of IIT Kharagpur, to look into the funny noise it was making. They agreed happily. In hindsight, I realise that they were a bit too happy. I passed out peacefully, confident that the matter was now in safe hands. A few hours later, I woke up to find my system spread over my table, while they were standing there looking at it, giggling, clutching each other so that they wouldn't fall down. They had taken it apart with gusto, but they had no idea how to put it back together. I put the fragments in a corner, where they stayed for the rest of my post-graduation.

The condition of my room did not go unnoticed. Our college

band, the Joka Bandstand, named after a local minibus route, had been worrying about where to store their instruments, and soon I was joined in my room by a full drum set, several guitars and two amplifiers. Seeing this, our cat got ideas. She lived with us on our floor. Her name was Stone. She was a lovely creature, and by far the most dignified person in the wing. She gave birth to her kittens in my pile. They were instantly christened the Pebbles. Subsequently, my pile was a mixture of clothing and kittens. The kittens enjoyed their stay. I would often wake up in the morning with a Pebble on my face, sometimes clutching a sock.

On the whole, my system has worked quite well. I still keep my clothing in piles, although I no longer recycle. My wife is very wonderful, and puts up with a lot, but she has very fixed ideas about hygiene.

The Hindu, 28 January 2019

A BRIEF HISTORY OF HERBAL CIGARETTES

A cigarette is a lot like a sausage: you're better off not knowing what's inside. You might think it's tobacco, but this is not true. According to experts, it contains a reconstituted tobacco product known as 'sheet', the ingredients of which include recycled tobacco stems, stalks, and floor sweepings, plus glue and chemicals. This is then sprayed with nicotine and shaped into curls. As a smoker, I'm okay with everything else, but the floor sweepings are a bit of a no-no.

I have personally observed the whole process, at the factory of a leading Indian company, who shall remain nameless because of lawyers. It was a vast and active enterprise, with two long chutes feeding into one massive hopper. One chute supplied the stems and stalks, while the other supplied tobacco leaves. I asked the manager what he did when the Government increased taxes on cigarettes, expecting to learn about economics. 'We just increase the amount of stalks we put in,' he said.

The cigarette was originally invented in Mexico. They had already invented tacos. They tried smoking them, but they were not very satisfying, so they invented cigarettes. By the 17th century, they had spread to Spain. The rest is history. Over the last couple of centuries, people have been putting other things in cigarettes, giving birth to the herbal variety. Mint, cinnamon and lemongrass are particular favourites. The more adventurous look beyond herbs and include things like rose and cloverleaf. Others add lettuce or cabbage, giving vegetarians the opportunity to smoke their meals. Most famously, a local entrepreneur in Indonesia added cloves to the tobacco, thus giving birth to the Kretek, named for the sound made by burning cloves.

It's important to note that none of these are particularly good for your health, because burning things and inhaling them is not the best thing to do. My only experience with herbal cigarettes was in college, with a Kretek. I was sitting in the back of a mini bus. This was a kinder, gentler era, when smoking was allowed in buses. I was sitting at the back, and I lit up my first Kretek. As the bus filled with the unmistakable sickly sweet aroma, several passengers towards the front started looking around, and said, 'Who is that? Who?' with various degrees of menace. One of them started rolling up his sleeves. I carefully dropped the Kretek down the side of the window, taking care not to make any sudden movements. Since then, I have stuck to regular cigarettes, floor sweepings and all. They kill you just as often, and the chances of getting beaten up are a lot less.

The Hindu, 11 March 2019

WHAT ARE YOU RUNNING FROM?

There are various reasons why people run. Sometimes they run from their demons. Sometimes they run towards the future. Sometimes they run because they've joined a company where everyone else is running. A friend of mine joined Nike, once. He lost 15 kilos in six months. His performance reviews were excellent, but he was always snappish and irritable.

Most commonly, they run from the police. This is sensible, because no good can come from being caught by them. They are empowered by the Indian Penal Code of 1860, one of the world's most durable pieces of legislation. It was designed by the British soon after the uprising of 1857, to ensure that if we tried to raise even a pinky in protest, that pinky would be crushed with maximum force. Its primary purpose was to suppress the natives. I'm not sure whether it allows them to blow you from the mouth of a cannon, but it might be tucked in there somewhere. They tried to cover every possible type of misbehaviour, and even thought up some new ones, such as sedition, which makes loving the government compulsory.

After two years of hard labour, the members of the drafting committee powdered their wigs and went to Queen Victoria and said 'Marm, kindly sign this, it's a little something for your subjects in India,' and she said, 'We shall be happy to do so, now kindly pour us some tea,' and ever since, in India, the police have been following her instructions. So if the police are chasing you, and you're a native, it's a good idea to run. Many of them do not look like they can run too far, but don't forget they have jeeps. In Delhi, they also have water cannons, but water supply in Delhi is intermittent, so it's 50-50.

Due to my deep knowledge of history, and a combination of extreme cowardice and a guilty conscience, I have always been mortally afraid of the police. I was once roaming around Dilli Haat, a local market with an endless supply of shawls, when I saw a sign which said, 'If you are being followed by a suspicious person, please report it to the police.' 'But what if the police are following me?' I asked a nearby shawl salesman. He pursed his lips and shook his head.

Of course, the police are not the only reason why people run. That would be ridiculous. There are many other reasons as well. One of my friends is a very successful former corporate person who now runs his own business. He's old as the hills and fit as a fiddle. He can run like a deer. If you're dying of thirst and you need someone to quickly fetch you a beer, he's your man. I asked him once about the secret of his speed. 'That's easy,' he said, 'I imagine I'm being chased by income-tax officers.'

The Hindu, 12 August 2019

ON HOW A 10-YEAR-OLD BOY MANAGED DEPRESSION

At the age of ten, I found myself suffering from deep depression. I was born in London, very close to where Paddington Bear was discovered. Soon after, I was taken to a village in Yorkshire, where my father became the local doctor. When I was ten, my parents felt a surge of patriotism, which is never a good thing. If they stayed in the UK much longer, they reasoned, their child would become a little Englishman, or even worse, marry an English girl. It was time for all of us to return to Calcutta, where the only danger was that I might marry a non-Bengali girl. It was a kind of reverse immigration. I was born English, with a high tolerance for cold, and a passion for bangers and mash. Then one day, they plonked me in Calcutta and said, 'Alright, now be an Indian!' My family has always had a knack for travelling in the wrong direction. My grandfather uprooted his whole family from Chittagong in 1945. Working on the assumption that the Japanese were on the verge of winning the war, he shifted to Calcutta, with his wife and eight children, just in time for Partition. Had my parents stayed in the UK, I would have been an immigrant, and could have written poignantly about the immigrant experience. Sadly, this was not to be.

So there I was, in Calcutta, suffering intensely from the heat. The only good thing was the *samosas*, and they made me break out in hives. The first thing I did was ask everyone where their telly was, because I needed Scooby Doo. All of them replied, unanimously, that it had gone for repairs. It took me several months to realise that this was not true. A cousin, addicted to *paan*, had a red mouth all the time. He explained that it was red because it was a delicacy that involved wrapping bugs and insects in leaves, and what I was seeing was their blood. To this day, I still feel slightly sick when I see one.

I used to show my little cousins my toys, and they stole them all, bit by bit. I had an Action Man, a sort of poor man's GI Joe, and its clothes disappeared one by one until it was completely nude. At school, things were worse. My Bengali was weak, and my Yorkshire accent was completely unintelligible. No one could make out a word I was saying. I was special. The girls used to point me out in the school ground, laughing and giggling. My school was unsympathetic. I was given a year to learn Bengali properly. This led to a crash course in Bengali. Material was limited, so I ended up reading all thirteen volumes of the *Complete Works of Saratchandra Chatterjee*, leaving me with fairly good language skills, a strong taste for melodrama, and a lingering fear of aunties. Whatever I am today, it's fair to say that it's thanks to him. Meanwhile, as time passed, I was able to eat *samosas* without breaking out into hives, and my depression lifted.

The Hindu, 26 August 2019

HOW TO IDENTIFY BURNOUTS AT WORK

It's easy to identify burnouts at work. They follow certain patterns, ranging from subtle to fairly obvious. The angry types get angrier. The emotional ones cry more. Socio-cultural forces often play a role. People from the hills often burn out in the plains. I had a colleague from Dehradun, a sweet and gentle lad, who resigned once a year for five years. Using my natural charm, I convinced him to stay back for four of them. When I asked him to stay back the fifth time, he said, 'Shovon, every day when I come to office, I walk to the bus stop, and I get on the bus, and I walk to the office, and I look at all the people all around me and I listen to them talk, and I look at their faces, and I can't stand it, I can't stand any of it, I can't stand it anymore. I want to kill myself.' That time I let him go. He left Delhi and went back to the hills.

Sometimes the signs of burnout are easy to spot. One of my colleagues, who felt he was suffering injustice, started taking his shirt off every evening. He would sit in the office, wearing a Lux Cozi banian and pants, and sing Robindro Shongeet very loudly. He did not know how to sing. Morale was plummeting, but luckily he resigned a few weeks later. One of my bosses would often start crying during review meetings. He would sob softly, and tell us how he was trying so hard, and ask us why none of us ever listened to anything he said. I wanted to point out that this was nothing personal, and that sometimes it was hard to make out what he was saying because of the sobbing, but he was already very upset, so I let it go. He left us soon after, to take up a senior position in American Express. I can only assume the employees there were more obedient, because he stayed on for three or four years.

Come to think of it, all the bosses I ever worked for burnt out at some point or the other. It's an amazing coincidence. Personally, I'm not a big fan of the long-drawn-out burnout process. I prefer it when it's quick. The ideal in this respect was Barun-da. Rain or shine, throughout the year, Barun-da would carry a long-handled black umbrella to the office. One afternoon, sitting at his desk, he opened the umbrella, and said, 'It looks like it's going to rain today.' For the rest of the day, he attended all meetings with the umbrella over his head. In the evening, he cordially bid all of us farewell, still holding the umbrella. We never saw him again.

The Hindu, 9 September 2019

THE PANCREATIC DIARIES:
BEING HOSPITALISED DURING LOCKDOWN

As a rugged individualist, I have never liked following the herd. Which is why, when everyone else was rushing or being rushed to hospital with COVID-19, I decided to be hospitalised for acute necrotising pancreatitis, which is about as bad as it sounds. In a nutshell, it involves your pancreas begging for mercy after years of abuse.

The whole thing was a new experience for me. I had never been hospitalised for anything before. It was a time of many firsts. It was the first time I had ever been put on a drip. Apparently I have delicate veins, like women from aristocratic backgrounds, or supermodels, so each time they tried to insert the needle, it was a voyage of discovery. By the end of the third day, I had more holes in me than a golf course. But it was all totally worth it, because these tubes were the mechanism through which they delivered pain killers.

After weeks of hugging my wife and promising to be a good boy in future, this proved to be a much better way of dealing with pain. The best part was that the pain killers were supposed to be as per requirement, so all I had to do was look pathetic and ask for more. It was brilliant. My childbearing years are probably over, but in case we have another one, Ketamine Chowdhury will be its name.

Soon after I was introduced to pain killers, I also received my first enema. The first time around, the enema man was quite reserved, but he warmed up as our relationship progressed. On the second occasion, he was quite chatty, inquiring about my family, and asking about my hobbies. I'm pretty sure he would have brought me flowers for our third date, but normal service was resumed soon after round two.

Since I'm in the middle of trying to write a book about Gandhi, this was all very useful. They say you should write what you know, and now, when it comes to enemas, I do. I also had my first ever CT scan, conducted by two men from Lucknow, who were extraordinarily polite. They injected me with blue dye, and kept asking me, with a mixture of concern and hope, whether it was hurting. They apologised repeatedly throughout the process. One of them may have kissed me on the forehead before sending me in, and periodically asked me to hold my breath in the nicest possible way.

During my stay, I was also exposed to different styles of nursing. Most of the nurses were from Kerala. They were competent, confident and multilingual, speaking both incomprehensible Hindi and incomprehensible English, depending on patient profile. Their contrasting approaches to patient care came out most vividly when the plaster and bandages connecting my needles needed to be removed. Some nurses were gentle and patient, coaxing off the sticky bits little by little, while others used it as an opportunity to strike a blow against patriarchy, yanking it off in one rapid movement, ignoring my high-pitched screams.

'This is what it's like when women have to wax,' said one of them, which was deeply unfair. I have never asked anyone to wax in my life. Nevertheless, a hospital visit is a strong argument in favour of being nicer to women. You may justify your innate sense of male superiority using a combination of statistics, gut feel and the laws of Manu. But Manu never went to hospital, whereas you almost certainly will. When you do, remember that at some point, you will be alone, in the dark, strapped to a bed, and a woman will be holding the needle. Be nice now, before it's too late.

Otherwise this is not going to end well. And whatever else you do, be kinder to your pancreas.

The Hindu, 4 May 2020

THE PANCREATIC DIARIES II

So here I am back in hospital again, partly because you can't keep a good man down, and partly because after paying health insurance for so long, it seemed wrong not to get anything back from it. The policy covered so many ailments, and I never seemed to get any of them. The lack of return on investment rankled deeply. This is no longer a problem. It turns out that my earlier diagnosis of acute necrotising pancreatitis was wrong, which is a pity, because it sounds so impressive. 'Something involving the pancreas or the liver' doesn't have quite the same ring to it. It feels more like an excuse to miss the Monday review meeting.

Either way, I was admitted to hospital again last week, where I am now a valued customer. The security guards salute when they see me. Events proceeded rapidly after admission. I was supposed to undergo tests on Saturday and Sunday. After reviewing the tests, I was supposed to have a stent put in my bile duct on Tuesday. This was news to me. I had always assumed stents were something you put in hearts, but apparently you can insert them anywhere, like Officers on Special Duty. I have never liked following schedules, so I screamed a lot from the pain on Sunday, and even more on Monday, by which time the doctors all had migraines, and said, 'Let's put that stent in right now!'

On Tuesday, I had a liver MRI, where the machine shut me up, because it was even louder than me. On Wednesday, they did an ultrasound, which is like what they did to my wife when she was pregnant, except it was with my liver instead of a baby. Both looked very similar. On Thursday, I had two plastic tubes inserted to remove fluid that I was leaking. I did not scream at all, and the doctor patted my head and said I was a good boy. I am now half human, half plastic, like a budget cyborg.

Throughout the whole process, Medanta hospital has been brilliant, and I'm not just saying this because I'm hoping Dr Naresh Trehan will give me a discount. The place is huge, and full of people. They never leave you alone. About three times a day, for example, a nurse comes into the room, stares at everything, and walks out again. The other day, three of them came in and did it together. I expect even larger viewing groups in the next day or two. They are also very helpful when it comes to bowel movements. They do not rest until they get results. Just the other day, I managed to have a dump after several days. The output was like the results of an archaeological dig. Various layers from various eras were visible. However, I have been blocked again for the last few days, and sense the shadow of the enema man lurking.

Nevertheless, surrounded by experts, I remain confident as my adventures continue. Will I be meeting the enema man soon? What will my first sponge bath be like? Should I be making a will? Does the striped hospital clothing make me look like a prison inmate, or is it just my imagination? And what language are the nurses all talking to each other in? These are some of the questions I have to consider in the near future.

The Hindu, 25 May 2020

A FEW OF MY FAVOURITE THINGS

It is surprising that Shovon, who loved books, films, and music, wrote so little on these topics. Was it perhaps because no one asked him to, even though he would have loved to? Because when the founder-editor of *Open* magazine did, Shovon responded enthusiastically and (as he mentions at the end of the last article in this section, on how avid soccer fans can avoid being divorced during the World Cup) the editor got away without paying him a penny. What follows is a selection of quintessentially quirky—and extremely knowledgeable—tributes to a few of his favourite things—science fiction, Asterix, the Beatles....

SPACE CADET

I was born in the UK, through no fault of my own, and one of my earliest memories, apart from the horrible food and the miserable weather, was of watching *Dr Who* from behind the sofa. Extensive research has shown that generations of British kids have been psychologically damaged by watching *Dr Who* while hiding behind the sofa, and it is well known that the decline in British society, economy, and culture started around the early 1950s—the same time they started showing *Dr Who* on a regular basis. This is no coincidence.

It's hard to explain how this TV programme, no doubt created with the best of intentions, has ended up horrifying so many innocent children. The production values are tacky, and the doctor seems amiable enough. Maybe it was the Daleks, who were vaguely conical robotic creatures with metallic voices and a limited vocabulary. They mostly trundled around slowly and repeated the word 'ex-ter-minate' at regular intervals. A one-legged granny on crutches could easily have outrun them at any time, but no one ever did. Instead, they hung around obligingly until they were exterminated. The programme ran for decades, with a brief hiatus when Mrs Thatcher came to power, triggering an economic renaissance. Unfortunately, when Tony Blair took charge, the good folks at the BBC sneaked the Doctor back in, and today the pound has almost the same value as whatever currency they use in Bangladesh. You can see a pattern here.

By the time Blair was ill-advisedly resurrecting *Dr Who*, I had moved on to Philip K. Dick, who was messing up my head in a whole new set of ways. But I'm getting ahead of the story. At the age of 10, I was suddenly transplanted from Yorkshire to Calcutta. Idi Amin was being mean to British Asians in Uganda, with little or no objection from the British government, and my dad figured that maybe a UK passport wasn't such a hot idea after all.

For me, Calcutta was like being teleported to a different planet, so

I could now relate to many of the stories I read in a deeply personal way. Plus, there was *no television* (this was the early 1970s). The agony was intense. I had no option. I had to read. I had to fill the void created by the sudden disappearance of Scooby Doo, the Flintstones and various puppets with squeaky voices. I had to escape the hell my life had become. The further the better, and that's where science fiction came in handy.

There's no better form of fiction for anyone with a taste for travel. I started my journey with Dr Asimov, switching doctors, so to speak, and my health improved remarkably. Today, he's somewhat unfashionable, because, like Enid Blyton or Agatha Christie, he's become almost synonymous with the form. But he was brilliant, and created many of the basic plotlines and conventions that define science fiction. His robot stories inspired many of the pioneers of robotics, and the Japanese named the first commercially produced robot, Asimo, in his honour, thereby proving that the Japanese cannot pronounce the letter 'v'. Or maybe they just don't like Russians.

The next time you see a bright-eyed 12-year-old who's wondering what to do next, hand him a copy of *I, Robot* or *Foundation*. You might convert a potential psychopath into a potential scientist, which is never a bad thing.

Once he seems like less of a menace to society, you could also introduce him to Arthur C. Clarke, who, apart from writing science fiction, invented the concept of geosynchronous satellites on a rainy afternoon. If, somewhat paradoxically, you like your flights of fancy to be grounded in scientific probability, then he's the man for you. Stanley Kubrick was deeply impressed and made *2001: A Space Odyssey*, a classic that you must only watch when sober.

By this time, I had acquired a taste for travel, and I discovered some pretty good tour guides. Robert Heinlein took me through dizzyingly interlinked alternate realities, and showed me the seamy side of military action in outer space with *Starship Troopers*. He was surprisingly right-wing, except when it came to sex, which he was fully in favour of. Since his books usually had spaceships on the cover, my mother could never figure out what I was actually reading, which was a major plus.

And then, in 1977, *Star Wars* happened. It's hard to explain the full impact of *Star Wars* to all you normal people. Spaceships! Robots! Giant furry creatures that talked! The coolest villain in the universe! Princess Leia in a gold bikini! (Okay, that came later.) Suddenly, you didn't have to imagine it any more. It was all there, all on the screen, all happening right in front of our eyes. I only managed to see it seven or eight times, funds being limited, but I spent weeks walking around in a daze. *Bobby* had a similar effect on most of my classmates, including one who used to see it every day, and quite literally wasted away in front of our eyes. He's walked with a slight stoop ever since.

Of course, I'm not a fanatic like so many other geeky losers, and don't want to get carried away, so I'll just end this bit by telling you that George Lucas is, to all intents and purposes, God. And if you don't agree, I'm afraid I'll have to come over to your house and beat you to death with my plastic light saber, which everyone thinks I bought for my son.

Once again, in my excitement, I have moved ahead of the story. Or perhaps it's just that I'm so used to time travel. But it's fair to say that science fiction fans are chronologically very similar to Christians—here's BSW (Before *Star Wars*) and ASW (After *Star Wars*). For example, in the years 1–2 ASW, I can remember doing very little else except waiting for the release of *The Empire Strikes Back*.

Okay, that's not true, strictly speaking. I was still reading too, since this was before VCRs had become popular, so I couldn't spend all my time watching *Star Wars*.

By this time, I was into Philip K. Dick, most of whose books should come with a health warning. In a strange, twisted field full of strange, twisted people, Dick was undoubtedly the strangest and most twisted of them all. He took me to worlds where time moved backwards, which is pretty handy if you're suffering from a hangover. Worlds where androids dreamed of electric sheep, which they turned into *Blade Runner*. Worlds where you took holidays by pretending they had happened, which became *Total Recall*. Worlds where criminals were arrested before they committed the crime (*Minority Report*). There were even worlds where 50 per cent of the population were drug addicts, who were kept in line by the other 50 per cent, who were mostly police, and where the hero, being schizophrenic, ended up spying on himself. You can achieve something similar with a Sony Handycam and a bottle of vodka. I've tried it. It works.

The funny thing is, for a man who inspired so many big ticket Hollywood movies, he spent most of his life starving. At one point, he was so poor, he and his wife were reduced to buying dog food, until one day the woman at the pet shop looked him in the eye and said, "You don't really have a dog, do you?", which Dick remembered as the scariest moment of his entire life. Luckily, soon after, Robert Heinlein gave him shelter in his garden shed and fed him three square meals a day, despite being at the opposite end of the spectrum politically. George Bush would still have been flunking junior school around the same time, so it was a kinder, gentler America.

It's fair to say Dick messed up my head completely, and blurred the lines between perception and reality so thoroughly that I have a hard time keeping track. But people can't see inside my head, so it's mostly okay.

Poverty is a recurring theme or motif in science fiction. Most authors never made a buck, and neither did most of us readers. I guess that's why we all needed to escape so much. Or perhaps that's what led to it. SF writers were also poor because they got paid by the word, a system which most publishers these days recall sadly as they weep into their beers. This had one great side effect. If those guys had to eat, they had to write. So they wrote a lot. Your typical SF author could grunt out a short story between trips to the bathroom, and a 200-page novel in the time his wife took to recover from the flu. So there's no lack of reading material. Which is great. I mean, let's face it, we all love J. D. Salinger, but do we really have enough of him? No one takes you seriously in SF until you've written at least a hundred books. Asimov, God bless him, wrote over 200, including *entire encyclopaedias*. (Check out *Asimov's Guide to Shakespeare*, which is large enough to be a murder weapon, and where he wrote copious notes on every play Shakespeare ever wrote. If my daughter passes Class XII English, it'll be thanks to him. And coffee.)

Having been sucked into SF during my misspent youth, I've never had to leave. There's just endless stuff to read. And watch as well, thanks to George, and his buddy Steven, whom some of us dislike for never mentioning Conan Doyle even once in any of the *Jurassic Park* movies. But then again, I remember my daughter, age three, gobbling popcorn and laughing hysterically as a T-Rex messily devoured a man sitting on a potty in the pouring rain. As I looked at her face, it was like coming home.

Open, 26 June 2009

HAPPY BIRTHDAY, ASTERIX!

I've got the brain, you've got the brawn/ Let's make lots of money/ You've got the brawn, I've got the looks/ Let's make lots of money!—'Opportunities', Pet Shop Boys

The first woman I ever loved was the voluptuous wife of Geriatrix, followed closely by Panacea. Like Obelix, the fact that Panacea was already engaged to Tragicomix (spelt with a T, as in '*Timeo Danaos et dona Ferentes*') did little to dampen my passion.

In other words, it was the art that first attracted me to *Asterix*. I liked the way people flew into the air, leaving their sandals perfectly upright on the ground. I liked the fact that in this world, the full measure of a man was reflected in the size of his nose. I liked how despite all the improbably graphic violence, no one seemed to actually get hurt, let alone die. And then, there's the magic potion. Who amongst us has not been in a situation when that wouldn't have come in handy? Even vegetarians can benefit, because after all, the lobster is optional, and only added for the flavour.

Asterix is 50. He first appeared in *Pilote*, a French children's magazine, on 29 October 1959. In initial sketches, Albert Uderzo had drawn Asterix as big and beefy, the way he thought a Gaulish warrior ought to look. But René Goscinny, the writer, was clear. He wanted someone small and clever. After all, Asterix literally means 'little star'. So Uderzo, unable to get the beefiness entirely out of his system, suggested that Asterix have a big, dumb companion. And so, Obelix was born. Since then, over 325 million of the 33 *Asterix* books have been sold worldwide, in 107 languages, making Goscinny and Uderzo the most successful French authors ever. No doubt Alexandre Dumas and Jules Verne are clinking glasses and saluting Goscinny as we speak.

Apart from the magnificent women, what is it that makes *Asterix* so appealing? Uderzo confessed to being puzzled himself, and once said they were like 'magicians who do not know how they do a trick'. For some, the fun is in all the historical and cultural references, which gives you the sneaky satisfaction of imagining that you're the only one getting all the clever jokes. If you're into statues, it's fun to see Impedimenta as Delacroix's *Liberty Leading the People*, Asterix as the Statue of Liberty, and a high priced slave impersonating, in rapid succession, *The Thinker* by Rodin, *The Lakoon* by Athanodoros and Polydoros, and *The Discus Thrower* by Myron. People have devoted years of their lives figuring out these things.

But it's not really about classical allusions, or even the fact that people have names like Titus Crapulus and Gluteus Maximus, which is a large buttock muscle. It's more about vital life lessons, like learning that it's okay to say 'Wkrstksft' when you can't think of anything else to say to a girl. Or that 'Zigackly!' is a wonderful way to demonstrate that you agree with someone, so long as you deliver the word with enough zest and panache.

You can also learn a surprising amount of history from *Asterix*. Their recreation of the ancient Olympic Games is extremely accurate, barring the declining and falling of all the participants (But then again, who knows?). Julius Caesar, who came from a genteel poor family, was born and raised on one of the upper floors of an insula exactly like the building described in *Mansion of the Gods*. He lived in the Subbura, a rough part of Rome now populated by Bangladeshis.

In France, *Asterix* is like Michael Jackson and Mickey Mouse rolled into one. The first ever French satellite was named Asterix, so he really did manage to become a little star. The three live action films are the most successful film series in French history, despite cringingly over-the-top performances by Roberto Benigni. They are partially salvaged by the perfect casting of Gerard Depardieu as Obelix, who gamely soldiers through the shambles, and probably deserves the Nobel Prize a whole lot more than Obama ever will. *Asterix*'s 50th anniversary in Paris will be celebrated with appropriate pomp, and will include concerts, exhibitions and an acrobatic display by elite pilots of the French Air Force, thereby revealing to an astonished world that the French have an air force.

It's strange to think that Goscinny passed away in 1977, over three decades ago, and it is entirely to Uderzo's credit that he has kept *Asterix* going. In fact, Goscinny handed in the script of *Asterix in Belgium* just before he died, but Uderzo was too upset to illustrate it, or even look at it, until he was sued by the publishers and forced to finish it. Since then, he has soldiered on. A little bit of zing may have gone out of the stories, but the artwork is always a joy. And there are still enough clever references, I might add. In the latest, the character Akoataki is a little touch of the hat to Takao Aoki, the creator of Beyblade. Pretty hip for a 50-year-old.

Rather touchingly, Uderzo has continued to give Goscinny full credit at every opportunity, and even refers to him in the present tense in interviews. In 2007, at the grand age of 80, he told BBC, "I find it completely normal to have both names on the album. I would be ashamed to only put mine on, even if it was only me who wrote them. Goscinny will intrinsically be a part of them as long as *Asterix* lives."

Goscinny's children are part of Albert René, the company Uderzo founded in both their names, although recently he has taken flak for letting other authors write and draw *Asterix*. In the meantime, you can look forward to *Asterix and Obelix's Birthday: The Gold Book*, published on 22 October, with the grand old man still in charge, and bits and pieces from Goscinny tucked away here and there.

What is it that makes so many of us love *Asterix*? Perhaps it's the little things, like the Belgian in *Asterix the Legionary* who has hair exactly like Tintin. Or the Egyptian who joins the Roman Army thinking it's a holiday camp. Or the shy barbarian looking for psychiatric help. In case you are reading this in a parental capacity, it's important to point out the educational benefits as well. You can learn important things about different countries by reading *Asterix*. The fact that the Swiss are constantly cleaning everything, for example. Or that all Greeks are cousins. And that Corsicans are very, very, very slow.

Fifty years is just a number, not such a big deal. Spiderman may fade into history, and Hogwarts become a distant memory, but as long as people still look at words and pictures, somewhere out there, our friends will always be at their banquet, where the jokes are simple, the laughs are loud, and they never ever run out of wild boar.

Open, 27 October 2009

COME BACK, ELVIS

My mother used to love Elvis with a passion that was deep and sincere, probably more than she loved me—something that I find perfectly understandable on a variety of levels. So did yours, most probably. Thousands and thousands of mothers lucky enough to be in Las Vegas between 1969 and 1977 threw their panties at him every night. In a spirit of scientific investigation and in order to get into the mood for this piece, I tried to do the same thing in the privacy of my own room, and I can assure you that it's not an easy thing to do. It needs extreme motivation and considerable flexibility.

What could possibly explain such inexplicable devotion? If you think about it, it's blindingly obvious. Elvis was an alien. Like Superman, his unearthly origin bestowed upon him superpowers barely comprehensible to mere mortals like us. Once you accept this, so many parts of the jigsaw puzzle suddenly fall into place. You gain new respect for estimable publications like the *National Enquirer*, whose frequent reports of Elvis broadcasting from Pluto, Elvis descending from flying saucers, and Elvis being spotted in the company of three-headed cows, John F. Kennedy and, more recently, Michael Jackson now assume a whole new significance. Instead of mocking them, we should congratulate them on their brilliant feats of investigative journalism. While their facts are correct, their analysis is slightly flawed. These are not acts of alien abduction. No, it's just that the King has gone back to join his own people, but occasionally he misses us, so he can't help coming back.

Consider the facts. He was born in 1935, and his twin brother Jesse was stillborn. People privately doubted his claims that he was in communication with him throughout his life, but obviously Jesse must have gone straight back to the mother ship, but stayed in touch telepathically. Elvis came from an unlikely background for a King, a dirt-poor Southern family with nothing but love to hold them together. His dad Vernon built their shack with his own hands and was arrested for forging a $5 cheque when Elvis was two. In an environment where White boys were taught to abhor Black music, Elvis used to sneak in to listen to B. B. King playing on Beale Street, and enjoyed gospel nights at the Memphis Auditorium. B. B. King still remembers him from those days, because first, he was White, and second, he was so good looking he hardly seemed human. No one taught him how to do his hair—the ducktail and the sideburns were entirely his own invention, and no one in high school could ever make him change them.

Once he decided to become a singer, in 1955, he struggled for approximately half an hour. The first few songs he sang at Sam Phillips' little recording studio sounded a little stilted, so Sam told him to loosen up. At which point, Elvis stopped trying to be like Bing Crosby, picked up a guitar, did 'That's All Right (Mama)', and pretty much blew everyone away. He continued to blow them away from practically the first time he got on stage, and never stopped doing so until the day he died. His hips quickly took on a life of their own, despite repeated warnings from the local police (I am not making this up), and a compromise was reached in the early years by ordering cameramen to shoot him strictly above the waist.

In 1956, between March and September, he did 'Heartbreak Hotel', 'Blue Suede Shoes', 'Mystery Train', 'Hound Dog' and 'Don't Be Cruel', and single-handedly created rock'n'roll as we know it. He also did 'Love Me Tender', just to show that he could. The National Guard was called out to control the crowd at a concert in Alabama. A deejay in San Francisco was fired for playing 'Love Me Tender' 14 times in a row. And Elvis bought his first pink Cadillac, thus turning it into an enduring American icon.

He was drafted by the US Army in 1958, and to the astonishment of almost everyone, he joined, since he thought it was his patriotic duty. He was an exemplary soldier, rising to the rank of sergeant, and receiving an honourable discharge in 1960. He never sang a note in public during that time. Within a month of leaving the army, he released *Jailhouse Rock*. In fact, in that one year, he released three albums, *Jailhouse Rock*, *GI Blues* and his first gospel album, *His Hand In Mine*, which went on to win a Grammy, and is still considered to be one of the best gospel albums. He recorded 16 songs for *His Hand In Mine* on one day, 30 September 1960. If you don't think that's superhuman, consider the fact that Queen took six months to record 'Bohemian Rhapsody'.

During the same period and, in fact, till 1969, he was doing an average of three movies a year, each of which was knocked off in two to three weeks, because his manager Colonel Parker really needed the money. This is the same Parker who never let Elvis do a concert outside the US, because Parker was an illegal alien, and he was afraid they wouldn't let him back in. He also renegotiated his contract with Elvis in 1972 so that he got 50 per cent (!) of his earnings, because, as he famously said, 'I have to earn a living too.' Despite being extra-terrestrial, Elvis always listened to Parker, because he didn't want to blow his cover as a good, decent Southern boy. Once you realise this, his actions become perfectly understandable.

Parker was always testing the limits of the King's superpowers. He put him in truly terrible movies like *Kid Galahad* and *Flaming Star*, and when that didn't drive the public away, he put him in even worse ones like *Roustabout* and *Harum Scarum*. Elvis never said a word, displaying a loyalty that was clearly inhuman. Despite all this, he had sold 50 million records by 1963. By 1967, he had hit 100 million. He also hit Las Vegas, at which point some hints that he was related to ET began to emerge.

For one thing, there were the jumpsuits, which he designed himself, and loved because they were loose and flowing and expanded when he did. There were over 25 different designs, with names like American Eagle and Cherokee Brave. Sequin manufacturers across the globe owe him an eternal debt of gratitude.

Then there were the drugs. By 1970, while he was having seven or eight different types of prescription drugs three times a day, he keenly felt the proliferation of drug culture in the US. It was an issue he was very close to. So he met Richard Nixon, and asked him to make him a Federal Narcotics Agent. In a move for which Nixon has never been given sufficient credit, he agreed, and gave Elvis a free hand to apprehend drug addicts. Elvis, in turn, told his bodyguards to keep a sharp eye out for junkies, saying, 'I'm tired of people like John Lennon talking about drugs. They're demoralising our youth. They're destroying our country. We've got to band together and stop this.'

It took his bodyguards some time to figure out that he was deadly serious. Despite their best efforts, though, they failed to apprehend anyone. It is obvious from this that by the early 1970s, we were failing to support the King in the way that we should have, and he was already leaving Planet Earth quite often, getting ready for the time when he would permanently shift to the mother ship. Further evidence emerged in 1975, when he met Eric Clapton. 'What do you do?' the King asked Clapton. 'I play guitar,' answered Clapton modestly. 'Well, if you'd like some lessons,' replied Elvis, 'Maybe my guitarist James Burton could give you some.' To his eternal credit, Clapton replied that he would be honoured. Also honoured were Led Zeppelin and George Harrison, who met him during this richly bizarre phase of his life, and showed him nothing but the greatest possible respect and affection.

Had Elvis been a normal human being, the years of drug abuse would have taken their toll. So he staged his departure very carefully. The last words he ever uttered to us earthlings were to his girlfriend in 1977. He said, 'Okay, I won't', because she told him not to fall asleep in the bathroom. What appeared to be his dead body was discovered some hours later.

You could say that his achievements were colossal, and that no one has ever brought more joy to more people than he did. Perhaps we should not disturb him while he is resting. But today, in his 75th year, as Jason Mraz takes centre stage and Bono hobnobs with Ban Ki Moon, I think we have to align those transmitters and send this message straight to the heart of the Milky Way: 'Come back, Elvis, our once and future King. We need you more than ever. We will try to be more worthy this time.'

Open, 13 January 2010

THE BEATLES ARE FIFTY

To me it's always been about the songs, and what they meant to me. I'm sure it's the same for you. It's about listening to 'When I Saw Her Standing There'—and the joy of actually seeing her standing there. It's about listening to 'She's Leaving Home', and completely unexpectedly, feeling a lump in your throat, even though you have no comparable experience to relate to—until many years later. It's about trying to sing 'She Loves You' in the bathroom, and discovering, on the last 'Yeah', that you cannot really sing. It's about listening to 'Come Together', and cringing at the thought of his disease, and wondering with a shiver what a 'joojoo eyeball' really could be.

Perhaps the full significance of The Beatles comes home to all of us when we view it through the lens of the death of John Lennon. Many individual deaths have affected many people across the world, from Princess Diana's to Michael Jackson's. But so many of us remember that awful evening in 1980, when that man walked up to John Lennon in a park in New York. That man whose name we will not mention because that's precisely why he did that sick and awful thing—so that people would remember his name. He walked up to John with a copy of *Double Fantasy* and asked him to sign it. John smiled and signed it, partly because over the years Paul had drilled into his head that it was important to be nice to fans, even if he didn't feel like it, and partly because he was fundamentally a nice person. That person took his autograph and then shot him, because he wanted to be famous.

That terrible night, in 1980, tens of millions of people felt deeply sad, from Kabul to Connecticut. Partly it was because they really loved John, and his music had touched them on a deeply personal level, and he'd never really hurt anyone at the end of the day, and he deserved much better. But for many of us, in the recesses of our hind brain, there was this little voice which told us, with a dull, indisputable finality, 'Now they're never going to get together again.'

But maybe that's too much like *Chronicle of a Death Foretold*. Maybe the end is not the right place to start. Maybe, like Julie Andrews ordered us to do, we should start at the very beginning, because it's a very good place to start. In 1957, John Lennon was regularly getting kicked out of the Quarry Grammar School, founded in 1926, for sundry offences, including 'throwing duster out of class window', 'gambling on school field during house match', and, my personal favourite, one word, 'insolence'. This is all verifiable truth, because it's all in the school records. Perhaps it's not surprising, because his mother Julia, whose blood flowed in his veins, and about whom he wrote one of his simplest and most heartfelt songs ('Julia'), used to do her housework wearing her knickers on her head, just because she felt like it. Clearly, the fruit didn't fall far from the tree.

Meanwhile, in a nearby school, James Paul McCartney was once more the head boy, having been the head boy in every class he had attended so far, an excellent student, and much loved by all his teachers, although the more perceptive ones noticed he was rather too charming, and frequently got himself out of tight spots thanks to his sheep's eyes and his gift of the gab. He was a tricksy one, our Paul.

Two more different personalities cannot be imagined. But although they didn't even know each other yet, suddenly synchronicity kicked in. They both discovered Elvis Presley. They both badgered their guardians until they got a guitar. And once they got a guitar, that guitar took over. They both played it day and night, with no one to teach them, learning the hard way. They played it in the bathroom. They played till late at night. That guitar became their life. And all of this happened individually, before they actually met each other. They were a few miles from each other, united by guitar, like a Liverpool version of 'The Corsican Brothers'.

In 1958, Paul joined the Quarry Men, John's band. Paul had worked harder at it than John had, and he knew more chords. Once he was in, he brought George Harrison, who was all of 14 at the time. George had one thing in common with the other two. The moment he got a guitar, he started playing it till his fingers bled. He wasn't as talented as the other two, but he worked at it with grim determination. John could see that the boy could play, and he'd furtively put on his spectacles to figure out what chords George and Paul were playing. He didn't like being second best.

So John, Paul and George were playing together by 1958, as the Quarry Men. Then they became Long John and the Silver Beatles, and finally in, 1960, The Beatles. Which is why this is their 50th anniversary. John was the early focal point, with his undeniable character and stage presence. John could have been the king of the heap, surrounded by friends and hangers on. Or he could have let Paul and George fully into it, knowing that he would be less of a king, but they would be a better band. He chose to be a better band.

Where did Ringo fit in? Until just before 1963, when The Beatles hit the big time, their drummer was Pete Best, described by a local paper as 'mean, moody and magnificent'. He was good, but didn't share the other three's strange sense of humour. In Ringo, though, they found a kindred spirit. Well before they were famous, the other three existed in a state of dynamic tension. Ringo played referee. Whenever John fought with Paul, or George was miffed with John, Ringo was there to soothe ruffled feathers, and to remind them that they were friends first and musicians second.

So much for group dynamics. What about the music? The white hot core of The Beatles was the songwriting team of Lennon and McCartney. It's quite simple, really. In the history of mankind, there have been never been better creators of music than them. This included a stream of hits for other people, such as the *Rolling Stones*, to whom they gifted their first hit—'I Wanna Be Your Man'.

Lennon and McCartney wrote songs and created music in three distinctly different ways, and their rivalry was always at the heart of it. One way was writing songs eyeball to eyeball, sitting in a hotel room or the back of a bus, which is how they did songs like 'Can't Buy Me Love', 'She Loves You', and 'Please Please Me'. The second way was when they just pretended to be a team, but actually wrote the songs individually, and then played and recorded them together, like 'Yesterday'

(Paul) and 'Across the Universe' (John). The third way was when they both had little bits and pieces, and they were too lazy to finish them, so they magically put them together, like 'Day Tripper' and 'A Day in the Life'. John and Paul had an unwritten agreement: whoever had contributed more to the song would then sing it, while the others would do backing vocals. They used to argue hotly about it, and it gives their harmonies on these songs a fierce edge, as if each one is saying, 'Listen to me. Listen to ME.'

This spirit of competition was what really drove The Beatles, and George was very much a part of it. He spent years as the grumpy younger brother, treated very off-hand by Paul and John, and grudgingly given a song or two. He complained bitterly and often, and even walked out during the making of *The White Album*. It's true that songs like 'Something' and 'Here Comes the Sun' were things of beauty. But it's worth remembering that George's first post Beatles solo effort, *All Things Must Pass*, was a majestic triple album consisting entirely of songs which he wrote while he was with The Beatles, but had been rejected by John and Paul. The quality of his material declined rapidly after this point. It was the competition that drove them. When else, ever, has the whole been so much greater than the sum of parts?

The Beatles were great performers. You could write a book just on their performances. The Royal Command Variety Performance in London in 1963, for example, where the 19 other acts included the dancing pig puppets Pinky and Perky, and John asked the Royals to rattle their jewellery. Unlike Queen Victoria, the Royals were quite amused.

Their first three years of fame involved enormous amounts of touring, because they needed the money. Thanks to a bum deal struck by manager Brian Epstein, The Beatles were getting 1 per cent royalty on their records. Despite this, their income was so high they were being taxed at 94 per cent by the UK government. This meant that The Beatles effectively got to keep 0.06 per cent of the total revenue earned from their music—a situation about which a bitter George wrote his first hit song for The Beatles—'Tax Man' ('So it's one for me, nineteen for you…'). This was the lead track on their 1966 *Revolver* album, which also included the kindergarten classic 'Yellow Submarine', Paul's brassy, upbeat 'Got To Get You Into My Life', and John's enigmatic and spacey 'Tomorrow Never Knows', the title being a phrase Ringo used often.

The upshot was, they had to tour, so they travelled the world and had many adventures, culminating with a legendary concert in 1965 at the Shea Stadium in New York, filled with 55,000 screaming fans, by far the biggest show anyone had ever done till then. They'd come a long way in three years, from backing a stripper named Shirley at the New Cabaret Artistes Club on Upper Parliament Street. But as musicians, they were demoralised. The constant screaming of teenagers could blank out the sounds of a jet plane flying overhead, and they could barely hear themselves play. On one occasion, Ringo was too wasted after a 72-hour binge to actually play the drums—and no one noticed. In 1966, after being bullied by Imelda Marcos (they refused to play for her guests) and burnt in effigy across the US Bible belt (after John said, injudiciously, that they were more popular than Jesus), they hung up their touring boots.

They never played together again as a band, except one memorable afternoon on the roof of the Apple building. Which left them at rather a loose end. John would rather have spent it on the sofa, but he decided to make the effort, before Paul took over everything. Particularly after Brian Epstein's death, it was Paul's energy and enthusiasm that pretty much kept The Beatles together. We should all be grateful, because the next thing they did was *Sergeant Pepper's Lonely Hearts Club Band*, and nothing was ever the same afterwards. Even the album cover was unique, featuring Karl Marx, Marlon Brando and Laurel and Hardy. Gandhi was removed from the original cover for fear of disturbing Indian sensibilities. It's unlikely Gandhi would have minded, and he certainly would have been a much better spiritual advisor than Mahesh Yogi, about whom John later wrote 'Sexy Sadie'.

The end wasn't far away, sadly. It began one day in 1967, when a little, dark haired Japanese woman walked up to John Lennon and silently handed him a little card with a single word: 'Breathe'. Thus began one of the great romances of the 20th century. It also made John start thinking about life beyond The Beatles, and consider bigger issues like world peace. He sponsored Yoko's Half Wind Exhibition, which consisted of items cut in half, such as half a chair, half a shoe, and half a toothbrush, and obligingly joined her inside a bag in Amsterdam, in an effort to get war-mongers to drop their weapons and climb into bags. Not a bad idea, if you really think about it. A bag is a lot cheaper than an intercontinental ballistic missile.

The Beatles stayed together for a couple more years. They made *The White Album*, and *Abbey Road*, and *Let It Be*. As well as killer singles like 'Hey Jude' and 'The Ballad of John and Yoko'. Only John and Paul played on this last track, because the others flatly refused to have anything to do with it. Ever obliging, Paul pitched in with John and laid down the drums and the bass, giving the song its cheerful, muscular rhythm.

The White Album was a colossal success, but it was made in a miserable atmosphere, with a lot of fighting, with John fighting to drop Paul's 'Ob-la-di, Ob-la-da' because it was embarrassing, and Paul fighting to drop 'Revolution No 9' because it was incomprehensible (true on both counts), and George fighting with everyone else. Even Ringo once walked out, because he was bored.

Paul tried to recapture their old spirit by suggesting they do a live album, which led to *Let It Be* (released in 1970, after The Beatles broke up), but that didn't work either. Not that we should knock it, including as it does the title track, and 'Get Back', which features a bass vocal from Paul, a cheesecutter sharp solo from George, and what John later said was the best rhythm guitar he ever played in his life. Forget about the songwriting, The Beatles were one helluva good rock band.

They wanted to end on a good note. So John temporarily suspended his Peace Campaign. George took a break from recording chants of the London Radha Krishna Temple. Ringo came back from Hollywood. They came together for the last time, in the middle of 1969, to make *Abbey Road*. They all knew it was the last time, somewhere in their hearts, and they all worked hard to bring back that old feeling, which is why we have 'Here Comes The Sun' and 'Come Together'.

Trust Paul to have the last word, though. At the end of the day, the reason so many of us love The Beatles is very simple, and it's explained in the last words, of the last song, on the last album The Beatles ever recorded together:

And in the end, the love you take / Is equal to the love / You make.

Open, 17 March 2010

HOW NOT TO END UP DIVORCED

Let's assume that some unfortunate woman made a huge mistake, and you are now a married man. Let's also assume that although India's Fifa ranking is around 337, you still want to watch the World Cup because you're not a narrow minded parochialist.

The combination of these two things spells trouble, and you are lucky someone is here to guide you. Unfortunately, that person got unavoidably detained elsewhere, so you'll have to settle for me.

Is this such a big problem, you ask? After all, she's used to the horror of being married to you, so her pain threshold must be pretty high. But therein lie the seeds of your own downfall. After all these years, if there's one thing she's learnt, it's this. Things can always get worse.

First, let's list out certain myths and misconceptions, some of which are myths while others are misconceptions. For your practical convenience and reading pleasure, I will point out which is which.

MYTH 1

She didn't throw anything at me while I was watching the Indian Premier League, so why would she start now?

Firstly, throwing things is not what you should be worrying about. I'm guessing that happens quite a lot already. Also, as one of my friends, an expert statistician who loses money for me on a regular basis, would say, you're comparing apples and oranges. IPL is cricket. She's used to cricket. Cricket is the old, familiar adversary, like Lucifer, or Mayawati. Plus, IPL involves Shilpa and Preity and that nice Mrs Ambani, so she may feel a certain pride in all that woman power. They carry themselves so much better than Shah Rukh and Mr Mallya. I'm hoping you didn't ogle the cheerleaders too much, though. In case you did, you really should think about not watching sports for a while.

MISCONCEPTION 2

Surely she'll understand that it's educational for the kids, and broadens their horizons and what not?

Newsflash! The kids have homework. They cannot watch football every evening, otherwise they will fail, and that means one extra year of school fees. Plus, none of the kids have the slightest interest in watching soccer. They like playing it. They like buying Manchester United jerseys. But they do not watch it. They have 23 different cartoon channels to watch. If you had those when you were their age, you would never have watched football either.

MYTH 3

It only happens once in four years, so she'll cut me some slack, won't she?

It depends on what you mean by 'some slack'. There is only so much slack one human being can cut another. If I were you, I would not test the limits of human endurance on this. There are scientists who are paid to do that sort of thing. In fact, this four year gap is the crux of the problem. You've been watching cricket non-stop since forever, India just got humiliated in the T20 World Cup, and it's reasonable for her to assume that you'll lose interest in cricket for a while. But she underestimates your capacity for humiliation. So, out of the blue comes this entirely new sport that you will now spend weeks watching. If you do not follow the excellent advice that I will soon be providing you, by Day 3, she will be calling her lawyer.

MISCONCEPTION 4

It's a beautiful game, loved by billions, so in good time, won't she come to love it too?

As the excellent Chinese General Sun Tzu said in *The Art of War*, 'Optimism not way to win battle. Instead emperor beats up your family and you end up running *wonton* stall on street corner.'

Ask yourself this. Is George Clooney on any of the teams? How about Hugh Grant? Personally, I'm not sure. Research has never been my strong point. But if the answer is 'no', why would she want to watch 22 hairy men running at each other, and occasionally kneeing each other in the groin? Does she like watching sumo wrestling? That might give you a clue. I'm not saying no women watch sumo wrestling, but I'm pretty sure most of them must be married to the wrestlers.

MYTH 5

I work so hard putting food on the table. Won't she let me enjoy this teenie-weenie little thing?

I'm not sure you should be raising the subject of teenie-weenie little things in a public forum. Why let other people in on the secret? And don't forget, the country is full of men who put much, much more food on the table. Mukesh Ambani, for example. Also, no one likes a whiner. Be a man. Which brings us to....

MISCONCEPTION 6

I'm the man of the house, so how does the question of her objecting to what I do arise?

Since you can read, and possibly even write, I have to assume that you are not a *khap* panchayat member. Also, you have probably read the title of this piece. If the above Misconception 6 was really true, how come you've read so far? Don't fool yourself. Other people are doing enough of that already, and they don't even have to try that hard.

MYTH 7

My wife really loves me, and we're so happy. Why would she even consider divorce just because I watch football for a month and ignore her completely, and come home from office early to watch matches, even though the pressure of work prevents me from doing so for the rest of the year?

As I said earlier, you've read the title. You're still here. There has to be a reason.

So now I've cleared up all the myths and misconceptions, which is half the battle. You are no longer ignorant. Ignorance is not bliss, it is merely ignorance. Because you are now less ignorant, you will avoid making elementary mistakes, like the ones listed above. If you did, your wife would be calling a lawyer almost instantaneously, which means you would be answering all his questions while you're half asleep from watching all those matches. This would lead to you losing your house, the children, the dog, and most of your salary, and you'll end up running the *wonton* stall that we discussed earlier. If the subject of divorce crops up later in the World Cup, at least you have the ghost of a chance.

What are the things you can do to avoid the inevitable? Here is a quick ready reckoner, which you should cut out and keep in your wallet for instant reference.

1. Make full use of half time

    In cricket, there's a commercial break every three minutes or so. So you have 30 seconds to shoot off a quick question, or nod your head, or (this is the safest) agree with whatever she just said. In football, there's only one 5 minute break—after 45 minutes. Make the most of it. Talk to her non-stop. Notice her hair. Get her a glass of water (keep talking loudly while you're coming and going). Do not under any circumstances watch the replays or the in-between analysis. If you cannot do this much, you had better start looking up *wonton* recipes.

2. Miss the matches involving Burkina Faso

    Yes, we all know you watched the India–Afghanistan match during the cricket World Cup. You may even be feeling a niggling sense of regret about it, once you discovered that they sucked. I have news for you. Some teams in this football World Cup will suck too. They sucked in the preliminaries. They sucked in the qualifiers. They only reason they're flying to South Africa to play the World Cup is that other teams sucked even more. Avoid these teams. Citizens of those countries feel compelled to watch them, which is understandable. In some countries, like China, it's compulsory, and you can get arrested for not switching on your TV. What's your excuse?

3. Use the Burkina Faso gaps wisely

   If you have the evening off, don't waste it. Take her to a swank restaurant. If you can't afford taking her to a swank restaurant, take her to a cheap restaurant. Try out places where they serve *wontons*. That way, in case things don't work out, you might lose a wife but you could gain one of your first customers.

4. For God's sake, get a schedule

   So you sit down to watch, and you discover Burkina Faso is playing. Then you say, 'Honey, I was thinking, why don't we go out for dinner?' This is a bad plan. She is clearly Plan B. You must not do this. You must tell her the same thing—but in the morning. It needs to be premeditated.

5. Involve her in matches with good looking guys

   Take a look at yourself in the mirror. Do you look like Prannoy Roy? If you do, then like Mrs Roy, she can look at you from time to time, and everything will be okay. If not, you need to involve her more closely in the matches involving handsome guys. Beckham is injured, which is a major setback for millions of men. You could involve her in matches with Cristiano Ronaldo. I think he plays for Portugal. I'm not sure, because I'm more of a marriage counsellor than a football expert, and they don't pay me enough to do actual research. In fact, they don't pay me anything. You could help by mailing Sandipan, editor-in-chief of the magazine you are reading, at [censored by editor], or just SMS 'Please pay Shovon something' to [censored by editor].

   Now that I've just realised this, I think I should stop writing now. I wish you all the very best. Enjoy the World Cup.

   Try to make sure your wife doesn't run away. But just to be on the safe side, take some stir frying lessons.

Open, 2 June 2010

Fiction

THE COMPETENT AUTHORITY

Shovon's first novel *The Competent Authority* (2013) holds a unique place among Indian novels for its bizarre dystopic imagination and laugh-out-loud humour.

It's a couple of decades from now. The Chinese have nuked large parts of India. Mumbai has been obliterated, Delhi is in the throes of rigorous reconstruction, Bengal has seceded and is now a protectorate of China. The most powerful person in the country is a deranged bureaucrat called the Competent Authority. Cloaked in anonymity, the CA rules the remnants of India with an iron fist.

Although, in theory, the government and the armed forces still exist, the Prime Minister and the Army chief are mere puppets in the hands of the Competent Authority. All they can do is watch in horror as he puts in motion a fiendish plan to annihilate everyone in the country, for reasons that are completely logical.

The following excerpt gives a glimpse of a very warped world.

'BARK LIKE A DOG'

Like a battle-scarred veteran returning from war, the Rajdhani Express groaned and creaked into New New Delhi Railway Station, riddled with fresh bullet holes, and dented in various places by stones and the odd grenade. It only went as far as Patna, since Calcutta was now in a foreign country, but even though its route was much shorter than it had once been, it was fraught with danger. The Maoists loved moving targets.

Personnel regularly sought transfer to Southern Railways, where the worst you could expect was having a stainless steel mug of coffee thrown at your head. The South had escaped largely unscathed in the war, except for the virus attack on Hyderabad, and the amphibious attack on Pondicherry, claimed by the Chinese in symbolic retaliation for historic French atrocities. This gave Southerners a healthy majority in parliament.

It meant very little, since the Competent Authority decided everything, but it felt good, and it gave them control over the canteen menu. The hospital car was packed to the brim, the arms and legs of the injured poking through the windows. Mr Chatterjee gaped at it, slackjawed, conserving his energy for when he would need it. He was completely exhausted and slightly weepy. He shook himself and started focusing on the disembarking passengers.

He was sitting on a bench on Platform No. 7 on the Paharganj side. He'd been at the railway station since morning. At first, as he went from platform to platform, he had made feeble attempts to dust off the benches before sitting down. Then he had compromised, and merely avoided the damp parts. Now he could feel a faint stickiness in the seat of his pants, seeping through the fabric and laying cold fingers on his buttocks, and he didn't care.

New New Delhi Station was a monument to normalcy in this time of reconstruction. The old station had been right in the middle of the Dead Circle. The new one was constructed as an exact replica, near the airport. The old station used to have a Paharganj Gate and an Ajmeri Gate, both of which had been vaporized. To compensate, the Northern Railways had nostalgically installed two small gates on either side of the new station, and named them Ajmeri and Paharganj, thus continuing the tradition.

Ajmeri Gate had two elephants with trunks intertwined. Paharganj was adorned with two stone lions, yawning. Most people called them the elephant gate and the lion gate. The station had been bright and new eleven years ago. Clean, shiny, and somehow wrong. The public had known what to do. So had the railway authorities responsible for it. After eleven years of hideous misuse and neglect, now it really was an exact replica. Until you took a closer look at some of the passengers, of course.

Which was one of the reasons why Mr Chatterjee hated railway stations. It was the crowds. Crowds made up of all kinds of people. And these days, 'all kinds' covered a fairly broad spectrum.

A few yards away a coolie was having an incident. A few people still had seizures, from time to time, though not as often as before. He had dropped the luggage he was carrying and sunk to his knees. He was trying to pry open one of the suitcases, gibbering. The fat auntie who had hired him was protesting, pulling feebly at his red tunic. By this time, the coolie had the suitcase open. He had found a tin of tooth powder. He pulled out the stopper and started pouring it down his throat, head thrown back, Adam's apple bobbing furiously.

Probably on drugs, thought Mr Chatterjee gloomily. A lot of them were. Maybe I should have done drugs, he thought. Maybe that would have been fun. He had never known anyone who did. He had had no idea where to get them from. Nobody had ever offered him any. Venky was the slick type. He would know. Perhaps he should ask.

On cue, Venky slid down on to the bench next to him. He looked at Mr Chatterjee, worried. He held out a paper cup. 'It has vodka in it,' he said, 'it'll do you good. I'll take this train. You relax.'

Now this was a caring side of Venky that he had never seen. Mr Chatterjee felt a lump growing in his throat. They could fight over cases, they could argue over money, but at the bottom of it all, in this dog-eat-dog world, Venky cared for him. Should he cry now? It seemed like the right thing to do. Perhaps a sip of vodka first.

Kutty and Mini Mom both passing out simultaneously at the Telepath Lab had been no coincidence, they had soon discovered. Telepaths across the city had been affected in various strange ways. They had soon found themselves in a briefing session with the CBI director, Mr Jogi Prasad Sinha, of the Bihar cadre. He was a shifty-eyed specimen with formidable white eyebrows and a walrus moustache. He was malcontented. His promotion had been delayed because of his involvement in a fodder scam. This was extremely unfair. He was very fond of cows. He had been due for promotion two years ago, but at the time they had said that seniority was not a criterion.

Subsequently, when the criterion was changed to merit-cum-seniority + suitability, he had been made director of the CBI. An officer on special duty from the Bureau of Reconstruction sat discreetly to one side. Director Sinha had first berated them for not anticipating the attack on the telepaths. It was a colossal failure of intelligence, and an inquiry commission of forty MPs would be set up, as soon as they were free from the other committees. One day's pay was to be deducted. A notation was being made in Professor Krishnan's file. As and when temporary staff like Venky and Mr Chatterjee came to deserve the recognition of a file, notations would be made in theirs also. Professor Krishnan himself seemed largely unaffected, although he was careful to look apologetic.

However, the Director had continued, fighting the enemy threat was currently higher priority. Punishment would occur subsequently.

Preliminary analysis had indicated four possibilities:

a) The Chinese had developed a new weapon targeting telepaths. This weapon was based in China. This would require action against China. CBI to procure evidence.
b) The Chinese had developed a new weapon targeting telepaths. This weapon could only be used locally, not long distance. One or more Chinese infiltrators would have entered New

New Delhi, carrying this weapon. CBI to identify infiltrators.
c) The Chinese had infiltrated and compromised the entire Indian telepath network. Chinese secret agents had been secretly meeting all telepaths, and implanting commands in their minds through hypnotic suggestion. All these commands had been programmed to go off at the same time, causing the incident of this afternoon. All telepaths and those associated with them to be subjected to thorough CBI investigation. Those who were contract workers, with no fixed loyalty to the BoR or the Republic of India, would be under particular suspicion. This meant them, the Director had pointed out with relish.
d) The Chinese had sent in a telepathic mutant with extraordinary powers. He was lurking somewhere in Delhi. CBI Telepath Team to launch an immediate city-wide sweep to locate the miscreant.

There was a brief hush as everyone digested the analysis. The Competent Authority had not yet indicated what the result of their investigation should be, said the Director, so they were to pursue all four possibilities until further notice. Venky had a question.

'Director sir, as per point c, are we not under CBI investigation? If so, how can we participate in point d?'

Director Sinha had gazed at him serenely. 'Both will proceed in a simultaneous manner. You will be both hunter and hunted.' His PA had guffawed, and then quickly subsided, his appreciation registered.

But Venky had more questions.

'There are only six of us. How are we supposed to sweep the city?'

Director Sinha had already thought of this and had a plan in place.

'Professionalism in the CBI is uncompromising! Even if six months is required, every inch of Delhi must be scanned. At the same time, urgency is also paramount, due to the emergency situation. Work smarter, not harder! Apply modern management principles.'

Professor Krishnan had led them back to the lab, pondering modern management principles. Logically, if this was a one-time attack, the evildoer would be trying to escape. New New Delhi Railway Station was a good place to start looking. They would scan all major departing trains, particularly those headed east, and look for evil. In case they happened to find evil, they would take it back to headquarters, and beat it up until it confessed.

So here they were, flopping on a platform bench, exhausted. Both Venky and he agreed they didn't have a hope in hell of catching anyone.

It was true that their brains were mildly sensitive to telepaths. Chatterjee could feel a slight tingling when he was near one. A strong telepath might project a bit further. But their main technique was sitting with a subject, visualizing things and testing them. You could hardly do that to a trainload of passengers. So they had settled on the technique of randomly testing anyone who looked suspicious. Or Chinese. Venky actually didn't give a shit, but Mr Chatterjee sincerely tried to feel that elusive tingle. Lives were at stake. Moreover, he wanted to make the world safe for Banani.

The passengers had started emerging from the Rajdhani. Venky's eyes lit up as he spotted a voluptuous young woman in a hipster sari, carrying a vanity case. 'See, Hemonto, that girl. Don't you think she looks suspicious? She looks highly suspicious to me. I think we should talk to her.'

'Give it a rest, Venky,' said Mr Chatterjee, covering his face with a wet handkerchief and leaning back. Hours of concentration had left him with a raging headache. Ignoring his advice, Venky leaped up with a single bound, and strode off purposefully. So this was Venky's idea of taking the Rajdhani for him? He closed his eyes, sighed and resumed searching, face still under the wet handkerchief.

His mind heard what his ears heard. No more and no less. Sometimes, on good days, he could pick up the odd stray thought. A person touching his mind once and then gone forever. He had followed a pretty secretary in the office around for weeks last year, after catching that one beautiful thought, convinced it came from her. She had stapled his tie to his shirt, and his pants to his underwear for good measure.

Today was not one of those good days. He would have to test

someone who looked suspicious. He pulled the wet handkerchief off his face and sat up. He steeled his gaze and focused on the passengers. Venky came back abruptly and sat down, a fraction of his former cheery self. 'Fish scales,' he said briefly, lapsing into broodiness.

None of the passengers looked suspicious to Mr Chatterjee. Some looked tired. Some looked hungry. Some looked innocent. Some looked angry. Some murmured to their Gods. Some grappled with babies. Some touched the ground. Some looked lonely. Some looked scared. Some looked hopeful. Most looked like they needed a cup of tea.

None of them looked suspicious. Welcome to the remnants of the big city, boys and girls, thought Mr Chatterjee. I hope you make it. He stood up. He was all clipped again, all of a sudden. One of his uncles had been a colonel, and sometimes he channelled him. He took the morose Venky by the arm, and pulled him up. 'Time to go,' he said, decisively. 'I have a wife to go home to. You need a bath.'

They picked up Professor Krishnan from Platform No. 6, forcing him to throw away his bhel puri, overruling his feeble protests.

Professor Krishnan took out his little notebook as they went down the steps to where their white Ambassador Classic Turbo was parked discreetly, next to all the other white Ambassador Classic Turbos. 'New New Delhi Railway Station—completed,' he said with satisfaction, and marked a flamboyant tick-mark in his notebook with his fat-barrelled pen.

◆

Director Sinha of the CBI was meeting with the Competent Authority and it was not going well. 'Bark like a dog,' said the Competent Authority, glaring at him.

'Excuse me, sir?' said Sinha nervously, wondering whether this was some sort of coded instruction which he was misunderstanding. He was expected to know all about code. Was he being tested on his ability as Head of Intelligence?

He wasn't. 'Get down on all fours and bark,' said the Competent Authority. 'And make it realistic.'

Sinha looked around the room. No one of equal or senior rank from the Bihar cadre was there to support him. Two of his subordinates were with him, as was the omnipresent Mehta, PA to the CA. Plus the PA to the PA. Plus the tea boy, who was serving tea with no expression whatsoever. He looked faintly Chinese. Probably a spy.

With some difficulty, he got down on his knees and barked. 'Arf,' he said, 'arf, arf.'

'Now wag your tail,' ordered the Competent Authority. Obediently, Sinha waved his fairly large backside from side to side. The only option I have, he thought as he wiggled, is to make those two subordinates of mine do the same thing once I get them in my durbar. Doubtless they would in turn do the same thing to their own underlings. Thus did the techniques of governance percolate down to the grassroots.

The Competent Authority had it all worked out. Like many of his lessons, this one too worked at many levels. Gautam Buddha had been very similar that way. He looked around at the others in the room. 'Can anyone tell me why the Director is barking?' he demanded.

This was a tricky area. The right answer could lead to immediate promotion. On the other hand, the wrong answer could, at the very least, lead to further animal impressions. After a brief pause, it emerged that none of them knew why the Director was barking.

The Competent Authority explained. 'This demonstration works at two levels. The people we are dealing with are dogs, and less than dogs. They are scum. They are filth. In Spain there is a saying—to be a bullfighter, you must learn to think like a bull. And it is important for us here in India to apply global best practices. Mehta,' he turned to his PA, sitting across the room, 'can you name any other global best practices?'

Mehta thought deeply. 'Usage of condoms, sir?' he said eventually.

The Competent Authority threw a paperweight at him. It missed. 'If we are fighting dogs, we must learn to think like dogs. And we are fighting dogs. Calling them human is an insult to humanity.' He made a gesture to Mehta, who noted down this last phrase. 'The Director has not been thinking like a dog. So I am helping him. But at another level, it is also a punishment. Can anyone tell me why this man is being punished?'

It turned out nobody could.

The Competent Authority smiled gently at the barking Director. 'You may stop barking now, Sinha,' he said kindly, 'for you have to listen.'

Sinha stopped barking and got off his knees. The tea boy, evidently a thoughtful fellow despite being Mongoloid, discreetly handed him a glass of water.

The Competent Authority got up and went to the map. 'The CBI analysis of the attack which the Director has presented is completely flawed and lacking in...lacking in what, Mehta, tell me? Begins with V.'

'Vision, sir,' said Mehta, hip to the boss.

'That's right—Vision. That is precisely what it lacks,' said the Competent Authority. 'I have a Master Plan, which I have not shared with you, but which you should have guessed.' He pointed to the right side of the map of India. 'What do you see here?' he asked, stabbing the map viciously.

That was an easy one. 'The traitorous slime of the Bengal Protectorate, sir,' said Sinha, eager to redeem himself.

'Correct,' said the Competent Authority, benignly, 'except that you should emphasize the word "traitorous" more when you say that. Not to mention the word "sir". Mehta, please make a note.' Mehta made a note.

'What is the history of the Bengal Protectorate?' asked the Competent Authority. This was a tough question. Luckily, it was rhetorical.

'I will tell you the history of the Bengal Protectorate,' continued the CA, to the immense relief of all present. 'Because Bengal was so pathetic, so insignificant, so unable to contribute to the well-being of India, so arrogant just because Rabindranath Tagore and Amartya Sen won Nobel Prizes, so unwilling to consume the various products manufactured by a thriving economy, so attitudinally opposed to any form of advancement, so infected and infiltrated by the anti-national Maoists, so keen to push inferior players into the Indian cricket team, so supportive of all forms of perversion and subversion that...that.... What was I talking about Mehta?'

'The history of the Bengal Protectorate,' supplied Mehta obligingly, dabbing some of the froth off the CA's mouth with the corner of his handkerchief.

'Correct,' said the CA, 'the state of West Bengal, due to its insignificance, was hardly affected by the war. They did not make the sacrifices that the rest of us did. The people of Bombay made sacrifices. The people of Delhi made sacrifices. Even the people of Jammu and Kashmir—they too made sacrifices. The Chinese missiles missed Bangalore, because they thought the airport was next to the city, otherwise they, too, would have made sacrifices. But not the mutinous dogs of Calcutta. And what was the result of this? Were they grateful? Were they relieved? Did they come forward to help the task of reconstruction? No, they did not. Instead they became traitorous pacifists. They demonstrated on the streets. They refused to be targets, not understanding the national interest. Their so-called leaders encouraged them in their cowardice. What was the end result?'

They all knew what the end result had been. However, they felt it was better not to mention it. It tended to put the CA in a bad mood.

The Competent Authority provided the answer. He was unveiling his grand strategy. Petty things like moods paled into insignificance. 'They indulged in sedition,' he said bitterly. 'They seceded from the Indian Union, like their treacherous Muslim brothers before them. Just because of a few bombs. Just because Delhi and Bombay were slightly damaged, and they feared for Calcutta. In any case, Delhi is now reconstructed, and in Bombay they are waiting for real estate prices to reach the right level. But did it help them?'

Everyone shook their heads regretfully.

'They were penniless, the stupid fools. They had no money to pay salaries even. They had no economy. What economy will a bunch of useless Bengalis run? They had not understood the whole basis of Centre–State relations, after complaining about it for years. So what did they do? They sold Darjeeling to China. Darjeeling! My brother-in-law had gone on honeymoon to Darjeeling. It was a nice place. And they sold it! It became part of the New Territories of China. And what did they do with the money? Wasted it! Within five years, they were back to square one, with no money, and no future. In their time of dire need, did they turn to us, their countrymen? No, because they are traitorous scum. They invited in a Chinese Governor, and became a Protectorate. A satellite state of China. Bloody communists. They betrayed us in 1942, they betrayed us again ninety years later. But why is this connected to yesterday's incident with the telepaths? Can anyone tell me?'

Once more, nobody could.

'On the face of it, it is not. Forget about telepaths for a moment. Let us consider strategy. This Bengal virus is a cancer which is gradually spreading west, in the form of the Maoist vermin. It has infected Chhattisgarh. It has infected Bihar. It has infected Orissa. It must be stopped, once and for all. Here, we must borrow lessons from the past. What did the last war teach us?'

'It taught us the art of reconstruction, sir,' ventured Sinha, still eager to get out of the doghouse. Literally. His wife was mad at him too. She felt his support for her NGO was inadequate.

'Of course, of course,' said the CA, secretly pleased. 'But that is not the main thing that the war taught us. It taught us the glory and the power of this nation that we call India or Bharat. It taught us that we can fight such a war and survive, even against the Chinese. It taught us that there is nothing that can destroy us as a nation. It taught us that there is nothing they can destroy that we cannot rebuild. If we can survive war with China, what hope does this puny Protectorate have? Filled as it is with evil Bengalis with unhealthy eating habits. They will be too busy getting the bones out of their fish to resist us.' The PA to the CA's PA, who was a Bengali himself, edged towards the door nervously.

The CA was on a roll. 'What does this have to do with the incident with the telepaths this afternoon, you may ask. You do not realize, do you?'

They nodded their heads, not realizing.

'A civilized nation like ours cannot just attack its neighbours, even neighbours who are treasonous ex-citizens with vile personal habits. Diplomacy demands a casus belli, which is a Latin term, meaning excuse.

Go out and get me my excuse. Do not be afraid. Even if the Chinese interfere, we will survive. Do you not see?'

They saw. They had seen nuclear war before, which made it easier to visualize.

'Now do you realize why I was so annoyed?' the CA asked Sinha. 'You come to me with a detailed analysis by your so-called analysts, giving four separate scenarios involving the Chinese. Who wants Chinese culprits? China's too big. China's not the problem. Give me Bengalis. Give me the Protectorate. Give me my casus belli. The time is ripe.'

There was silence as everyone digested this.

Sinha went first. 'Clearly, sir, we have been misguided. On reflection, it would appear to me that the culprits are the Protectorate, not the Chinese.'

The CA looked for his paperweight. Mehta picked it off the floor and passed it back to him, but the moment had passed.

'I don't know who the culprits are, you moron,' he thundered, 'that is what you are paid to find out. But we can officially blame it on the Protectorate, and take the necessary action. Maybe you would like to go to Calcutta and deliver our strongly-worded protest personally?'

'No, sir,' begged Sinha, 'please not that. Anything but that. Don't send me to Calcutta, sir. Some of them are cannibals.'

Once more, the Competent Authority was secretly pleased. Due to contamination, the supply of non-vegetarian food in the subcontinent had become somewhat restricted. At his suggestion, the CBI had for several years been spreading rumours and news reports that the citizens of the Protectorate, unable to curb their base cravings for flesh, had begun to eat each other (Daughter-in-law consumed in hideous dowry death scandal!).

'Whether you are sent to Calcutta or not depends on your performance,' he told Sinha sternly. 'Find me the culprits of this attack. Find me the real culprits. And dig out a Protectorate connection. We will find out the truth. Then we will twist it. Then we will take action. Is that clear?'

Director Sinha had many questions, but some sixth sense warned him that now was not a good time to ask them.

As they trooped out, the CA turned to Mehta. 'What is next on my agenda?'

'One of the victims of the Haryanvi Horror case would like to meet you, sir,' said Mehta, 'both he and his BMW have suffered severe damage, sir, mainly at the backside. The investigating officer is also with him.'

'Send them in,' said the Competent Authority. BMW ownership guaranteed a five-minute audience. He could hardly spend all his time discussing strategy, tempting and appropriate though it might be. What kind of a leader was he if he lost touch with his people?

THE MAN WHO TURNED INTO GANDHI

This short story was written for *The Gollancz Book of South Asian Science Fiction* (2019), edited by Tarun Saint. Shovon had become fascinated with Mahatma Gandhi while researching his first novel *The Competent Authority*, and it is almost certain that the novel that he had been planning and making notes about on his iPhone but never got around to writing, would have featured Gandhi in a major way.

Shovon saw Gandhi as an extremely complex character—wily, autocratic, possessed of a strong moral centre, and a unique personality who unified as well as divided. However, in balance, he interpreted the Mahatma as a unique force for good.

THE MAN WHO TURNED INTO GANDHI

1 AUGUST 2017

Clumps of hair in my comb this morning. Am shocked. Have been secretly using my wife's hair oil, but hair loss continues. Perhaps Keo Karpin does not suit me. Talked to the barber, he suggested coconut oil.

3 AUGUST 2017

Coconut oil was a failure. Patches of my scalp are now visible. Feel embarrassed. The men in my family are famous for their hair. My father had flowing locks at age 72. My wife is blaming the rum. I do not agree. Have enjoyed Old Monk with many, most of them have full heads of hair.

4 AUGUST 2017

Hair loss continues. Spat out a tooth while brushing this morning. Several others are loose. Why am I decaying like this? What else is going to fall off? Have lived a reasonably blameless life. Never raised my hand in anger. Gave only one or two bribes, did not steal anyone's money. Have even donated to others, when able. If I am being punished, what is it for?

5 AUGUST 2017

Caught one of my students staring at me. There are five of them, they come after school. Their Class X exams are next year. I've spent my whole life teaching. After retirement, this is what I do. The lights are dim in my single room. Was hoping they would not notice. 'Sir, have you seen a doctor?' he asked. I probably should. Have been too shocked by the speed of my disintegration. My wife has been surprisingly unsympathetic. She seems to feel I'm doing it on purpose. She has also hidden her hair oil.

This evening, I felt ants crawling all over my skin. It was unbearable.

I tore off my shirt, but there was nothing there. It must be the shirt. It was a gift from a foreigner who stayed with us once. He was one of the many reporters who came when our village was in the news. I seem to have developed an allergy to foreign clothing.

I am definitely seeing the doctor tomorrow.

6 AUGUST 2017

Doctor said it's some kind of viral, and prescribed some antibiotics. He said I should brush my teeth more. He seemed quite confident. I am not convinced by his diagnosis, but I had to pay him nevertheless.

7 AUGUST 2017

Suddenly, I am able to write with my left hand. The letters are tighter when I use my left hand, the writing full of flourishes. I can write with both hands now. A useful skill. If I believed in any god, I would have considered it a blessing. As it is, I am wondering whether it has anything to do with the radiation from my mobile phone.

8 AUGUST 2017

Today, I was unable to eat chicken. My wife had made it as a special treat.

We can barely afford vegetables. I pushed the bowl away. It made me feel ill. What is happening to me? The odd piece of chicken was one of the few remaining pleasures of my twilight years. 'Can you get me some goat's milk?' I asked, without thinking.

'You're losing your mind,' said my wife. 'I knew it would happen. There's a history of insanity in your family. Your uncle in Ghaziabad used to talk to furniture. I can't look after you, I'm warning you. I've done a lot. It's been 40 years. Enough is enough.'

It's probably just as well. In any case, I have just 11 teeth left. Chewing solids is becoming difficult.

9 AUGUST 2017

I have become a public spectacle. When I walk on the street, people make way for me. Sometimes they point at me and whisper. I saw a little boy standing on a boundary wall, trying to beat down mangoes with a stick, his tongue sticking out in concentration. He paused briefly to salute me, teetering precariously.

'Where did you learn to do that?' I asked.

'In school,' he said, 'on Indypindy Day.'

10 AUGUST 2017

Saw a picture of Nehru in the paper today. Felt an overwhelming rush of affection. Am surprised. Never been a big fan. He was the father of Indira Gandhi, an unpleasant woman who misguided her sons.

11 AUGUST 2017

Realized this morning that the toilet is filthy. Spent the rest of the day cleaning it. In the evening, I gave my wife a lecture on our lack of a moral compass. We were discussing the Akhlaq case and how the young men had just been released after local politicians said they had been unfairly targeted.

There was much celebration in the village. All my life I have believed that education will transform this country. I have dedicated myself to this.

But now it is becoming clear that moral values are what we lack. Unless every child receives moral instruction from an early age, this country has no future. Late into the night, after I finished my lecture, I asked my wife for her opinion. 'All these years, you used to talk very little,' she said, 'It was one of your few good points.'

12 AUGUST 2017

The shape of my face seems to be changing. Of all the things that are happening to me, this is the most peculiar. My wife felt my forehead. 'Are you suffering from dengue?' she asked. 'Maybe you should get a blood test.' I probably should, but I'm nervous. I'm not sure this is normal. 'My chin is pointier, isn't it?' I asked. 'It's definitely pointier,' she said. 'Plus your smile is sweeter than it used to be.'

I am now almost completely bald.

13 AUGUST 2017

Today my vegetable seller refused to take money from me. 'It's okay,' he said. 'It's okay.' He folded his hands.

Finished my course of antibiotics. They had no effect, except on my bowel movement. Meanwhile, my chest has become slightly concave. My rapid degeneration continues. What is happening to me?

14 AUGUST 2017

This evening there was no power. In the light of the kerosene lamp, I saw my shadow on the wall. It looked very familiar.

15 AUGUST 2017

I woke up this morning and found that my spectacles have changed. They are round now. I'm not an idiot. I know what this means. Even a child can recognize those spectacles. But why him? If I had to mysteriously turn into someone, I would much rather become Shashi Tharoor. How wonderful his life is! Fate has given him everything. But this? What is the point of this? Just because my name is Mohandas?

My father named me after him. He was a genuine admirer. Personally, I never thought much of the man. He was feudal and reactionary. He never did enough to break the caste system. He did not save Bhagat Singh. He was unfair to Netaji, forcing him to tie up with Hitler. He preferred worship to genuine democracy, establishing the principle that what we require is a Maximum Leader, who must always be followed. We are still suffering because of it. We already had a tendency for worship. Thanks to him, we gaze up at our leaders, instead of looking them in the eye. And why is every main road in every city in India named after him? Was there no one else in the country?

17 AUGUST 2017

The vegetable seller came to my house with a plastic packet full of vegetables. It was a gift. 'Why should you go to all the trouble?' he said. 'You just do the leadership.' I examined the packet after he left. The vegetables were slightly rotten. There are limits to his devotion. On the other hand, they are free.

He's not the only one. Salim from across the road has left a goat tied in front of my house. He's doing well as a dealer of aluminium foil for wrapping food items. It's becoming quite popular in the village, as people realize that it can be used for a variety of purposes. In his spare time, he drives an Uber. 'Whenever you need her milked, just call me,' he said. 'Plus I'll come once a week and give her a bath, otherwise the milk will taste funny.'

If the community is feeding me, I may have to do something for the community in return. It's only fair.

18 AUGUST 2017

None of the villagers have directly approached me about my transformation, until today. Today, Naresh-ji came to my house. It makes sense that he would be the first. Naresh-ji is a big man, perhaps the biggest man in the village, apart from Chaurasia the sand trader. I was given advance notice by three of his followers, who took one look at my room and said, 'He won't be coming in.' He arrived in a big car, followed by several smaller cars. They stopped in front of our little house, blocking the narrow lane.

A traffic jam of rich Delhi people formed behind him. They soon realized that Naresh-ji was a minister and stopped complaining, re-dedicating themselves to their mobile phones.

Naresh-ji stood outside my house and addressed me, so that his followers could hear him. 'Sir, we have the utmost respect for you,' he said, 'but kindly do not interfere as we transform society. All this time, relations between people were of a particular type. Now, we are trying to create new kind of relations, and in this way we will build a new nation. Efforts have been going on for many years, now we are beginning to see lasting success. At this crucial point in our history, you have come. We humbly request your blessings, and ask you to allow our work of nation-building to continue, otherwise I cannot answer for the consequences. Sometimes, the boys get excited.'

Why would I object to nation-building? I'm not looking for any trouble. I thanked him for his advice and offered him a cup of tea. He declined. He climbed back into his luxurious vehicle and left. The rich Delhi people resumed their journey to Delhi, eyes glued to their mobile phones, not seeing the village they drove through. We could see them, though.

19 AUGUST 2017

My next visitor was Sunil, and I was happy to see him. Most people in the village are happy to see him. He is the only son of a farmer who has just enough land to be middle class, especially if the weather is good. He is always full of bright ideas about how to improve the village and what new businesses we should start. No one ever pays him the slightest attention, but this does not stop him. He believes very strongly that our lives will get better. He knows we live in a time of opportunities. All we have to do is grab the right ones. He is confident that his time will come. He loves Narendra Modi more than life itself, and votes for him all the time.

'Uncle, we're very lucky. This is the chance to lift up our village. It's not the first time this has happened. One gentleman in a village near Faridabad was the duplicate of actor Naseeruddin Shah. People were constantly bringing him sweets, and he never said no. But what did they do after that? Nothing! At least they could have started a film academy. We will not make their mistake. God has given us this chance; we should make the most of it. We should start a Living Gandhi Museum. There are many museums, but none of them have a Living Gandhi. People will come from far away. I have already asked my father for land. My mother helped me to convince him. After two-three days, he agreed, saying, do what you like. We'll charge Rs 150 for admission, Rs 300 for a selfie. Every morning we'll do a Salt March on the Agra Expressway. For less than the price of a movie ticket, people can see the Living Gandhi and participate in the Salt March. In addition, we'll make money from food items. I was thinking of Gandhi Cola, which will contain water, lemon and honey and bottled milk from goats blessed by you. We can charge extra if you milk the goats. Please say yes and

I'll start the construction.'

I hated to dampen his enthusiasm, but I declined firmly. The last thing I need to do is attract more attention.

21 AUGUST 2017

The villagers have started coming to me for judgement. My first case was a good one. It was the case of Chumki, who ran away with the butcher's son, from a lower caste than them. Her father and uncles, accompanied by her brothers, who looked nervous and shifty-eyed, approached me with a simple question: should they hang her from the nearest tree? They were angry and forceful. More than judgement, they were expecting my blessing. I suggested they shave her head, to remove temptation for potential sinners. 'So long as you keep shaving her,' I said, 'your honour will forever be safe.' I was a little disappointed in myself. I used to be more honest than this, less willing to compromise. I imagined Chumki undergoing this indignity on a regular basis, her head bowed, tears coursing down her cheeks. Nevertheless, these are the words that popped out of me. The villagers left, satisfied.

This story had a happy ending, as Chumki, clearly different from what I had imagined, promised to scratch out the eyes of any barber who tried to shave her. 'I'll come to your house late at night while you're sleeping,' she promised. One of the brighter young men suggested cutting her tongue out and then shaving her head, to prevent her from threatening the barbers, but her mother said it was too late, she had already said what she had to say, and the barbers had heard, and they knew and she knew that she did not need her tongue to scratch their eyes out. I predict a bright future for the girl. She will either become a master criminal or a minister. Possibly both.

Later on, I met her during my morning walk and I apologized to her.

'Are you joking?' she said. 'You were so clever. I was getting *latkaoed* from that tree for sure. I'll remember you. When I become chief minister, I'll make you a minister.' She gave me a quick hug. 'So much gravy you'll see in your old age, Uncle!'

22 AUGUST 2017

The local boys are planning to do a *jagran* in front of a mosque. There is only one reason to do such a thing. Hopefully, the police will stop them. I ask Salim the foil-dealer-cum-Uberwala. 'Things are getting pretty hot here in Dadri,' he said. 'The boys are getting restless. Our local leader is coming regularly and exciting them. He has become a big man in Delhi, but he hasn't forgotten us. Sometimes I think I really should shift to Pakistan, but it's very far away, and I'm not sure the food would suit me.'

24 AUGUST 2017

The district magistrate came to visit me. Once more, there was a traffic jam in our lane. He must be a good officer. The good ones know that if something strange is happening in a village, at least five minutes need to be allocated for a personal look-see. First, two policemen came. They entered our home and went through our meagre belongings. Since they were not beating anyone up, I did not raise any objections. One of them looked at my books, piled on the table and the floor. 'There are no Naxal books in this, I hope?' he asked, semi-humorously. Actually, there was a copy of *Jangalnama,* but I said no.

The district magistrate himself was a cheerful fellow, and surprisingly young. He looked at my books. 'Ah, books!' he said, approvingly. He took a moment to look at me. 'The resemblance is truly uncanny.' He beamed with pride. He was clearly filing it away in his mind as a major achievement for his administration. 'Carry on, carry on,' he said, as he turned to leave.

My five minutes were over. 'Keep up the good work.' He twinkled at me roguishly. 'Of course, I have several orders for your arrest on charges of sedition ready on my desk, I just have to sign them. As I recall, last time we had to use it frequently.'

It's true what they say—India is timeless and eternal.

25 AUGUST 2017

Today, two young girls barged into my room and took a selfie with me. They left, giggling.

Sunil must have gone ahead with his plans. It's annoying, but I suppose I should support him. It does represent an opportunity for the local youth. I've been teaching them all these years, how can I not help them earn a living?

It looks like anonymity is no longer an option.

27 AUGUST 2017

Chumki has become quite popular amongst the local youth, for outwitting the elders. People talk about love jihad and honour killing, but everyone loves a good love story. Her boyfriend the butcher came back and, in another move that was clearly innovative, offered to publicly shave his own head, to compensate for the misbehaviour of his fiancee. The boys refused his offer, but they appreciated his gesture. Even though he was of a low caste, they said, he wasn't such a bad chap.

Of course, Chumki had to contribute to the discussion. She claimed the whole thing was irrelevant, because she was not even Hindu. 'My only religion is Virat Kohli,' she declared. I have heard of Virat Kohli. He is a fine young cricketer, but technically not yet a god. The local leader of the good boys, a shrewd young man who always gets bail, could see that youth opinion in the village was swinging her way. From this point on, I am fairly sure, no one will bother the young couple.

30 AUGUST 2017

Today, I helped an old lady get her rations. I don't really know her, but she lives a few doors down the lane. 'They're not giving my rations, sir,' she said. 'They're saying my fingers are wrong.'

On the whole, I think this Aadhaar system is a good thing. Many people are getting their rations, more than before. If you live in a city, you do not see this. But a few are getting left out, and those few are the weakest.

We live in a big country, and for thousands of years village officials have preyed on the weakest. The only solution is moral instruction and stiff jail sentences. I can't do much about such things, but at least I can help one person. I went with her to the ration shop. In front of me, she tried again.

Once more, she was refused.

'Show me the computer,' I said, 'let me also see.'

'Who are you?' asked the dark-eyed boy behind the counter, all vinegar and insolence.

I looked him in the eye and said, 'I'm her neighbour.' This is an important point. I want him to think about it. We fight for caste and religion, but how often do we fight for our neighbours?

'So, what will you do?' he demanded, a little less confident.

I was very sweet. I smiled and put my hand on his arm. 'I'll call the police and say someone is refusing a fingerprint without showing the computer.'

'Polis,' said the boy, gaining some confidence at the mention of their name. 'I'll stand here. You'll refuse to show your computer, your *malik* will come with Aadhaar Act, saying that in order to see such things I require written permission from the adhaar authorities. Police will go away, saying, "Let us look into the matter." But do you know how many youngsters have cameras on their phones in this village? All of them will be here, shooting. In all their films, you and your *malik* will be heroes. In addition, there's me. Look at my face. How many people will look at those videos? You should consider that situation.'

The boy considered it. 'Ask her to put her finger on the machine again,' he said sulkily. 'These machines sometimes make fools of us.'

I'm beginning to think there is some point in fighting after all.

3 SEPTEMBER 2017

'Sir, I think your band is going to get *bajaoed* pretty soon,' said Nirupam the chaiwalla. This is not encouraging. Being the local chaiwalla, he is very well-informed. Whenever I see the local police trying to investigate a crime, which does not happen very often, I keep thinking, *why don't they ask the chaiwalla?* He knows everything.

'The local Naxal *dada* is seeing you as the return of a powerful advocate of feudal reactionary petit beurjosis. They want to eliminate you immediately, even before the district magistrate, whom they intend to do the same to when the time is right, and the socio-political winds are blowing in the right direction.'

I looked at Nirupam thoughtfully. He is always particularly well-informed about Naxals. The Naxals are hiding among us. They will reveal themselves when the time is right. Who is to say he is not one of them, perhaps the leader even. Currently he is a chaiwalla, but perhaps he has bigger plans. This would not be the first time that this has happened.

'So, you think I should run away to Delhi immediately?' I asked.

'There's no guarantee that it could help,' said Nirupam. 'You're still an enemy of the revolution, but they don't want to do *ghadar* in Delhi at this stage.'

This does not suit me. I can't do any good in Delhi. Not yet. The sin runs too deep, it has seeped into the foundations.

6 SEPTEMBER 2017

Yesterday, Salim was beaten up for attempting to abduct a Hindu girl. He tried to point out that he was an Uber driver and she was a passenger, but they refused to listen. He has received his final warning.

8 SEPTEMBER 2017

I visited the local councillor, whose house is like the Taj Mahal, and suggested that he should give his servants a holiday once a week and clean his house himself. It would be good for his soul and also teach him about the dignity of labour. I have decided that society needs to be reformed from the top. His security guards chased me away. One of them was apologetic.

'It's not that what you're saying is wrong,' he said. 'At the very least, it will help him lose weight.'

Had a cup of boiled vegetables and some carrot juice in the evening.

10 SEPTEMBER 2017

Salim knocked on my door late at night. His clothes were torn. He looked frightened. 'Can I stay in your house for a few days?'

I glanced at my wife. She nodded, her lips pursed grimly. I felt a certain sympathy for anyone who might try to come and get him. 'Promise you won't eat any meat,' I said.

'I promise,' he whispered softly.

I opened the door and let him in.

13 SEPTEMBER 2017

Today, I received a letter from Fabindia. They want me to model for their khadi range. They are offering me Rs 50,000. I showed the letter to my wife and asked her what she thought. 'Is anyone else offering Rs 50,000 for your picture?' she asked. No, I admitted. 'Then go get a camera and send them your photo.'

The Fabindia people subsequently clarified that this would not be necessary. They would send a photographer and some clothes. Apparently, I can keep the clothes. This is encouraging. It looks like I won't have to pay for anything anymore.

Salim offered to make me a charkha. He says he knows the basics of carpentry; the rest he will Google under the lamp post near Agarwal Sweets, which is the only place we can get Wi-Fi. He will wear a sari, so that people don't recognize him. He is a boy of many talents. It strengthens my resolve to protect him. Beating him to death would be a loss to society.

15 SEPTEMBER 2017

Sunil came and asked me for my signature. I know what he's up to. The number of people who come and take selfies with me is increasing every day, and they display the entitled behaviour of paying customers, never asking permission and rarely saying thank you. Business is in full swing.

'You want to put my signature on the label for Gandhi Cola, don't you?' I said.

He looked sheepish. 'I was going to pay you your share, but collections have been poor, and there are overheads. Not to mention advertising.'

'Build a new roof for your local school by December,' I said.

'Otherwise, I'm calling my lawyer.'

My lawyer used to be my cousin's classmate Chunilal, who died in Banaras in 1996. But Sunil does not know that.

18 SEPTEMBER 2017

There was much excitement in the village. A large group of people came and interviewed me for TV. They tried to put powder on my face, but I refused. The reporter was clearly a big man, and he seemed to be in a bad mood. He was the kind of person who is aggressive with poor people. He was sweating in his expensive suit. His hair is remarkable. Ever since I turned bald, I have begun to appreciate other people's hair.

'Can you sing "Vande Mataram"?' he demanded. It's a complex and patriotic song, saluting the nation.

'Excuse me?' I replied nervously.

He fixed me with his piercing gaze. His nostrils flared. His spectacles shone with menace. 'You are pretending to be a great man,' he said, 'but don't think that we are fooled by you. Can you sing "Vande Mataram"?'

'Certainly,' I said, and did so. I did it slowly, so that I could get it right.

I can no longer hit the high notes, but I can still carry a tune. I stopped once or twice to explain the lyrics.

I have to give the anchor credit. He digested it all very quickly. You don't get to his position by being a fool. He turned to the camera, his lips quivering. His expression was soulful. 'Ladies and gentlemen, you have just witnessed a miracle. The miracle of patriotism, flowering in this small village in Uttar Pradesh. One day, soon, it will transform India into the glorious nation that it deserves to be.' He brushed away a tear. He reached out and clasped me by the hand. I clasped right back.

19 SEPTEMBER 2017

This morning, another tooth fell out. I now have six.

20 SEPTEMBER 2017

Today, I found a note slipped under the door. 'You have been found guilty of promoting a feudal reactionary mindset, which is hampering the progress of the revolution. Also, you have been demonstrating petit burjeoisie thought processes. Marx was never clear who the petit burjeoisie are, but he did know that they must be eliminated. Accordingly, you have been declared an enemy of the people. Unless you immediately cease your activities, you will be sentenced to death and executed. You are also cordially invited to a performance of the revolutionary play, *Eklavya,* by the People's Theatre Collective, in which the ending has been changed to reflect proper revolutionary values, and Eklavya cuts off Dronacharya's head. Musical accompaniment will be provided by Suhasini Rao and Dilip Mahato.'

That's what I like about the Naxalites. They lay emphasis on culture.

After all, without culture, what are we? The death sentence is an area of concern. For a moment I think of informing the police, before I come to my senses.

21 SEPTEMBER 2017

'I've signed up for a sperm bank,' said Sunil.

'I would expect no less,' I replied.

'I mean for you, Uncle,' he said. 'I have already thought of the advertising campaign. "Let the father of the nation be the father of your child!" So many couples are unable to conceive; now their liability will turn into an opportunity. We'll auction the first lot online, that way we'll be able to estimate a price range.'

I considered the youth unemployment scenario, and the livelihoods such a project could generate, but nevertheless I was unable to comply.

'What you are asking for, I only have a limited supply of,' I informed him.

He is not going to give up. I shudder to think what he will do to make me more productive.

22 SEPTEMBER 2017

Today, I did not wear my shirt. I went out wearing just my dhoti, and my Quovadis sandals from Bata. The sun was warm on my skin.

It felt good.

23 SEPTEMBER 2017

They came this morning and banged on my door, a whole crowd of young men with nothing better to do. People often ask 'Don't these boys have anything better to do?' but that's the wrong question, because the answer is always, 'No.' Of course, it's not really true. If they just got together and cleaned the village every day, this place would be like heaven on earth.

But their thoughts are clouded by tradition. Dispelling these clouds may take some time. I may need to start some kind of ashram, where they can be trained in a closed environment. Discipline will be required, and purity of intent. But this was not a good time to raise the subject. They had come to beat me up.

'Send Salim out, or things will be the worse for you,' cried one of them.

I peeped through a crack in the door. There were at least 20 of them. Two or three were from among those arrested in the earlier case. They were brimming with confidence. My wife emerged from the kitchen, with a saucepan in her hands. Salim was hiding under the bed. He slipped in surprisingly quickly. He must have some kind of technique. He spent a few years in the army. I must learn it from him. My wife moved forward with the saucepan. I waved her back.

'What did he do, son?' I asked through the door.

'He was doing love jihad with a Hindu girl from Greater Noida. He says he was doing Uber, but his intentions were otherwise.'

'But if he was driving his Uber, he must have been in the front seat, no?' I replied. 'If she was in the back seat and he was in the front seat, how could he do love jihad?'

There was silence outside for a while. I heard them whispering to each other. Some of them were semi-convinced. But the ringleader was made of sterner stuff. 'You think you're clever, but you're not,' he said. 'Send Salim out or your house will burn. We can do it very easily. My uncle has a kerosene dealership. Remember, when your house burns, you may not be able to escape. The lane is very narrow.'

'It won't look good though, will it,' I said. 'Because we're Hindus. Should you be burning down the homes of Hindus?'

They were genuinely puzzled. Having been part of the school system, I know what the problem is. We don't teach them how to think. It's too much effort. They slunk away down the lane, muttering. I know that it is not the last time I will see them.

25 SEPTEMBER 2017

The friendlier of the two policemen who came last time came again. 'Sir, you are not cooperating, there could be trouble. You created *ghadar* at the ration shop. The district magistrate has made a note in your file. You interfered in the case of Chumki, although god knows that girl needs no help. She will go far. You told the councillor to do *jharu pochha*. He's a tall leader and he's very annoyed. In the matter of Salim, you are not being helpful. The good boys are getting upset. The Naxalites are also up to something. My snitch was more nervous than usual. Obviously, if something happens, we will take action, but sometimes we arrive too late. You seem like a good fellow, I thought I should warn you.' He looked around quickly, checking for exits. I thanked him and ushered him out.

26 SEPTEMBER 2017

I caught one of the good boys checking out my window. He opened and closed the shutters and checked how it locked from inside. 'If you want to come in, my door is always open,' I told him. 'Whatever your problems, we can solve through discussion.' I genuinely believe this. It's the democratic way.

'That's your problem,' he said. 'You're doing too much discussion.'

27 SEPTEMBER 2017

Nirupam the chaiwalla refused to look me in the eye today. When I thanked him for the tea, he grunted. I think a Naxalite attack is imminent.

28 SEPTEMBER 2017

I am becoming obsessed with my bowel movements, which are now quite regular. Today was good, rich golden-brown, firm in its consistency.

30 SEPTEMBER 2017

They entered at night, the good boys. A group of five. Two of them had guns. The others carried sticks. It looked like my time was up. I thanked my stars that my wife was visiting my sister. She had taken Salim with her. He had worn a sari. When I thought of her, I felt regret. What will she do on her own? I stood in the middle of the room with my hands up.

They went through my things, hoping to steal something. 'Books!' said one of them, annoyed. 'All he has is books.'

The leader raised his gun. I closed my eyes. What had the real one said?

'Hey Ram.' Those were his last words. *What should mine be,* I thought. I wished I had thought about this before. I should plan things in advance.

'Long live the revolution!' said a voice from behind the door. It burst open and three young men burst in, carrying automatic rifles. This was a lot of weapons in close proximity, I thought as I hit the ground flat, the way Salim had taught me, and rolled myself under the bed. My ears rang with the sound of gunfire, punctuated by the sound of lathis breaking skulls.

1 OCTOBER 2017

The friendly policeman was quite cheerful. 'Three Naxalites and four of the good boys,' he said. 'For a person devoted to non-violence, you got yourself quite a score. Half the village is in mourning.' He did not seem too devastated by their deaths. I requested him to take me to the hospital.

My ears were ringing terribly.

'You look very fine, what can happen to you?' he said. 'Who Hari is keeping, no one can take away.'

Nevertheless, I insisted. He took me on the back of his motorcycle. We made quite a sight, the pot-bellied police officer and the little old man in a dhoti balanced precariously behind him. We were stopped several times for selfies. One of them offered me money. 'Talk to my manager,' I told him.

The doctor confirmed what the policeman said. The ringing should stop by this evening. If anything, my health has improved. This could well be true. I feel much more energetic these days. He advised me to brush my teeth regularly, since I have only five left, and gave me some drops for my ears.

'Eat more, keep your strength up,' he said. 'Have an extra cup of boiled vegetables.'

2 OCTOBER 2017

It's late in the evening. My brain is buzzing with ideas, but I must go to sleep. I have to get up early in the morning.

There's work to be done.

I LOST MY TROUSERS IN TILJALA

Going through Shovon's papers, Urmila discovered this story written in long hand in a notebook. It refers to certain events that took place around 1989–90, with minor embellishments. For instance, it was not a mango tree in the garden, but several coconut trees, that the local boys would lay bare. We have not been able to ascertain when the story was written, but bits of it found its way into *The Competent Authority*. Clearly the forces of justice in the Kolkata suburb of Tiljala had made quite an impression on Shovon and appealed to his sense of humour.

I LOST MY TROUSERS IN TILJALA

This is the story of how my trousers were stolen, and how I got them back. They were stolen from my father-in-law's house. He has this huge house in Tiljala, with a garden the size of half a football field and a mango tree in one corner. The mango tree is because of his father—he had one in his garden. It's not that any of us actually got to eat any mangoes. They got stolen by the ragged kids of the neighbourhood before they were much bigger than ping pong balls, which is not the recommended size for consumption. They can hardly have enjoyed eating them, but it was the principle of the thing. Stealing mangoes has been a proud part of Bengali heritage—it features prominently in the literature.

My father-in-law shifted to Tiljala because of real estate prices in Kolkata. He'd been born and brought up in a zamindari mansion, with sprawling grounds and plenty of loyal serfs. Corporate life found him in a swank flat in Tivoli Court, but when the time came to build a home of his own, his roots called out to him, faintly but incessantly. So he bought a huge plot of land in Tiljala and built a huge pink house, with embossed pink lotuses over the main entrance.

Tiljala was still pretty much the Wild West in those days, so there was open space as far as the eye could see. Various houses in various stages of construction, which never actually seemed to get completed. Single-storied shanties in various stages of dilapidation. And, of course, the cowshed, which was the local landmark. And which meant that you generally got cow dung on your shoes while getting to the house.

We used to spend our weekends there, my wife and I. It made a pleasant change from the congestion of the city, and it was nice to be waited on hand and foot. We used to sleep in the first-floor guest bedroom, which had a nice view of the cowshed. In fact, it was this very window through which my trousers left me, thereby setting off a trail of events which led to my interrogation in a temple, an emergency meeting of the Communist Party of India (Marxist)—Tiljala Wing, a riot at the police station, and of course, my falling out and subsequent reconciliation with the forces of justice.

The evidence suggests that my trousers vanished somewhere around four in the morning. We were chatting in bed till one, and got up at seven, to discover that somebody had burned a hole through the mosquito net in the window, reached a fairly long arm through, and removed my trousers from the hook on the nearby wall. He didn't take anything else, and he was thoughtful enough not to wake us up in the process.

'Well, they were pretty old anyway,' said my wife, who usually sees the bright side of everything. I thought so too, so I quickly got ready for the office, and went downstairs. I'd lost my watch and my wallet as well—they were in the trousers. But the watch wasn't such a good one, and I had only two hundred rupees in the wallet, so I adopted a philosophical air and sat down to breakfast.

There was a bit of to-do downstairs. After all a break-in is a break-in, however minor. My father-in-law mumbled something about bars on the window. My mother-in-law looked vaguely worried. Remati, the maid servant, hinted darkly that the culprit had to be Ramu, the security guard next door. She had never liked his face, and besides, he had bad habits. 'This might well be true,' I said, 'but unless you catch him wearing them there's not a lot you can do about it.'

It seemed like a closed chapter. I went off to work. I was basically an errand boy at an advertising agency, so I ran errands long and hard the whole day, and wound my weary way home—stepping in cow dung on the way as usual.

So there I was, sitting in my father-in-law's living room, wondering whether he was going to offer me anything to drink. You could never be quite sure. I blame Hindi movies for this. In Hindi movies, only bad people drink. Really bad people tap cigar ash in their whiskey, swirl it around, and knock it off. Sometimes they even manage an evil cackle while swallowing, without choking, which I personally find very impressive. You can tell a good woman from a woman of loose morals by the fact that the loose woman drinks, while the good woman shudders and covers her eyes whenever she sees a bottle. In real life, Western influences have made it more acceptable of course, but in middle class families like ours, there's still an element of uneasiness. Images of villainy flash across our eyes, sly and subconscious.

I was giving meaningful looks to the bottle of scotch in the corner, when we heard sounds of a commotion outside. Remati burst in, her eyes alight with excitement. 'Dada, dada, they're here,' she said breathlessly.

'Who?' I asked.

'The local pada boys,' she said, 'And they've got your pants, dada.'

I had a brief flashing vision of a host of them parading down the streets, my pants aloft on a flagpole. Not good. I went out to check. It was late evening, and there were no street lights. I could make out a group of five or six dim, shadowy figures. The pada boys. They came into our lives only in times of celebration—like Durga Puja or a Mohun Bagan victory—or crisis, as in when you got hit by a speeding motorist. Otherwise everyone kept their respective places, barring the occasional catcall.

The leader came forward to meet me. He was thin and dark, and his shirt was unbuttoned to the waist. Calcutta has always been full of thin, dark men with their shirts unbuttoned to the waist. This usually reveals a very weak chest. 'I may be thin,' this chest seems to say, 'but just come on and try to hit me. See what happens to you.'

I dragged my eyes away from his chest because he was speaking to me. 'My name is Parimal,' he said, 'Are you Shovon-babu?' He had a serious, formal air about him.

'Yes, I am,' I said, smiling to ease things up a bit. He didn't smile back.

'Have certain goods been stolen from your house last night?'

'Yes, they have' I said, eager to be helpful, 'A pair of—'

He raised one hand in a magisterial gesture, cutting me off.

'Please don't give me the details right now. That's for later,' he said. 'We've caught the thief, and certain items have been removed from his possession. You have to come with us to the Kali temple to identify them.'

I agreed readily, since after all I did want my trousers back. Also, even at that stage I had a premonition of a situation full of bizarre promise.

We walked off into the darkness, through narrow lanes and by-lanes, which got progressively muddier. The small buildings and huts all around were dark, and no one seemed to be around. I wondered where everyone was. I found out when I reached the Kali temple.

It was a small enough place—a small courtyard with an arching roof. The walls were dull grey and stained with the smoke of many prayers, and quite a bit of ganja too I guessed. At the moment though, the gathering wasn't very religious. A throng of young, plus a few grey haired eminences of the locality. There was a pile of clothes on a small table in the centre. Everyone was very silent.

I spotted my trousers and went for them, happy to see something familiar in this somewhat forbidding atmosphere. Parimal pulled me back by the elbow.

'Wait,' he whispered urgently, 'Let Jaga-da come.'

As if on cue, Jaga-da emerged, pushing his way through the motley throng. He wore the same kind of uniform as Parimal—a shirt unbuttoned to his waist, but with a red handkerchief wrapped around his throat. He had about him the air of a general, weary after a long day of battle, but determined to carry on his duties.

He came straight to the point. 'Mr Chowdhury,' he said, 'There have been several thefts in the locality yesterday. Naturally we were most unhappy—the reputation of our locality was being questioned, and some of my innocent boys were being suspected. So we made a thorough investigation and found that a person from another pada was the culprit. We launched a raid into that pada, and the goods have been forcibly recovered. They will now be returned to the respected owners.'

'Good show, I must say,' I said, and I really was impressed. I'm even more impressed now when I think about it. I live in Delhi now, not Kolkata, and the chances of anything remotely like this happening there are low, to put it mildly. Almost everyone in Delhi is a thief, in one way or another, and if people started recovering stolen goods from them, things could get pretty confusing. The whole basis of the city's economy would be undermined. Complete turmoil would be the result, and we can't have that in the nation's capital, can we?

I moved forward to grab my pants—I could see a corner popping out of the pile seductively—when the magisterial hand stopped me.

'I'm sorry, but some formal identification will be required.' said Jaga-da. 'We don't want to doubt your word, but frankly anybody can say anything. And if the real owner comes later, the case will become even more complicated. Deepak will ask you a few questions.'

Deepak came forward. He wasted no time on preliminaries, launching immediately into a sort of quiz contest or viva voce.

'What was the label on your trousers?' he asked.

'Levi's,' I said, in a clear, firm voice.

'Correct,' he said, at which a pleased murmur ran through the crowd. 'What was in the pockets?'

Easy one, I got it right.

'Which pocket was the watch in—back or front?'

'Front,' I said, making it three out of three.

'How do you know Sanjay Saxena?'

Having lulled me into a false sense of security, he sprung his trap.

'Sanjay who…?' I was stumped by this one. He fixed me with a piercing gaze. 'There is a visiting card in your wallet—it says Sanjay Saxena. What is the company?'

An acquaintance, a ritual exchange of cards, in a place very different from this one—a different country in more ways than one. 'American Express,' I said, relieved to be able to remember.

'But that's a bank, you work in advertising,' he said, and now he looked dubious. I began to feel extremely guilty. 'Well actually…' I began—but the crowd was on my side.

'Don't be silly Deepu!' said a voice from the crowd, 'He can know people in other professions also, do you mix only with ticket blackers?'

Much laughter, and a glare from Deepu. 'You can take your things.' he said curtly, acknowledging defeat with rather poor grace, I thought. I gathered up my belongings.

Jaga-da came back into the fray. 'One more thing,' he said, with a defiant note to his voice. 'There was 200 rupees in your wallet. We've kept it.' I was about to mumble something to the effect of professional fees etcetera, when the magisterial hand went up again. 'I am afraid we had to beat up the thief severely to get the location of the stolen goods. Afterwards, he needed medical treatment. We used your money to pay for it. After all, why should we pay—they're not our trousers.'

The logic was irrefutable, so I reassured him on this point, and we parted as friends. A brief nod and a wave to the crowd, and off I was, on the way back home.

Poems

POEMS

Shovon's *India Update* blog was marked by his natural humour and characteristic whimsy. However, he had made it clear what his blog stood for:

'Many physicists today postulate the existence of multiple universes, even when sober. We used to live in a world of infinite possibilities. Now we live in an infinite number of worlds. India shines. Democracy thrives. The economy booms. A hundred flyovers bloom. This is not that India. If you see your picture here one day, don't worry. That's not you.'

What follows is a selection of his 'pomes'.

MIDDLE MEN

In between
The beginning and the end
Are lots of men
Who know the men
Behind them

                                                  6 July 2012

TOMORROW NEVER DIES IN DELHI

I want it tomorrow
I said
He agreed
Two weeks later
I yell, I beg, I plead
He's shocked, and full of sympathy
And conscious of my need
'I said tomorrow, Sir-jee
Tomorrow it will be'

16 July 2012

BIG RED FLASHIE LIGHT

Mama, can we get the car
A big, red, flashie light?
Flish! Flash! The light will go
Such a pretty sight
If police are on the lookout
It can keep us out of sight
Also very useful
If we have to catch a flight
Look, look there goes one of them!
Quick, get to the side.
If he comes and stops here
You don't want to take a ride
Why can't we be more like him?
And make them all give side?
Even when he gets out, see
He's walking very wide
Mama, what does papa do?
Is our future bright?
Please say we can get one too
A big, red, flashie light

11 August 2012

MAMA'S PIZZA

Come to Mama's Pizza shop
Pizza very nice
Drool at all the things on top
But never ask the price
You can come and stand outside
And smell the mozzarella
If it's raining don't forget
To bring your own umbrella
Watch as Mama's friends go in
Don't get in the way
If they kick you in the shins
Be careful what you say
Watch out! Here comes Sonny Boy
Did you bring a sheet?
Lie down, let him walk on you
He mustn't wet his feet
Mama cuts the pizza up
Mama feeds her friends
Will you get some crumbs as well?
Well, it all depends
Were you nice to Sonny Boy?
Did you kiss his tushie?
Were you gentle, full of joy?
He hates it when you're pushy.
Mama's pizza, hot and fresh
Pizza very nice
If you bend down far enough
You could get a slice.

18 September 2012

MAN OF GLASS

Upper class, man of glass
Totally transparent
Easily, see through me
It's all quite apparent.

A gives money
Straight to B
There's nothing to hide.
Nuts to you
Go and sue
Gorment's on my side.

Mummy-ji, loving me
Playing games with fruit
You can shout
I'll just pout
And chill out with my loot

Mummy see, ragging me
Can't you make them stop?
Why so mad? What's so bad?
They gave you the shop

Salman-bhai, said he'd die
Why has he not done it?
In this fight, might is right
How come you've not won it?

Mummy G, let me be
I have golf and gym
One-two flats, minor stats
Grandkids need to swim

I see you, through and through
It's all crystal clear
I blame you, yes I do
They're losing all their fear

                                        12 October 2012

STITCHING

I stitch myself together
I use the needle well
It hurts, I scream
I hide the seams
So nobody can tell

                                                           22 March 2013

THE GRUMBLIES OF THE NO-NO
(TRANSLATED FROM SUKUMAR ROY, RAMGORURER CHHANA)

The Grumblies of the No-No
Frown upon the ho ho
Say anything funny, they go
'Ho ho? No no! No no!'

They live in mortal fear
That laughter could be near
They peer around suspiciously
To check the coast is clear

They hardly ever sleep
Their vigilance is deep
'If I smile,' they warn themselves
'I'll beat me till I weep!'

Near woods they'll never be
Nor leap from tree to tree
For fear the tricksy south wind
Could tickle out some glee

No rest can be allowed
When every passing cloud
Is chock-a-block with funny drops
They hear them, oh so loud!

In bushes, left and right
On dark and gloomy nights
Glow worms glow in unison
Like mocking laughter lights

Oh you who laugh around

And roll about the ground
Don't you see the agony
You cause them is profound?

The Grumblie house is full of ways
To make you shut your face
No funny wind can blow there
And laughter has no place.

1 July 2012

UNCLE'S INVENTION
(TRANSLATED FROM SUKUMAR ROY, KHUROR KAL)

Chandidas's uncle made a really weird machine,
The local people cheered, it was the best they'd ever seen.
When he was very small, perhaps a year, if that at all,
His baby cry of 'Goonga!' would echo through the hall.
While babbling 'Mama Gaga' is the baby drivel norm,
Uncle going 'Goonga' raised quite a local storm.
'This boy will surely shine,' is what everybody said,
'If indeed he lives, he'll turn the world upon its head.'
Now, today, we see it, the product of his brain,
Five-hour trips in under two, with very little strain.
I went and had a look, and I understood it fine,
Five hours of fiddling, and its secrets could be mine.
How can I explain to you, how strangely it's designed?
It fits you on your shoulders, and it grips you in its bind.
The food hangs in front, you can choose yourself a treat,
A cutlet, or a chop. A loochi, or a sweet.
Your mind will think 'Yummy!' Your mouth will move to feed,
Food and mouth will scurry, at a solid rate of speed.
Pulled along by greediness, staring at the food,
Delirious with happiness, you'll run as if pursued.
Cheerfully and easily, you'll cover many miles,
Smelling all the goodies, and drooling all the while.
History will thank him. So will we, of every age,
For Chandidas's uncle, has written a new page.

17 June 2012

LIFE

Hey!
Wait!
No!
Damn!
Shit!
Really?
Over.

                                                29 August 2012

SOURCES

Many pieces included here were first published in the *Hindu Business Line, The Hindu, Open* magazine, *swarajyamag.com, scroll.in,* and *newslaundry.com.* The 'Ask Uncle' columns and poems first appeared in the author's blog, *India Update.*

COLUMNS

The Investigator

'Defence Ministry Authorises Use Of Files As Weapons', *Hindu Business Line*, 14 March 2014.
'Govt To Provide List Of Words To Describe "Govt"!', *Hindu Business Line*, 11 November 2016.
'27 Resolutions for 2017!', *Hindu Business Line*, 6 January 2017.
'Will Protect Cows From Romeos, Says UP Police!', *Hindu Business Line*, 31 March 2017.
'New Acronym Launched To Fight Maoists!', *Hindu Business Line*, 26 May 2017.
'Man Without Aadhaar Refused Toilet Facility!', *Hindu Business Line*, 23 June 2017.
'Grouse Of Cards', *The Hindu Business Line*, 13 October 2017.
'Law Min To Launch Self-Service App!', *Hindu Business Line*, 8 December 2017.
'A Brief History Of R-Day Floats', *Hindu Business Line*, 26 January 2018.
'Director Of Nirav Modi Biopic Reveals All!', *Hindu Business Line*, 20 July 2018.
'Patriotic Channel Launches Wide Range Of Merchandise!', *Hindu Business Line*, 24 August 2018.
'Tatkal Scheme Announced For Absconding Promoters!', *Hindu Business Line*, 12 October 2018.
'Transparency Officer Selected In Secret!', *Hindu Business Line*, 4 January 2019.
'Judge Receives Global Speed Reading Award!', *Hindu Business Line*, 1 February 2019.
'Bollywood In Peril Due To Declining Birth Rate!', *Hindu Business Line*, 1 March 2019.

'Revealed! Pollution In Delhi Due To Smoking By Nehru!', *Hindu Business Line*, 8 November 2019.

'Public Shocked After Delhi Police Arrests Criminal!', *Hindu Business Line*, 7 February 2020.

'Bihar Leader To Be Secular On Tuesdays, Thursdays And Saturdays!', *Hindu Business Line*, 6 November 2020.

We the People

'Excuse Me, But What is Right Wing?', *swarajyamag.com*, 27 September 2014.

'Why Modi's US trip is like "Amar Akbar Anthony"', *scroll.in*, 28 September 2014.

'How the Sedition Law Makes India a More Loving Nation', *scroll.in*, 16 October 2014.

'An Ardent Plea to a Publisher to Consider an Original Series on Youthful Love in India', *scroll.in*, 21 December 2014.

'We Need More Transparency in Corruption', *scroll.in*, 5 October 2015.

'Obituary for Indian National Congress (1885-2016): "Death Was Slow in Coming"', *scroll.in*, 22 May 2016.

'Nobody is on the Rampage in India and It's Hight Time He is Brought to Justice', *scroll.in*, 23 October 2017.

The 4-Minute Manager™

'The 4-Minute Manager™', *newslaundry.com*, 16 January 2014.

'Blanket Marketing', *newslaundry.com*, 24 January 2014.

'How to Become a Management Guru', *newslaundry.com*, 12 February 2014.

'Management Classics Made Easy', *newslaundry.com*, 25 February 2014.

What If

'What If Gandhi Hadn't Been Thrown Off the Train?', *swarajyamag.com*, 14 November 2014.

'What If *Ramayana* Had Never Been Telecast?', *swarajyamag.com*, 27 November 2014.

'What If the Marathas Had Won at Panipat?', *swarajyamag.com*, 6 December 2014.

'What If the Chinese Had Stayed on in 1962?', *swarajyamag.com*, 8 February 2015.

'What If Madhuri Had Not Done Ek Do Teen?', *swarajyamag.com,* 7 May 2015.

Health is Wealth

'In Pursuit of Wellness', *The Hindu*, 20 February 2017.
'The High Way to Health', *The Hindu*, 6 March 2017.
'Evidence That Gyms Are Unnatural', *The Hindu*, 17 April 2017.
'This Slimness Fetish Must Stop!', *The Hindu*, 1 May 2017.
'Can You Handle the Diet of the Gods?', *The Hindu*, 29 May 2017.
'Why I Will Avoid Bosu Workouts', *The Hindu*, 7 August 2017.
'My Experience as a First-time Runner', *The Hindu*, 18 September 2017.
'Is Social Media Making Us Fitter or Fatter?', *The Hindu*, 2 October 2017.
'Posture Can Make You a Winner!', *The Hindu*, 30 October 2017.
'Why Syringes Should Not Be a Surprise', *The Hindu*, 11 December 2017.
'Please Read This Before Using Your Hands', *The Hindu*, 4 June 2018.
'Which Cow Product Is Best for Me?', *The Hindu*, 30 July 2018.
'Did Someone Say 1984?', *The Hindu*, 13 August 2018.
'Why Delhi CEOs are Super Fit', *The Hindu*, 8 October 2018.
'How to Correct Your Sleep Cycle', *The Hindu*, 15 October 2019.

42

'Why Men in Beards Should Never Be Trusted', *scroll.in,* 16 December 2014.
'Why My Wardrobe Is Almost Empty', *The Hindu*, 8 January 2018.
'Exam Stress Decoded', *The Hindu*, 26 February 2018.
'Why "Active Holiday" Is an Oxymoron', *The Hindu*, 12 March 2018.
'Men Over 40 Who Gym', *The Hindu*, 14 January 2019.
'Tidiness – The Piling Method', *The Hindu*, 28 January 2019.
'A Brief History of Herbal Cigarettes', *The Hindu*, 11 March 2019.
'What Are You Running From?', *The Hindu*, 12 August 2019.
'On How a 10-year-old Boy Managed Depression', *The Hindu*, 26 August 2019.
'How to Identify Burnouts at Work', *The Hindu*, 9 September 2019.
'The Pancreatic Diaries: Being Hospitalised During Lockdown', *The Hindu*, 4 May 2020.
'The Pancreatic Diaries II', *The Hindu*, 25 May 2020.

A Few of My Favourite Things

'Space Cadet', *Open*, 26 June 2009.
'Happy Birthday, Asterix!', *Open*, 27 October 2009.
'Come Back, Elvis', *Open*, 13 January 2010.
'The Beatles Are Fifty', *Open*, 17 March 2010.
'How Not To End Up Divorced', *Open*, 2 June 2010.

FICTION

The Competent Authority, New Delhi: Aleph Book Company, 2013.
'The Man Who Turned into Gandhi', *The Gollancz Book of South Asian Science Fiction* (ed. Tarun Saint), Gurugram: Hachette India, 2019.